The door swung open silently.

The distant, high-pitched cry of a gull echoed in Horatio's ear like a warning.

He entered the house, Glock held rock-steady in front of him, sighting down the barrel. Delko was no more than a step away. Horatio moved slowly through the large living room, noting that it had been cleaned up since the last time he'd been here; the blood on the walls had been washed away, the splintered furniture removed.

He could see a seated figure through the doorway to the kitchen, its back to him.

"Place your hands on top of your head!" Horatio called out.

The figure turned slowly, the chair itself swiveling.

Abdus Sattar Pathan regarded Horatio with a slight smile on his face.

Other ***CSI: Miami*** books

Cult Following

Riptide

Harm for the Holidays—Misgivings

Also available from Pocket Books

CSI: Crime Scene Investigation

Double Dealer

Sin City

Cold Burn

Body of Evidence

Grave Matters

Binding Ties

Killing Game

Snake Eyes

and

CSI: NY

Dead of Winter

Blood on the Sun

CSI: MIAMI

HARM FOR THE HOLIDAYS

PART TWO: HEART ATTACK

DONN CORTEZ

CSI: MIAMI produced by CBS Productions, a business unit of CBS Broadcasting Inc.
and Alliance Atlantis Productions Inc.
Executive Producers: Jerry Bruckheimer, Ann Donahue, Carol Mendelsohn, Anthony E. Zuiker, Jonathan Littman
Series created by Anthony E. Zuiker, Ann Donahue, and Carol Mendelsohn

POCKET STAR BOOKS
New York London Toronto Sydney

An *Original* Publication of POCKET BOOKS

A Pocket Star Book published by
POCKET BOOKS, a division of Simon & Schuster, Inc.
1230 Avenue of the Americas, New York, NY 10020

ISBN-13: 978-0-7434-9952-1
ISBN-10: 0-7434-9952-2

This Pocket Star Books paperback edition February 2007

10 9 8 7 6 5 4 3 2

Cover design by Patrick Kang; Cover photographs by Getty Images

Manufactured in the United States of America

To Steve Forty,
keeper of FRED
and friend of Wreck Beach

CSI: MIAMI

HARM FOR THE HOLIDAYS

PART TWO: HEART ATTACK

1

THE DAY AFTER CHRISTMAS, thirteen men died in Miami.

Two perished in an accident on the freeway, victims of too much holiday cheer and not enough judgment. One died in a fire caused by a string of faulty Christmas tree lights, and one was shot in a drunken family dispute over a football game on television.

The other nine had gathered in a junkyard on the outskirts of Homestead. Two guarded the gate, two were situated in hidden positions with sniper rifles, and four provided heavily armed protection for the last man. He carried no visible weapons, only a large metal suitcase with scarred, khaki-green sides.

The man's name was Marcello Fratelli, known as Miami Marko to his associates. Marko favored extremely tight T-shirts that showed off his steroid-enhanced, overly tanned physique, coupled with the most expensive, custom-tailored trousers he could find. Marko was naturally fair-skinned—blue eyes, blond hair—but generous applications of Florida sunshine, hair dye, and tinted contacts had given him a swarthier look. He wore his jet-black hair slicked back over a thick-browed, bullet-shaped head, and scrupulously shaved the pale stubble that sprouted every morning on his square chin.

Marko was that most dangerous of men, a wannabe. Like wannabes all over the world, he was desperate to be recognized for more than what he was—but Marko didn't want to be a rock star or a model or an actor. Marko wanted to be a Made Man, a Mafioso with the power of the Five Families behind him. And like every security guard who dreamed of becoming a real cop, Marko was willing—more than willing—to take bigger risks and use more extreme methods than any real professional ever would. This made him useful, in the same way a rabid dog was; you never allowed him to get too close, but he was handy to throw at an enemy when more disciplined techniques were unavailable. Marko himself would never be allowed into the Family, but an effort was made to convince him the possibility was there.

Marko knew this was the case. And in typical wannabe fashion, he had decided the only way to circumvent the situation was to do something so dramatic, so groundbreaking, that the Dons would be forced to change their minds. It had taken him a long time to broker this deal, and some of the people he'd had to work with made even Marko hesitate; but everything had come together in the end. Tonight, he would make history.

Marko's first thought when the man walked out from behind a stack of wrecked cars was that he was a bum. He wore what Marko thought of as the Bum Uniform, a long coat over a hooded jacket and jeans, but he wore military-issue boots instead of dirty sneakers, and his jeans weren't nearly grimy enough for someone living on the street.

"Lenny," Marko snapped. "Thought you said you cleared the yard?"

Lenny, a man with shaggy sideburns streaked with gray, shrugged. "He must have been sleeping in a car."

"You were supposed to *look* in the cars."

"I was not sleeping in a car." The voice was rough, slightly muffled by the black scarf wrapped around his face. "I am here to complete our deal."

Marko was instantly alert. He had expected the man to arrive with his own backup, and the fact that he hadn't made him more than a little nervous. "Where are your people?"

"There is only myself."

"Yeah? Where's the product?"

"Nearby. I will tell you where it is hidden once I see what you've brought."

"Fair enough,"said Marko. He walked over to the rusting chassis of an old pickup and set the case down on the hood. He snapped open the latches, lifted the lid, and stepped back. "As specified," he said.

The hooded man stepped forward and examined the contents. "I will need to examine it to verify authenticity," he said.

"Go ahead. It's the real deal."

While the hooded man went to work, Marko debated contacting his men at the gate, letting them know the deal was in progress. But it was a bad idea to make a call in the middle of a transaction, especially one this sensitive. No, he decided; if the lookouts spotted any potential problems at the gate they'd call him on his cell, just like they'd prearranged. Trouble that realized its potential before a call could be made would also certainly announce itself, probably in a hail of gunfire.

And as for his two men with rifles, there was no need to talk to them—they were watching right now through telescopic sights outfitted with night-vision. If the hooded man so much as twitched wrong, he'd get a Teflon-coated armor-piercing round right through the heart.

The man finished what he was doing and closed the case with a snap. "I am satisfied," he announced. "Sadly, you will not be."

"Excuse me?" said Marko.

"I will be unable to provide the payment promised," the hooded man said. He stood loosely, his arms at his sides. Calm brown eyes above a black scarf met Marko's unbelieving stare.

"Look, pal," said Marko. "You want what's in that case, you better produce fifty kilos of Afghani smack real quick, or you're going home empty-handed."

"I think not," the man said quietly.

Marko snapped his fingers. The four men standing behind him produced machine pistols and leveled them at the hooded man.

"If you're about to pull out a badge," said Marko, "it's the last thing you'll ever do."

"I am not a police officer."

The calmer the man was, the more nervous Marko got. "Okay," he said. "Open that coat, and do it slow."

The man complied. There were two bulky-looking automatics stuck in the waistband of his jeans.

"Pull 'em out, thumb and forefinger only."

The hooded man did so.

"Throw 'em over."

The man tossed both at the same time. The guns arced through the air and landed at the feet of Marko's men.

"Okay," said Marko. "I got your weapons, I got you outnumbered, I got the drop on you. If you don't have the heroin, what the hell *do* you have?"

"A small switch," the hooded man said, "held between my teeth."

The handles of both automatics were packed with plastique.

Four of the men were killed instantly. Marko

was slammed face-first into the ground; only the hooded man managed to remain standing.

Somehow, Marko held on to consciousness. There was a monumental ringing in his ears, as if he were standing on top of a gigantic bell that had just been struck.

That's why I can't hear the shots, he thought groggily. *When Carlo and Little Henry put a bullet through this guy's head, I won't hear a thing.*

He raised his head, pushing himself up on his elbows, hoping to maybe see the top of the guy's head come off. He couldn't feel anything below his waist.

The hooded man stood there as if nothing had happened. He made eye contact with Marko, then pointed with his finger—first to the right, then to the left.

Directly at the places Marko's snipers had concealed themselves.

The hooded man brought his index finger up to his throat and drew it quickly across.

Marko understood. Somehow, he knew that the hooded man had killed them without help—quickly, silently, efficiently. And when the two guards at the gate came running to investigate the explosion, he'd kill them, too.

It was the last thing Miami Marko ever got right.

Lieutenant Horatio Caine surveyed the carnage grimly. Seven bodies, abandoned like the junked vehicles around them. Alexx had examined four that apparently died in twin explosions and was now inspecting a fifth.

"This boy worked out," she said. "But from the acne, I'd say he had a little chemical assistance, too."

"I'm sure you're right," said Horatio. "But I don't think steroids were the primary drug involved here."

"Don't see too many cases of 'roid rage involving high explosives," she admitted. "But this man wasn't killed like the others—he was injured by the blasts, but he was still alive when his throat was cut."

Horatio nodded. "I recognize him, Alexx—his name is Marcello Fratelli, known as Miami Marko on the street. He's a player in the local mob scene, but not a major one."

"Think he was looking to move up in the world?"

"If so," said Horatio, "all he managed was a distance of six feet. In the wrong direction . . . what about the last two?"

She checked the first of the two bodies that lay sprawled a short distance away. "Gunshot wound to the chest," she said. "Through-and-through."

She moved on to the next. "Huh," she said. "Horatio, take a look at this."

Horatio peered at the corpse. "Looks like the same thing," he said.

"Yeah. *Exactly* the same thing. One shot, straight through the heart."

"Which suggests our shooter was either very good or very sure of himself. Maybe even a sniper . . ."

"H," Delko called out. He stood on the other side of the crime scene, taking photos. "Got a blood trail."

Horatio walked over to inspect his CSI's find. "Not only that," he said, "but it looks like the donor was traveling toward, not away from the murders. Let's see where this leads . . ."

They followed the trail away from the bodies, into a rusting maze built of vehicles crushed into cubes and stacked like a giant toddler's building blocks. It ended on top of a pile of the blocks themselves, where another body lay on top of a blood-soaked blanket, still clutching a rifle with a telescopic sight.

"What do you think, H?" asked Delko. "Maybe this guy shot the two down below before getting killed himself?"

"I don't think so, Eric." Horatio lifted the barrel of the rifle carefully with one gloved finger and sniffed the end. "This weapon hasn't been fired. He never got off a shot."

"Well, there's only two reasons for him to be here. Either he was insurance against a double cross—"

"—or part of a double cross himself," Horatio finished. "Either way, this has all the markings of a deal gone extremely wrong. The question is, who walked away . . . and with what."

"So far, all the vics seem to belong to the same set," said Delko. "I think three of them are even wearing the same brand of shoes."

"Which means there was a clear winner in this dispute—but that blood trail tells us the other side may have taken some hits, too. Let's do a thorough search of this entire yard, Eric; this may not be the only body we find."

It didn't take long to locate the other sniper, positioned inside the cab of a wheelless semi-trailer. "Looks like the work of the same person," Delko said. "Throat was cut from behind."

"Yes, and the killer had to reach through the window to do it," Horatio pointed out. "Without alerting the victim or any of his friends."

"Sounds like a pro."

"So are we, my friend. So are we . . ."

Horatio Caine *was* a professional, one of the best in his field. He was also deeply troubled.

What was on his mind wasn't the nine bodies in the junkyard, though he knew it should be. No, what was bothering him was a man named Abdus Sattar Pathan.

Pathan's stage name was the Brilliant Batin. He performed primarily on cruise ships, and though most people would describe him as a magician, Batin himself would not. He was a devout Muslim, following a branch of Islam that regarded the practice of magic—even stage magic—as blasphemy. He had reconciled this seeming contradiction by hiding his faith his entire life—even from his family, who were also devout Muslims.

Horatio had uncovered Batin's secret in the course of an investigation, but he had been unable to prove that Batin had faked his own kidnapping in order to extort money from his father, a Saudi Arabian oil magnate. That was what Horatio had initially believed, anyway; after being manipulated into a wild-goose chase all over Miami, he'd realized that the kidnapping was just a diversion to occupy his attention.

It was a conclusion he reached just in time. A landmine planted in a Miami nightclub claimed the life of an FBI agent instead of its intended victim—Horatio. *What,* he'd wondered, *was so important that Pathan would murder a federal officer just to draw attention away from it?*

He still didn't know—but Pathan had "escaped" from his supposed captors on Christmas Day. The day before nine men had been efficiently slaughtered in a Miami junkyard . . .

These were the thoughts running through Horatio's mind as he pulled his Hummer into the parking lot of the Miami-Dade crime lab. He was so preoccupied he didn't see Calleigh Duquesne until he almost walked into her at the front door.

"Horatio,"said Calleigh, nimbly sidestepping her boss. "You look a little distracted."

"I suppose I am," he said, giving her a self-conscious smile. "You heard about the junkyard shooting?"

"I did," she said. "Delko told me there were a lot of guns involved, but hardly any bullets."

They fell in step beside each other down the hall. "That's true," said Horatio. "I believe Delko managed to recover both of them; they should be waiting for you in Ballistics."

"Great. Holidays are nice, but I always find I'm eager to get back to work. Of course, I guess I could solve that problem by just never leaving . . . you know, like some people?"

He stopped, cocked his head to the side, and gave her a look. She returned it—as usual—with an open-eyed, innocent stare, but she couldn't maintain it.

"All right, I'll stop mother-henning," she said with a smile. "Besides, I know you go home every night—your appearance is never less than dapper. I was referring more to your mental state."

He gave her a single, slow nod. "I know. And I appreciate your concern. But these shootings . . . I can't help but wonder if they're connected to the Pathan case."

She frowned. "What makes you think that?"

"I'm not sure. I'm convinced Pathan was trying to distract me from something, so my radar is extremely sensitive at the moment . . . It could just be a drug deal gone wrong. But something about it just doesn't sit right . . ."

"You recover anything else of interest?"

"Some blood that may be the shooter's. Valera's running the DNA now."

"Well, I'll get right to work on those bullets."

"Good."

Horatio watched the CSI walk away and reflected on how lucky he was to have her on his team. Calleigh Duquesne was smart, resourceful, and had an internal thermosat that was under her complete control; she could go from radiating warm, Southern hospitality to having ice water in her veins in the blink of one of her long-lashed eyes. Anyone who thought the blond beauty got by solely on her looks and charm soon found out otherwise . . . although there was no question both of those attributes were part of her arsenal.

He headed for the DNA lab. Maxine Valera looked up from the test results she was studying and said, "Horatio? I don't have anything for you yet."

"I know," said Horatio. "I just wanted to ask if you still had the blood data from the Pathan kidnapping." Pathan's residence had been splashed with blood from an apparent arterial wound, but Horatio believed the magician had faked it with a small pump and fluid from his own body.

"The FBI took all my files, Horatio," said Valera. "You know that."

"I do. But I also know that files can be copied . . . and if there's one thing a scientist hates, it's losing information."

"That's true. You know another thing a scientist hates? Getting in trouble with federal authorities." Valera was a good tech, but an unfortunate mistake had put her in legal hot water a while back, leading to much of her work being called into question. Horatio knew she hadn't done anything wrong, but it had made her a little gun-shy.

"I understand," he said. "And I would never ask you to do anything you might be blamed for. However, the other thing about files is that—sometimes—they find their way mysteriously from one place to another, with no apparent human agency responsible."

She studied him frankly, her large brown eyes unblinking. "I suppose that sort of thing happens," she said. "Even in Miami."

"*Especially* in Miami . . . so here's what I want you to do. Get me the analysis of the blood from this morning's crime scene ASAP—and maybe by that time this hypothetical file will give me something to compare it to."

Valera sighed. "Okay, Horatio. For you."

"Not for me, Maxine. For the nine dead men we found today in an auto graveyard."

Someone had tried to kill Horatio.

This was the single thought going through Ryan Wolfe's mind, over and over. Wolfe's obsessive-compulsive tendencies were largely under control, but every now and then something would lodge itself deeply in the grooves of his psyche and be impossible to get out. If he was lucky, it was simply a song or phrase, something of relatively minor importance that he could suppress or ignore. However, if he was unlucky what would get stuck would be something completely irrelevant, like a sequence of numbers. Numbers could be like burrs, getting under the skin of his condition and producing a mental itch that could seriously impair his concentration. That only happened in extreme situations, though; Wolfe hadn't had a number attack in years—even though he now worked with all sorts of numbers every day—and he doubted he ever would.

But—*someone had tried to kill Horatio.*

Wolfe had been deep in his own case when it happened, and his single-mindedness had prevented him from really focusing on the assassination attempt. But it had started to gnaw at him on Christmas Day; visions of Horatio's body lying on Alexx's table kept intruding into the whirl of presents and food and family. Now, he was determined to do whatever he could to help nail the assassin.

"Horatio?" said Wolfe, standing in the door to his boss's office. "Got a minute?"

Horatio looked up from some paperwork. "Certainly, Mister Wolfe. What's on your mind?"

"I was just wondering about the status of the Afterpartylife investigation."

Horatio raised an auburn eyebrow. "The nightclub bombing? That's a federal case, Mister Wolfe—the FBI don't take losing one of their own lightly."

Wolfe put his hands in his back pockets and shifted his feet. "I know that. But the bomber wasn't after the agent that died—he was after *you*."

"So it would seem," Horatio acknowledged. "But I'm still here . . ."

"No offense, H, but—if someone tried to kill *me*, I wouldn't leave the investigation in the hands of the Feebs."

Horatio smiled. "None taken, Mister Wolfe—though I'm sure our esteemed colleagues at the Bureau would feel otherwise. But this particular case—despite the appearance of a personal threat to me—is not the important one."

"It's not?"

"No. Like every other facet of the Pathan kidnapping, it was simply meant to direct our attention elsewhere. However, with the FBI now pursuing those avenues, we are free to concentrate on other aspects of the case."

"Such as?"

"Such as Francis Buccinelli."

Francis Buccinelli was the name of Pathan's lawyer—at least, it had been the name on his falsified credentials. He had shown up to talk to Pathan after the man had been arrested for assaulting a convenience store clerk, apparently incensed by a picture of a nude Middle Eastern woman on the cover of a men's magazine. Pathan had refused to have his fingerprints taken—until his lawyer had talked to him. After that, he had become extremely cooperative, blaming his previous behavior on a mild concussion.

The evidence, once processed, proved contradictory. Footage from a security camera seemed to show Pathan assaulting the clerk, but it also showed him leaving a print on the magazine—a print that Calleigh proved wasn't Pathan's. The assailant also used a scarf to cover his face, further confusing the issue. When the store clerk refused to identify Pathan as his attacker, he was released.

"So," Wolfe asked, "you think this Buccinelli smuggled something in that let Pathan doctor his own fingerprints?"

"Pathan's a professional illusionist," said Horatio. "I haven't figured out the specific mechanism yet, but if he could fake almost bleeding to death from a cut throat he could fake his own prints."

"Well, I just wanted to let you know I'm available," said Wolfe. "Now that the Patrick case is closed, I mean."

"Thank you," said Horatio. "As a matter of fact, I was planning on assigning you to that very thing . . ."

"So where do we start?"

Horatio got up from his chair and walked around the desk. "We start," he said, "at the beginning. We go back and talk to the subject of the initial assault, see if we can learn anything new. If nothing else, maybe we can discover what he's so afraid of."

"Hey there, Calleigh," Frank Tripp said as he walked into the Ballistics lab. He had his suit jacket slung over one beefy shoulder and his shirtsleeves rolled up.

"Oh, hey, Frank," Calleigh said. "How was your Christmas?"

"Well, my house is still standing and nobody shot me, so I guess it went all right," he said. "How about you?"

"About the same," she said. "Mom behaved herself, so that's something."

"Those the bullets from the junkyard shooting?"

"They are. You have an interest?"

"I busted Miami Marko a couple times—always knew he'd come to a bad end. He used good sense and judgment like a hurricane uses diplomacy."

"Well, it looks like his choices finally caught up with him," said Calleigh. "Whoever killed him and eight of his associates was definitely not the forgiving type."

"What do you figure—mob hit?"

"I don't know," said Calleigh. "Most gangsters—whether they prefer Tupac or Sinatra—aren't known for their restraint. They apply bullets the way some people apply insecticide."

"I know what you mean—I've cleaned up my share of spray-bys. Don't seem to care who gets hit, as long as their target takes a bullet."

"Exactly—and in an isolated place like an auto salvage yard, there's even less reason to be careful. But the two GSW vics were both killed by a single shot to the heart."

Tripp frowned. "Wait a minute. I thought you said they found nine bodies?"

"They did. Two were shot, four were killed by explosives, and three had their throats cut."

Tripp's frown deepened. "That doesn't sound like

any gangland killing *I've* ever heard of. Sounds almost—"

"Military?" said Calleigh. "I was just thinking the same thing. But here's the really strange thing. These bullets came from a MAC 10 machine pistol."

"So you're saying the shooters could have used full auto to blast away—but decided *not* to? Why? If they were setting off explosions they couldn't be worried about noise."

"Maybe," said Calleigh thoughtfully, "they thought two bullets were all they needed."

Talwinder Jhohal, the man Abdus Sattar Pathan had supposedly assaulted, was already back at work. Horatio had decided to talk to the shopkeeper at his store—hoping that being in familiar surroundings might give the man more confidence in talking about the incident—and took Wolfe with him.

"Mister Jhohal," Horatio said to the man behind the counter. "I'm glad to see you're back on your feet."

"I am fine," the man said curtly. "And I have nothing to say to you."

"Mister Jhohal, just hear me out. I know you're worried for your family, and I'm not going to try to convince you to do anything that would put them in jeopardy."

"No?" Jhohal asked suspiciously.

"No. If you don't want to press charges against the man that attacked you, I respect that."

The hardness in the man's eyes eased off a little. "Then why are you here?"

"Because I think you're a good man," said Horatio. "And I don't think you want to see anyone else's family get hurt, either."

The shopkeeper looked away. "There is nothing I can do."

Wolfe had been hanging back, letting Horatio talk, but now he interjected, "Well, what if you could? Without testifying, without anyone ever knowing?"

Jhohal frowned. "What do you mean?"

"All we're looking for," Wolfe said, "is a little information. Nothing official, no written statement. Anything you can tell us about the attack or attacker, anything at all, might help."

Jhohal sighed. "I do not know . . ."

"Mister Jhohal," said Horatio, "I'm not asking you lightly. We have reason to believe that the man who assaulted you is an extremely dangerous individual, and if we don't stop him he is certainly going to hurt others. I know you don't want that on your conscience . . ."

Horatio paused and made eye contact. "I promise you," he said softly, "that no harm will come to your family as a result of this."

"I—I don't want anyone else to get hurt."

"Of course not."

Jhohal glanced around, as if he were afraid someone were watching; there was no one else in the store except for a white-haired woman in a pink dress. "All right," Jhohal said. "I will tell you what I remember, but I do not think it will do much good."

"You let us worry about that," said Horatio. "Now . . . tell us exactly what happened."

"It was about eleven o'clock. I was working alone in the store. This man came in—dark-skinned, about six feet tall. He wore a long, dark coat. He had a black scarf wrapped around his neck, but not his face. He did not cover his face until he approached the counter with the magazine."

"The angle on the security camera didn't catch his face when he entered," Wolfe said.

Horatio pulled a picture from his pocket. "Is this the man?"

Jhohal looked at it, hesitated, then said, "Yes. That is the man."

"Did he go straight to the magazine rack?" asked Horatio.

"No. He walked down several aisles, looking for something. He had it in his hand when he walked past the magazines and one of them caught his attention."

"Security footage didn't show him holding anything but the magazine," said Wolfe. "He must have put it down before the attack."

"Mister Jhohal," said Horatio, "do you remember what it was?"

Jhohal shook his head. "Something small. That's all I remember."

Wolfe walked over to the magazine rack, a head-high wooden structure against one wall. "If it were something small, he probably would have put it down right here," said Wolfe, pointing to the narrow ledge the bottom row of magazines rested on.

"Nothing there now," said Horatio. "But that's also the place people invariably put down a magazine they've been leafing through and decide not to buy . . ." He lifted a copy of *Rolling Stone* that currently occupied the spot—revealing a small, rectangular box beneath it.

"Toothpicks," said Wolfe.

"Bag it, please," said Horatio. He turned back to Jhohal. "Now . . . please describe what happened next, Mister Jhohal."

"He approached the counter with a magazine in his hand. He had pulled the scarf up over his mouth and nose. I did not know what was happening at first; if he was going to rob me, why did he have the magazine? But then he began to shout, waving the magazine around and thrusting it in my face."

"And what was he shouting?" asked Horatio.

"That it was blasphemy, a sin in the eyes of Allah. That I was a, a *whoremonger* for selling such a thing. That was the word he used."

"I see. Did he say anything else?"

"Yes. He said that this country was a disease on the face of the world, and that God would destroy it and everyone in it."

"Strong words."

"I told him he was crazy, to get out of my store. That's when he attacked me. I fought back, but he was strong—very strong. I thought he was going to kill me."

"He very well might have, Mister Jhohal, but you got lucky; after knocking you out, he slipped on the blood from your broken nose and wound up unconscious himself."

"So I have been told," said Jhohal. He reached up to touch the bandage on the back of his head gingerly. "Do you want to know what I think? I think God was looking out for one of us . . . and it wasn't him."

"I hope you're right, Mister Jhohal. But in the absence of divine intervention, you can definitely count on my help. Okay?"

Jhohal nodded. "Okay."

"Now, I understand why you might be reluctant to discuss this next part, Mister Jhohal, but if I'm going to help you protect your family, I need as much information as you can give me. I need to know about how you were threatened."

"They—they called me. In the hospital."

"I don't mean to contradict you, Mister Jhohal, but hospital staff told me the only call you received was from your family."

Jhohal nodded again, and now Horatio could see the fear in his eyes. "Yes. Somebody called me—from *my own house*. He described things in my living room, told me my children were upstairs asleep. My wife never heard a thing. He said if I were to press charges, that terrible things would happen to them. *Terrible* things."

"I understand. Did this person identify himself in any way?"

"He said—" Jhohal swallowed. "He said he was *mujahideen.*"

Horatio's eyes narrowed. "*Mujahideen.* You're sure?"

"Yes."

Wolfe had finished bagging the box of toothpicks and had walked up to stand beside Horatio. "All done."

"Good, let's get that right to the lab. Mister Jhohal, I'm going to have a patrol car do a regular check on your house. Here's my card—call me if you think you or your family are in danger. I promise you, no one will ever know you talked to me."

"Thank you," Jhohal said. "Thieves I can deal with. But this . . ."

"I know. Don't worry, Mister Jhohal. You did the right thing."

Once they were back on the sidewalk, Wolfe said, "Did I hear that right?"

"You did, Mister Wolfe. Whoever threatened that man's family is claiming to be a member of an underground Islamic militia."

Horatio took out his sunglasses and put them on. "Or as they're usually called, a terrorist cell . . ."

2

"You really think Pathan's involved with terrorists?" Wolfe asked. He stared thoughtfully out the window of the Hummer as Horatio drove them back to the lab.

"When it comes to Pathan, there are few things I'm certain about," said Horatio. "This could just be more smoke and mirrors. But the landmine that killed Agent Hargood *was* an Iraqi model . . . and Delko turned up information linking Pathan's father to Islamic extremists."

"So whatever's really going on, it's a lot bigger than just a faked kidnapping."

"Definitely. And I suspect our friend, Special Agent Sackheim, knows more about the situation than he's letting on . . ."

Dennis Sackheim was the FBI agent in charge of their investigation into the Pathan kidnapping. He and Horatio hadn't exactly gotten along—and Sackheim had eventually pulled rank and yanked the entire investigation away from Horatio, including confiscating all the evidence his lab had collected. By that point Horatio had already concluded the kidnapping itself was a dead end, but Sackheim's high-handed behavior still rankled.

"You think the guy that called Jhohal was the same one who posed as Pathan's lawyer?" Wolfe asked.

"Possible, but not proven." Horatio didn't mention a possible connection to the shootings at the junkyard; so far, he had nothing more than a hunch to justify his suspicions. "We need to verify Jhohal's story. Check his phone records, go to his house and see if there's any evidence of a break-in."

"You got it. What about the box of toothpicks?"

"I'll process that myself."

Toothpicks, Horatio thought. He'd found toothpicks in Pathan's house, as well—it was one of the clues that tipped him to the fact that Pathan was a practicing Muslim. Certain sects forbid the use of toothbrushes, insisting on the more traditional toothpick—but the box in Pathan's residence was the large size, holding at least five hundred, and had been half-full. *Why would he be buying another?*

He didn't know, but at least it was something. Maybe the box itself would tell him more.

He dropped Wolfe off at the lab so the young CSI could get his own vehicle, and headed inside to get the toothpicks to the lab. He ran into Frank Tripp just coming off the elevator.

"Horatio, you got a minute?"

"Sure, Frank. What's up?"

"More like who's down. I heard about Marko and his boys."

"You've had dealings with him in the past, right?"

"Yeah, I busted him a few times on weapons charges. Never got anything major to stick."

"You want one last swing at him?"

"Guess I do. Thought I'd sniff around, see if I can find out what he had his fingers into."

"Much appreciated, Frank. I'll keep you in the loop."

"All right, then. I'll talk to you later."

Horatio had just gotten the box to the lab when his cell phone rang. "Caine."

"Lieutenant." The voice belonged to Dennis Sackheim; his usually flat tone was edged with something else. Anger? "I have some information for you regarding the Pathan case."

Now, *that* was a surprise; Horatio had thought the only way he'd ever learn anything new from Sackheim was from an autopsy. "Is that so? I'm listening . . ."

"The FBI is no longer in charge of the investigation. You'll be contacted shortly by a woman named Quadiri, who will have full access to any and all evidence collected in the case by your people and mine."

"And who would this Quadiri be, exactly?"

"She can explain herself," said Sackheim bluntly.

"Second, as part of Abdus Sattar Pathan's debriefing, we took his fingerprints. We were extremely careful."

"And?"

"And the prints still don't match the one you took from the convenience store assault. Either Pathan is innocent—or your people were the ones who screwed up."

Sackheim hung up.

Well, well, Horatio thought to himself. *Do I detect the flavor of extremely sour grapes, Special Agent Sackheim? Whoever this Quadiri is, I get the feeling she didn't make a very good impression on you . . .*

He liked her already.

Ryan Wolfe checked out a Hummer and proceeded to Talwinder Jhohal's home, a tidy two-story house in Hialeah. Before knocking on the door, he called Jhohal's store. "Mister Jhohal? This is Ryan Wolfe. I was one of the officers you just talked to . . . right. I know you don't want to alarm your family, but it would greatly assist our investigation if I could take a look at your home and see if the person who broke in left any traces behind. I promise I'll be discreet . . ."

As it turned out, discretion wasn't necessary. Afraid for his family's safety, Jhohal had sent them to visit relatives; the house was empty. Jhohal gave Wolfe his permission to enter and look around, and even told him where to find a key.

He didn't waste time checking the phone for

prints—at this point, all he'd find would be those of the family. Instead, he concentrated on possible points of entry, checking all the doors and windows. He found what he was looking for in the dining room, a window with some scrape marks at the bottom of the frame and a cheap, latch-style lock that had been forced open. He took some pictures and then went outside.

He was lucky; it hadn't rained in several days, and there was still a footprint in the dirt below the window. He took more pictures, then cast the footprint in quick-setting plaster. He dusted the window for prints, too, but wasn't surprised when he got nothing; whoever broke in had no doubt worn gloves.

It wasn't much, but at least it was consistent with Jhohal's story. Somebody had broken into his house and called Jhohal while he lay in a hospital bed, all without rousing his sleeping family.

No wonder the guy's scared, Wolfe thought. *I'd be terrified . . .*

"Horatio Caine?"

Horatio looked up from the toothpick box he was examining. "Yes?"

The woman who'd addressed him stood in the door to the lab, a briefcase in one hand. If he'd seen her in the hall, he would have assumed she was a lawyer; her jet-black hair was drawn back in a tight braid, and her black business suit and white blouse were typical of what he often saw down at the courthouse.

"I'm Nadira Quadiri," she said. Her skin was a light, dusky brown, her eyes dark and serious. "Homeland Security." She stepped forward and offered her hand.

Horatio stripped off one blue glove first. Her grip was strong and confident, the handshake quick and professional.

"Ms. Quadiri," Horatio said. "Would I be right in assuming you're now the federal officer in charge of the Pathan investigation?"

"That's correct." Her tone, while businesslike, held none of the cold formality Sackheim's had. "And—like you—I believe in doing my homework. Special Agent Sackheim didn't have a very high opinion of your lab, but I checked out your jacket; your conviction record is impressive."

"Thank you. I work with good people."

"You don't seem too surprised that Homeland Security is stepping in." Her eyes studied him frankly.

"Considering who's involved, I'm surprised you didn't show up sooner."

"We've been monitoring the situation. We didn't think our direct involvement was warranted until that landmine blew."

"I see."

"Do you? It can be hard to see when you're kept in the dark." She smiled, but there was no malice in it.

Horatio smiled back. "That's true. Are you offering me a flashlight, Ms. Quadiri?"

"Call me Nadira. Lack of cooperation between different law enforcement agencies—both federal and local—was cited as one of the contributing factors to nine-eleven. Homeland Security was created to eliminate those factors; we have a very different approach to interagency communication."

"I'm glad to hear it. Does this mean we'll be sharing information?"

"I'll tell you as much as I can," she said. "But this concerns national security, Lieutenant; on certain matters, my hands are tied."

"I understand. Can you confirm this involves an Islamic terrorist group?"

Her face betrayed no emotion, but she studied him carefully for a second before answering. "We have reason to believe one may be involved, yes. What led you to that conclusion?"

It was Horatio's turn to pause. "I'm sorry," he said. "I don't mean to start our relationship off on the wrong foot, but I can't disclose that."

"Why not?" She didn't sound angry, just curious.

"I made a promise," said Horatio. "My source had his family threatened; any information that comes from his direction will have to be handled by me."

"That's acceptable," she said. "As long as you don't mind passing that information along, you can keep your source as private as you like, Lieutenant."

"Good. Thank you, Nadira . . . and please, call me Horatio."

"All right, Horatio. Why don't you tell me what you've learned so far, and I'll see if I can fill in the blanks."

Horatio told her his theory: The kidnapping was staged to draw attention away from something bigger. He told her about Francis Buccinelli, and his firm belief that—despite the evidence—Pathan had managed to fake his fingerprints while in custody.

"I'm willing to believe that's possible," said Quadiri. "Maybe his lawyer smuggled in a fake ten-card and he used sleight of hand to switch them."

"Right now I'm less interested in how he did it than in what he plans to do next," said Horatio. He told her about the bodies found in the junkyard.

"I'll see what I can find out about that," said Quadiri. "By the way—I heard about that stunt you pulled with the feather. Nicely done."

After deducing that Pathan was a Muslim, Horatio had confronted him with a piece of rope tied in a knot and challenged him to blow on it—something he knew Pathan couldn't do; the Quran defined a magician as "one who blows on knots," and no magician would be allowed through the gates of Heaven. Pathan never billed himself as a magician, and always declared his illusions to be works of skill—but when Horatio placed a feather on top of the knot, Pathan's skill had failed him. Knowing he couldn't defeat Horatio's simple test, he had refused to try.

"Well," said Horatio, "science doesn't always require a lab."

"Indeed it doesn't," she said. "Science is an approach, not a catalogue of equipment."

"'In the creation of the heavens and the earth and in the alternation of the night and the day there are indeed signs for men of understanding,'" said Horatio.

Her smile grew broader, revealing even, white teeth. "You quote from the Quran. Are you a scholar, or merely showing off your research skills?"

"You got me," he admitted. "My knowledge of Islam is fairly recent and not that extensive—though what I've learned so far has proved intriguing. I wasn't aware that so many scientific disciplines have their roots in the Muslim world."

"It surprises most people," Quadiri said. "Do you mind if I sit? I've been traveling since five A.M."

"Please."

She pulled an office chair on wheels over and lowered herself onto it gracefully, setting her briefcase down beside her. She crossed her legs, then clasped her hands lightly across one brown knee. "Religion and science are seen, for the most part, to be at odds. You can have faith or you can have knowledge. The apple in the story of the Garden of Eden is widely regarded as a symbol of knowledge, and by choosing to partake of it Adam and Eve lost their innocence and were banished."

Horatio leaned against the table and crossed his arms. "But the Islamic tradition is different."

"Yes. Despite the restrictive rules of the more traditional sects, Islam as a whole has always embraced science. The universe was created by Allah; how then, can knowledge of His creation be wrong? Islamic scholars see the hand of God in all things, and this knowledge makes their faith stronger, not weaker."

"It all comes down to what you do with that knowledge, doesn't it . . ."

She nodded soberly. "Always. Some faiths suppress scientific inquiry because they feel an informed populace poses a threat to their authority; almost every major religion—including Islam—has done this at some point in its history. Even during the enlightenment of the Renaissance, scientists like Galileo were persecuted by the Catholic Church. What most people don't realize is that before the Renaissance—during what the Western nations call the Dark Ages—the torch of science was being carried by the Muslim world. In fact, this period is referred to as the Islamic Golden Age; it's when the Abbasid caliphs of Baghdad established an academy to translate and study Greek and Sanskrit manuscripts of scientific interest. Many important works by Greeks like Euclid and Aristotle only survive to this day because they were recorded in this manner."

Horatio nodded. "Some people claim the scientific method actually originated with a man named Ibn-Al-Haitham, in his book on optics."

She raised an eyebrow in approval. "That's true. Roger Bacon, the man the West usually credits with creating the scientific method, was known to be familiar with his work. Mathematics, in particular, has much to thank the Muslim world for: words like algebra, zenith, and even zero were coined by Islamic scholars."

"I sense, Nadira," said Horatio, tilting his head slightly to the side and studying her, "that your expertise in this area is not a coincidence."

She met his eyes calmly. "Again, correct. I have a degree in Islamic studies, speak four Middle Eastern dialects fluently and two more passably. I was born in Tehran and came to the U.S. with my family when I was thirteen. I am currently head of a Special Interdiction Unit for the Atlantic coastal border, tasked with the surveilling and prevention of terrorist activity connected to or based in the State of Florida. I hope that answers a few of your questions."

"Some, but not all . . . most of which have to do with Khasib Pathan."

She nodded again. "Abdus Sattar Pathan's father. Yes. He is, in fact, the reason I am here. How much do you know about him?"

"Mostly, what's in the public record: he's wealthy, a member of the Saudi royal family, has four wives, nine children, and a mansion on Fisher Island. One of my CSIs turned up a possible connection to a radical Islamic group, but nothing concrete."

"Your CSI must be good—Khasib usually covers his tracks carefully. He's funneled financial aid to terrorist groups for years, but we've never been able to prove it."

"And his son?"

"That's the strange part. Abdus and Khasib are estranged, have been for years—they see each other rarely, only for important family functions, and even then barely acknowledge each other. Abdus's faith was something we never suspected; it raises many questions."

"It certainly does. Such as what Abdus's real relationship with Khasib is—and whether or not they share the same politics as well as the same faith."

Nadira picked her briefcase off the floor, set it in her lap and opened it. "Exactly. Which is why we need your help." She pulled out a thick manila envelope sealed with tape that bore the insignia of Homeland Security. "We don't want to tip our hand," Nadira said. "If they suspect an antiterrorism unit has been alerted, they'll suspend whatever action they have planned. But you're already involved; any further investigation on your part will be seen as standard operating procedure."

She offered him the envelope. "This is all the intel we have on Khasib and his activities over the last six years. If we can assist you behind the scenes in any way, we will."

Horatio stripped off his remaining glove before accepting it. He turned the envelope over in his hands, but didn't open it. "Are you telling me I'm in charge?"

"Consider this a partnership. We both want the

same thing—to prevent whatever Khasib and his son have planned."

"Us against them, Ms. Quadiri?"

"No, Horatio. Life against death. Regardless of whatever flag or faith it tries to hide behind."

"I believe," Horatio said slowly, raising his eyes from the envelope, "that we are on the same page, Nadira."

"Good," she said. Her eyes held Horatio's for an instant, then moved to the box he'd been examining on the light table. "Is this connected to the case?"

"It is." He told her about where it had been found. "I was just about to dust it for prints."

"Then I'll let you get back to work. I'm staying at the Graciana Hotel; you can contact me there or on the cell number on my business card. It's in the file."

"I'll do that," said Horatio. He reached into his pocket for one of his own cards, but she stopped him with a raised hand.

"No need," she said, smiling. "I've already got your number . . ."

3

The folder Nadira had given Horatio proved interesting reading.

Khasib Pathan was a very dangerous man—dangerous in the sense that he was a fanatic with a great deal of money. When they'd first met, Khasib had seemed to Horatio an imposing figure, used to having his orders followed; and the concern, the worry he showed when his son was apparently kidnapped had seemed genuine.

Now, Horatio wasn't so sure.

Khasib had channeled funds to a number of terrorist organizations in Afghanistan, Palestine, and Iraq. Like any movement fueled by zealotry, such groups were volatile and often split into different factions. Disturbingly, every time one of the groups he patronized underwent a schism, Khasib always switched his funding to the more radical splinter.

The file contained a list of attacks the groups had

undertaken: beheadings, car bombs, assassinations. The style of the report was as dry and clinical as any scientific study, and Horatio had the sudden feeling that Khasib Pathan was doing exactly that: conducting research. Offering cheese to a variety of rats, and seeing which way they ran. Always rewarding the one that was willing to go further, commit worse acts.

And he'd been doing so for over thirty years.

Thirty years. That's a long time—a long time to study, to learn, to test out theories.

A long time to plan . . .

But plan what? What was it that had taken Khasib Pathan three decades to shape?

The report didn't speculate on that, nor did it mention Abdus except in passing. Whatever Khasib had in mind, either it didn't involve him—or the Pathan family's capacity for deception went deeper than anyone realized.

Sean Daltry stared at the case sitting in the storage locker before sliding it out. He had never thought he would be handling such a thing, let alone be entrusted with its safekeeping and transport. From what he'd heard, those in the very highest levels of the RIRA had argued both for and against it, and it had caused such bitter divisiveness that the final decision was to sell it and use the money for less controversial ways to support the organization's goals.

That was why Daltry was here in Miami, to

arrange the transfer. Daltry was a hard man, a soldier born, willing to do whatever it took. He was responsible for many casualties on the other side, and it mattered little to him if the body growing cold was that of a British soldier or a Protestant child; he killed in the name of his God, and that was enough to erase any doubts from his mind.

What he was feeling now wasn't doubt. It was fear.

He slammed the white metal door shut. The storage locker was in a health club in Coral Gables, a place where the middle class came to sweat away their fast-food lunches and beer bellies. He had a lifetime membership courtesy of a local sympathizer, and it made an ideal place to keep items hidden but close at hand. He had planned to keep the case here until it was time to hand it off, but now he was forced to change his plans.

He knew about the deal with Miami Marko. And when he'd heard about the slaughter at the junkyard, he knew who had to be responsible, too.

The Hare.

Daltry went straight from the locker room to the parking lot, putting the case at the foot of the passenger seat in his rented Taurus; there was no way he was letting it out of his sight. He got in and drove east, toward Miami.

He wasn't sure what to do. If the Hare was on his trail he was as good as dead, and only the Hare could have dispatched Marko's crew with such ruthless efficiency. The IRA had always had contacts in law enforcement—there was a long tradition of Irish cops in America, especially on the East Coast—and one of them had leaked a description to Daltry. "It was god-awful," he'd said. "Nine dead—two shot, four blown to hell, and three with their throats cut. Pure butchery."

And a pure butcher is what he is, Daltry thought as he pulled onto the highway. *No wonder he wants what I've got.*

From what his source had told him, it didn't sound like a deal gone wrong—the Hare had eliminated every target methodically, which meant that had been his intention all along. Money couldn't be the objective; the Hare's backers had plenty of that. No, the only reason for a mass execution like that was simple: he was making sure that he remained invisible by killing everyone who could be traced back to him.

Which meant he was going to kill Daltry, as well.

There were precautions he could take, of course. While he had no choice in whether to deliver the case—that had been decided by his superiors, and he prided himself on obeying orders—he could certainly take steps to ensure his own survival. The Hare wouldn't kill him as long as he was the only one who knew where the case was, and right now that was true.

He drove, past what seemed to him to be endless strip malls, the same outlet stores and chain restaurants and gas stations over and over; like God was grabbing them up behind him, shuffling them like a deck of cards and dealing them out in a different order ahead. America seemed to Daltry the most unreal place he'd ever been, a country made entirely of concrete, asphalt, and brightly colored plastic. Even the lushness of Florida vegetation didn't seem authentic—the grass and leaves all had the smooth shininess of high-gloss magazine paper.

He tried to find something on the radio that wasn't rap, country, or gospel. He settled for an eighties station and some old Devo, which fit the prefabricated landscape perfectly.

He cranked the air-conditioning up a notch, too. The Florida heat and humidity was all too real, and Daltry wasn't used to it. He couldn't wait to finish his business and get back home.

Yes. Once the Hare had the case, Daltry wanted to get as far away from America as possible.

He might never have known he was being tracked if he hadn't stopped for gas. The cap for the gas tank slipped out of his fingers when he undid it, hitting the ground and rolling beneath the car. He went down on his knees to retrieve it—and that's when he noticed the small electronic device attached to the underside of the chassis.

Daltry had planted his share of car bombs, and he knew immediately that what he was looking at was too small to be that. It was a GPS tracking beacon, broadcasting his position to a network of satellites that anyone with the right hardware could use to tell exactly where he was.

He considered his options. Destroying the device or leaving it behind would tell his tracker he was aware he was being hunted. He could use it to try to draw his follower into a trap—but if the follower was the Hare, that was unwise in the extreme.

The best strategy would be to transfer the beacon to another vehicle, letting him escape. A large parking lot, preferably underground, would be ideal.

He filled the tank, put the gas cap back on carefully, and paid for his purchase. Getting back on the highway, he kept an eye out for anyone who seemed to be following him; if someone was, he was too good to be detected.

He selected a large mall with a multilevel lot and circled the block it squatted on. The lot had two entrance/exits on opposite sides from each other, which made it perfect. He pulled in.

He drove to a level one away from the top, which seemed to have the fewest cars. He parked beside a black SUV and made sure he wasn't in the line of sight of any security cameras.

He pulled the small folding tool case he always carried out of his pocket and slid beneath the car. It was only the work of a minute to detach the device, and not much longer to attach it firmly to its new host.

There. Now all he had to do was leave, and he should be safe.

He hesitated. There was always the chance he was being monitored directly as well as remotely. No one had followed him into the lot, but he might have been observed entering it. To leave immediately would arouse suspicions that would quickly be confirmed.

Better to leave the car here and proceed on foot. He could catch a bus or a cab from one of the mall's many entrances. He grabbed the case, left the doors unlocked and the keys in the ignition; with any luck the car would be stolen, further confusing his trail.

His footsteps echoed hollowly as he walked toward the elevator. The Miami sky showed in strips of brilliant blue between the concrete pillars that separated the levels, and the air smelled of exhaust and hot rubber.

He got to the elevator, hit the button. The doors opened almost immediately, revealing a single passenger. The man held a cell phone to his ear and was saying, "Hello? Hello? Damn!"

He gave Daltry a frustrated smile. "Reception in these concrete boxes, huh?"

"Yeah," Daltry said noncommittally, and pushed a button for the mall level. He leaned back against the wall, trying to act casual but still keeping a watchful eye on the man. The other passenger wore a cream-colored suit cut from tropical-weight linen, with a green silk tie and brown leather shoes shined to a high luster. He frowned at his cell phone, then slipped it back into his pocket. "Maybe I should switch providers," he sighed.

Maybe you should drop a few dollars on a new cell phone, Daltry thought. He'd gotten so used to seeing phones the size of a deck of cards that the businessman's seemed clunky in comparison; it was at least twice that big.

He smiled to himself, suddenly bemused by the thought; a technology that had seemed miraculous when he was younger was now not only taken for granted but had evolved secondary characteristics more concerned with style than functionality. *Like any beast. First it has to survive, has to find a niche and eat while trying not to be eaten. Once it's managed that, it's time to get sexy.*

The door opened on the mall level and he got out, along with the businessman. Daltry strolled along, keeping an eye out for anyone who might be following him. The crowds of shoppers, though, seemed as blank-eyed as sheep, overloaded by the holidays and caught in the swirl of post-Christmas, preinventory markdowns.

All just a big mating dance, he thought. Engineering was about functionality, but marketing was about seduction. *Brightly colored feathers and birdsong come-ons, all of it. No wonder people talk about getting screwed by salesmen.*

But then, that was the nature of the world, he reflected. Screw or be screwed.

There was a large crowd of people in front of him, apparently waiting to be let into some sort of outlet store. They reached all the way across the mall corridor, an impassible wall of humanity.

He stopped. There was a mall exit just on the other side; he could either backtrack to the elevator and strike off in another direction, which he really didn't feel like doing, or he could find a way through and be outside in a few minutes. He decided to forge ahead—if he stuck close to the wall, he could probably slip by. It was slow going, but he just nodded and smiled and muttered "Excuse me" a lot.

The stacatto burst of gunfire came from behind him.

His head snapped around. He found himself staring into the calm brown eyes of the businessman in the cream-colored suit, only inches away. Midway through the fusillade of shots, Daltry felt an explosion of pain in his chest; somehow, in the middle of a crowd, one of the bullets had found his heart.

As he slumped to the ground, the last thing Daltry saw was the businessman, raising his unfashionably large cell phone to his ear and quickly turning toward the sound of the shots like everyone else.

The case slipped from Daltry's fingers as he collapsed. Nobody noticed the businessman retrieving it and quietly slipping away.

"From the stippling and the wound pattern, I'd say he was shot at close range," Alexx said.

Ryan Wolfe knelt beside the ME. "That's strange. According to witnesses, the shots came from farther down the mall."

Calleigh strolled up, holding a clear evidence bag in one gloved hand. "Which is exactly what our shooter wanted them to think." She held the bag up. "Firecrackers, wired to a remote activator and tossed into a planter. While they were going off, everybody's attention was focused on that—one more shot wouldn't be noticed, especially if the barrel were pressed right against the victim's body. Alexx, is there a muzzle stamp?"

Alexx peered closely. "Looks like, but it's awfully small."

"Twenty-two caliber, maybe?" Calleigh leaned over, studied the wound. "That's interesting."

"Poor guy," Alexx said. "See, this is why I don't set foot in a mall between December and February."

"Well, this was no case of shopper's rage," Wolfe said. "More like an assassination."

"You think it's related to the junkyard shootings?" asked Calleigh.

"Could be," Wolfe said, checking the body for ID. He pulled a wallet out of a pocket and flipped it open. "Sean Daltry. Looks like he was visiting from Ireland."

"From Italian mobsters to Irish tourists?" said Calleigh. "Seems unlikely."

"If this guy was a tourist," said Wolfe, "he was a paranoid one." He pulled a gun from the man's pocket

"SIG-Sauer P250," said Calleigh. "That's a serious weapon. Not the kind of thing you take through customs, either."

"So he must have gotten it here . . . and that's not all." Wolfe was patting down the body as he spoke, and now he pulled up the right trouser leg to reveal a long-bladed knife in an ankle sheath. "Looks like a K-Bar," he said. "Commando blade."

"Mister Daltry was prepared for trouble."

"Not prepared enough," said Alexx.

"I'm going to talk to mall security, see if any of their cameras picked up anything," said Wolfe.

"I'll finish processing the scene,"Calleigh replied.

Wolfe approached the nearest security guard keeping curious shoppers behind the crime scene tape and got directions to the mall's security center. It was located on the administrative floor, just another office with an unobtrusive sign on the door.

The door opened before he knocked. A black man with a prominent gut bulging the buttons of his mall security uniform stood there, a smile on his face.

"Saw you coming," he said, motioning Wolfe inside. "Wouldn't be much good at my job if I didn't, would I?"

"I guess not. I'm Ryan Wolfe, Miami-Dade crime lab."

"Ernie Driver. I'm head of security here."

"Ernie, I'm going to need to look at—"

"Any of the footage of the shooting, I know. I've got it ready to go, but I don't know how much good it'll do you."

"Why's that?"

"Let me show you." A bank of monitors from waist-to-ceiling height covered the far wall; Ernie pulled out an office chair in front of the screens and sank into it, gesturing for Wolfe to do the same.

Wolfe hesitated. He knew he should just grab the footage and take it back to the lab, but he knew how much it would mean to the guard to play cop in a genuine investigation—besides, the guard might have noticed something that someone unfamiliar with the mall wouldn't. Wolfe took a seat beside him.

"Okay," Ernie said, tapping away at a keyboard, "here's the shooting itself. It's a bad angle, the shooter's facing away from the camera, and the crowd obscures most of what's going on. But you can still tell who shot whom."

Wolfe watched the replay. At the same moment everybody else looked in one direction—presumably at the sound of the firecrackers going off—one man turned the other way. Almost instantly, Daltry's face registered shock, then disappeared from view as he collapsed. The man beside him quickly turned to face the firecrackers as well, raising a cell phone to his ear at the same time.

"Wait—where's the gun?" asked Wolfe. "Did he drop it? There wasn't enough time to put it away—"

"I figure someone in the crowd must have picked it up," said Ernie. "I've been going through the footage, trying to spot some likely suspects—"

"No, that's not it," said Wolfe. "Play it again."

Ernie tapped a few keys.

"There," said Wolfe. "Go back and freeze it right when he lifts the cell phone to his ear."

Ernie did so.

"See?" said Wolfe. "Rising up from the aerial?"

"Sonofagun," said Ernie. "Is that a wisp of smoke?"

"Yeah. I'm guessing that model of cell phone isn't exactly standard . . . where does he go after that?"

"Right out the front door," said Ernie. "But it's what he has with him that's interesting." He played the footage.

"The suitcase?" Wolfe asked. "What's so special about that?"

"The fact that the victim was the one carrying it when he arrived on the premises." Ernie called up some more footage, showing both Daltry and the shooter exiting an elevator.

"They got off together," said Wolfe. "But it doesn't look like they know each other. So the shooter must have been stalking him the entire time. Can we tell when he got on the elevator?"

"Sure. He gets on at eleven-twenty-seven, on the top floor. Then he just rides up and down for the next ten minutes . . . waiting for his victim, I guess."

Wolfe studied the screen. "Every shot of this guy is obscured," he said. "He keeps his face turned away from the camera the entire time."

"I know," said Ernie. "And once he leaves the elevator and follows the victim, he's almost never *on* camera. It's like he knows where they are and avoids them." Ernie shook his head. "I must have a good twenty minutes of tape on that guy, and you can't see his face in a single frame."

"No offense, Ernie," said Wolfe, "but the guys in

our AV lab can see things nobody else can. Thanks for compiling the footage, though."

"My pleasure. Hope you catch the guy."

"Me, too," said Wolfe. *And find out what's in that case.*

"A cell phone gun?" Calleigh said, arching her eyebrows. She studied the image on the lab monitor intently.

"You don't sound that surprised," said Wolfe.

"The list of things that firearms have been disguised as is long and strange," said Calleigh. "And it's been going on a long time, too—poachers used to build rifles that looked like canes. I've seen guns built into pens, rings, key chains, and umbrellas. A cell phone isn't much of a stretch."

"Well, it's certainly a distinctive weapon. Think we can trace it?"

"I don't know. Most of the disguised weaponry floating around comes out of countries like Croatia or Bosnia—it's all underground, strictly black market. I might be able to tap a few local sources, see what I can come up with."

"Okay. You find anything else of interest at the scene?"

"The car the vic was driving. I ran the plates of the vehicles on the level he took the elevator from and checked them against his ID—it's a rental. I also noticed some stains on the vic's pants; they match grease I found beside his car."

"Suggests he was doing something under his vehicle," said Wolfe.

"That's what I thought, but I couldn't find anything obvious. I'm having the vehicle towed in to the lab to take a closer look."

"Well, I've been doing some checking on the vic himself. Sean Daltry was ostensibly in the U.S. for a vacation. No priors—at least here—and he was staying at a hotel in North Miami. Passport lists his occupation as 'Laborer.'"

Calleigh frowned. "So, no obvious reasons why anyone would want him dead, or what he was carrying in that case."

"Nope. The killer was obviously a pro, though—no trace of him once he left the mall. He managed to keep out of sight of most of the security cameras, too; even the one in the elevator never gets a good shot of his face."

"Well, " Calleigh said with a shrug, "if we can't track the killer, we'll have to backtrack his victim. Want to go check out a hotel room?"

"Sure. But if the phone there rings, I'm not answering . . ."

Detective Frank Tripp hailed from Texas. He had been compared, more than once, to a Brahma bull; his preferred method of dealing with problems was head-on, and he had the muscle and determination to back it up.

He was also smart—but, like many cops, he'd learned the value of projecting a certain kind of street persona. His straightforward, no-nonsense approach gave him a folksy kind of trustworthiness on one hand, and a tough, don't-get-me-angry attitude on the other; one of his partners had once called him "Dr. Phil with a baseball bat." He preferred not to use the "Aw, shucks, I'm just a country boy" act if possible—he hated pretending he was stupid—but he would if that was the approach that worked. At heart, Tripp was a pragmatist.

Which is why, when he spotted Little Pooch Berretano down by the rail at the Calder Race Track, he didn't waste any time. He headed straight over and wedged his large frame in beside the man.

Berretano glanced over in annoyance. Despite his nickname, he was a tall man, as tall as Tripp himself—but where Tripp had the shoulders of a linebacker, Berretano looked like a skeleton in a suit. An extremely well-tailored, expensive suit, but one that hung loosely on his lanky frame nonetheless. He scowled when he realized who had shouldered his way in.

"Hey, Pooch," Tripp said. "How's business?"

"How should I know?" Berretano growled. He had a voice like a rusty blender. "I'm a gentleman of leisure."

" 'Course you are. That's how I know you always have time to answer my questions."

Berretano turned back to look out over the track. "Yeah, right. What makes you think I got anything to say to you?"

"Maybe 'cause you don't want to wind up like Miami Marko."

"And how would that be?"

"Don't play dumb, Pooch. You know Marko's on a slab down at the coroner's office along with eight of his friends, and I bet you know how he got there, too."

"I can hazard a guess."

"Guess away."

"Marko suffered from a lack of perspective. He didn't understand where he stood in the bigger picture, and he was always acting like he had more clout than he did. That's the kind of thing that attracts the wrong kind of attention."

"That why he got whacked—he didn't know when to keep his mouth shut?"

"It wasn't his mouth. It was his judgment."

"What's that supposed to mean?"

"It means," said Berretano, "that Marko was associating with an unsavory element."

"You're a funny guy."

"No, I'm not. I am, in fact, a very scary guy, Detective." There was no threat in Berretano's gravelly voice; he was simply stating a fact. "You know it, I know it, anybody with an ounce of street smarts between here and Key West knows it. And I'm telling you right now, there are guys even I won't deal with."

"But Marko would."

"Marko tried. I heard he didn't do so well."

"You got that right. And who might these too-scary guys be?"

Berretano shrugged. On him, the gesture looked like someone poking the inside of a jacket with a bent coat hanger. "That's not really for me to say. These guys keep a very low profile—invisible-man low."

"Yeah? Then how'd a loser like Marko find them?"

"He didn't. They found him. And if Marko had kept his mouth shut about his deal, right now I'd be giving you a whole lot of nothing. As it is, though . . . I feel a certain obligation."

Tripp snorted. "Sure. Just doing your civic duty, huh?"

A slight frown crossed Berretano's bony features. "Despite the difference in our career paths, Detective, there are certain things we have in common. Like patriotism."

It was Tripp's turn to frown. "Hang on. You're saying these guys are from another country?"

"Not just another country," said Berretano. "A whole 'nother world . . ."

The hotel Sean Daltry had been staying at was neither a dive nor one of South Beach's decadent palaces. It was the kind of midlevel chain that had an ice machine on every other floor, a coffee shop, and a bar that catered to lonely businessmen on overnighters.

Calleigh opened the door with the card-key she'd retrieved from Daltry's body. "After you," she said to Wolfe.

They stepped inside and closed the door. Wolfe put down his kit and opened it up. "I'll take the bathroom."

"Okay, I'll tackle in here."

Calleigh started by using an Alternate Light Source to check the bed; the ALS used ultraviolet light to detect traces of bodily fluids. "No signs of sexual activity," she said. "Not on the sheets, anyway. I know I've said this before, but I'm never sitting on a hotel bedspread again."

"Oh, come on," Wolfe said from the bathroom. "I'm sure they wash them every couple of years or so . . ."

"I've got nothing unusual so far," said Calleigh after a few minutes. "Pretty standard stuff for a tourist, actually. Some clothes, pair of sandals, guidebook to Miami. How about you?"

Wolfe walked out of the bathroom. "*Nada.* Toothbrush, shaving kit, deodorant. Think we should look a little deeper?"

"Well, our guy was definitely mixed up in something nasty—you don't carry weapons like that around unless you know how to use them. But if we assume he was a pro—"

"—he's not going to leave anything incriminating laying around in his hotel room."

"Incriminating, no. Indicative, maybe . . ." Calleigh picked up the Miami guidebook and balanced it on her palm by the thick spine. She kept it from toppling over with her thumb and forefinger, which she slowly spread apart; a gap appeared as the book's pages fell to either side. She opened the book to the gap—and smiled. "You think Mister Daltry was the type to appreciate Renaissance furnishings?"

"The Vizcaya Museum and Gardens," Wolfe read over her shoulder. "Think that's significant?"

"Only as a placeholder," said Calleigh. She pointed to the opposite page, where a phone number was written in the margin. "I'm guessing this might be his contact in Miami."

"And now," said Wolfe, "it's ours . . ."

4

Eric Delko, as he would freely admit, loved beautiful women—emphasis on the plural. Sometimes, he couldn't decide whether Miami was the best place on Earth for him to be, or the worst; it was like being a foodaholic confronted with an endless buffet table. It wasn't that he was incapable of commitment, he told his friends. He just wasn't sure which flavor he wanted to stick with for the rest of his life. And there were so many to choose from . . .

And then he met Marie.

She wasn't like most of the women he dated. She had a quirky sense of humor, along with a ferociously intelligent mind. She was the only woman he'd ever met who could get him so wrapped up in a discussion about politics or books or science that he almost forgot about sex.

Almost.

Because Marie was just as lovely to look at as she was to talk to—long, gorgeous legs, rich chestnut hair that reached to her waist, luminous blue eyes and a dimpled, snub-nosed face that always seemed to be smiling. Delko had spent a lot of time with her in the last few weeks, and he was hoping to spend even more.

Tonight, they were having dinner at a Japanese restaurant, the kind where the chef chopped and cooked everything right in front of you. Marie watched the chef intently, clearly fascinated by his skill; Delko was busy watching her. When she caught him and stared back frankly with a smile on her lips, he laughed.

"Busted," he said.

"Should I read you your rights?" she asked.

"I have rights?"

"Depends on how well you feed me."

"You heard the woman," Delko told the chef, grinning. "Chop till you drop." The chef grinned back and spun his knife like a baton.

"So how are things at the lab?" she asked.

"Kinda crazy," he said. "Working on that multiple shooting that was on the news."

"At the auto graveyard?"

"More than just autos, believe me."

Despite the sometimes gruesome nature of his job, Marie never reacted squeamishly. "Was it messy?"

"Not too bad. Gore doesn't bother me as much as decomp."

"On the news they said explosives were involved."

"Yeah, couple guys got themselves blown up. I was collecting body parts for an hour."

The chef slid plates of finely sliced steak in front of them. "You guys have a funny way of building an appetite," he said. He glanced pointedly at another group that had just sat down at the other end of the counter.

"Sorry," said Delko. "We'll try to keep it to ourselves."

"Well, I've got some news," said Marie. "I'm in a new show on the *Heart's Voyage*." Marie was a dancer, working in Vegas-style reviews on the many cruise ships that put into Miami.

"Yeah? What's the theme?"

"It's around Valentine's Day, so with the name of the ship and everything, naturally they're going with Cupid. Lots of togas and high-heeled sandals."

"*I'd* pay to see you in a toga."

"*You'd* pay to see me in sweatpants."

"Uh-oh. You've discovered my flannel fetish."

She picked up her wineglass and smiled mischievously at him over the rim. "Really? Any other fetishes I should know about?"

"Just beautiful, intelligent women."

"Is that all? 'Cause you wouldn't *believe* some of the outfits I've had to wear onstage."

Delko took a sip of his own wine. "Yeah? They let you keep any of them?"

"I'm not telling. Guess you'll have to investigate . . ."

"I guess I will . . . say, there's something I've been meaning to ask you. You ever work a cruise with a magician called the Brilliant Batin?"

She raised her eyebrows. "Batin? Sure—he usually works in one of the smaller lounges, but we've been booked on the same ship at the same time before. Why?"

Delko hesitated. "I can't really say," he said. "He's involved in an ongoing investigation. You ever talk to him?"

"Not personally, no—he pretty much keeps to himself. The entertainers on board usually hang out together, but not him. Which is probably a good thing."

"Oh? Why do you say that?"

"He doesn't play well with others. I saw him lose his temper at a porter once—the guy was helping him haul some equipment on board and dropped a box. Batin just lost it—started cursing the guy out in some other language, even shoved him. If the purser hadn't come over, I think Batin would have—well, I don't know what he would have done, but it would have gotten ugly. And the really scary thing? As soon as the purser showed up, he just became a different person. Totally calm, totally under control. Apologized to the porter, turned on the charm."

Delko wasn't smiling anymore. "Yeah. That's pretty much how a sociopath acts."

Her eyes widened. "A sociopath? You mean he's some kind of killer?"

Delko realized he'd said too much. "No. I mean, we think he's involved with something, but there's nothing to suggest he's guilty of murder."

"But you can't tell me what you think he *is* guilty of."

"I'm sorry, I can't. Just tell me he won't be on this Valentine's cruise."

"I don't mean to be a smart-ass, but—I'm sorry, I can't." She put down her wineglass. "He's doing two shows a night in the Anchor Room."

Delko nodded. "When does the cruise leave?"

"Three days before Valentine's. I'll only be gone a week."

"All right. Guess we've got over a month to put this guy away."

"Are you sure he's guilty?"

"My boss is. I think so, too. Look, it'll probably be fine—but promise me you'll stay away from Batin if he does make it on board, all right?"

She gave him a rueful smile. "Are you kidding? For all I know, he's a mass-murdering cannibal with Hitler's brain. I wouldn't go near him if he were covered in puppies and chocolate."

Delko laughed despite himself. "You know, that's not an image I really associate with most criminals."

"Good. Because as far as I'm concerned, those are things that should really be reserved for upstanding, law-abiding citizens. Like us."

Delko speared a piece of steak and popped it in his mouth. "Really. Sounds a little sticky, if you ask me."

"That's not a very scientific attitude."

"I don't have a lot of data to work with."

"Then, obviously, experiments are called for."

He chewed while he considered. "You have access to the necessary equipment?"

"Not exactly—but I've got some Häagen-Dazs chocolate chocolate chip at home."

He raised his eyebrows. "No puppies?"

She took a forkful of her own steak. "I'm sure," she said thoughtfully, "that we can find an appropriate substitute . . ."

Nadira Quadiri opened her hotel room door to find Horatio Caine standing in the hall, his hands on his hips. He didn't look happy.

"Horatio," said Quadiri. "I wasn't expecting you quite so soon."

"May I come in?"

"Certainly." She stood aside and Horatio stepped into the room. She closed the door behind him.

"That file made for interesting reading," said Horatio.

"Khasib Pathan is a very dangerous man."

"What was even more interesting," said Horatio mildly, "was what *wasn't* in it."

"I'm not sure I take your meaning."

"I just had a long conversation with a friend of mine. He has his own sources of information, sources a lot closer to the street—and one of those sources gave him a name that isn't even mentioned in your report."

She shrugged. "This is why I want us to work together, Horatio. You have local resources we can't access—"

"The only access this has to do with, Ms. Quadiri, is what *you* are withholding from *me*." Horatio crossed his arms. "The name that came up . . . was the Hare."

"I see." Her face gave away nothing.

"Do you? Because according to my source, the Hare is a *very* heavy player . . . and I find it hard to believe that a Homeland Security antiterrorist detail isn't aware of his involvement."

"Of course we're aware," she said. She took a deep breath, then let it out slowly. "Look, Horatio—I meant what I said about cooperation. But you don't expect me to give you detailed intel on every op we have running, do you?"

"If they're in my backyard," said Horatio, "I do."

"We didn't think you'd ever cross paths with him."

"Well, it seems that I have . . . and now, I want to know everything *you* know about him."

She matched his flat stare with one of her own—then shrugged and strode over to the corner of the room. She took a thin file out of her briefcase and offered it to him. "Here. It isn't much."

Horatio didn't take the file. "Then why don't you run it down for me . . ." He sat down in an overstuffed chair and studied her expectantly.

"All right," she said. "The Hare first surfaced in Afghanistan in 1986. He was responsible for a series of daring sabotage attacks against the occupying Russians, but even the CIA—who were financing the rebels at the time—didn't know anything about him. He was rumored to be young, but that was all. Between '87 and '89 he relocated to Beirut, where he was credited with at least a dozen brutal attacks against Christian factions. When the Lebanese civil war ended, he moved again—to Palestine. Some of the worst attacks in the region during the nineties—including the bombing of a hospital and a school—were supposedly orchestrated by him. Since nine-eleven he's been active primarily in his old stomping grounds of Afghanistan, and recently in Iraq."

Horatio leaned forward intently. "And why," he asked, "do they call him the Hare?"

"Because of his ability to disappear into the underground. No photo or even description of him exists. There's a sizable faction in the intelligence community that thinks he's a shared identity—that there is no one man called the Hare, just a legend deliberately crafted to create fear and confusion."

"Is that what you believe?"

"No. I think the Hare is just one man. He's very good at what he does, but he can't hide forever."

"What's his connection to Khasib Pathan?"

She picked up a bottle of mineral water from a small table against the wall and poured herself a glass. "Pathan contributes to extremists, and they don't come any more extreme than the Hare."

"Are they planning to meet?"

"Not that we know of. If that were the case, we'd have informed you."

"You'll forgive me if I take that with a grain of salt."

She picked up the glass but didn't drink from it. Instead, she just swirled the liquid inside around and stared down at it. "I don't blame you. But you have to understand, Horatio—when you work in intelligence, everything is compartmentalized. Secrecy is a way of life. Homeland Security is trying to break down the barriers, get us all on the same page—but it's not easy to tear apart a structure so firmly entrenched."

"Are you talking about the DHS . . . or the terrorists?"

She smiled ruefully, but didn't look up. "Believe me, I'm aware of the parallels. When hunting monsters, be careful not to become one. When you stare into the abyss, the abyss also stares into you . . ."

"Part of the job. You know what I find helps?"

Now she did look up. "What?"

"Not staring into it alone. There's more than one kind of strength to be gained in numbers . . . and monsters are notoriously short on friends."

She shook her head. "Depends on the monster. You know the Greek legend of the Hydra?"

"Sure. Cut off one head, and two more grow in its place."

"That's what hunting *mujahideen* is like. For every one that blows himself up, two more proclaim him a martyr and join up in his place. It's like fighting homicidal lemmings."

Horatio smiled. "At least you still have a sense of humor."

She sighed, and put the glass down. "I suppose. What I don't have is any idea why or how the Hare is involved."

"Maybe I can help with that," said Horatio. He told her about the junkyard shootings, and Berretano's claim that the Hare was responsible.

By the time he was done, she was pacing back and forth, an intense look of concentration on her face. "I need to know what Marko was moving," she said. "The murders sound very much like the Hare. He used a similar technique at a checkpoint in the Gaza Strip—let two soldiers disarm him and then activated explosives concealed in his weaponry."

"Misdirection," murmured Horatio. "Interesting . . ."

"The Hare isn't just a killer," said Quadiri. "He's smart, he's experienced, he's patient. Fanatics willing to die for their cause are a dime a dozen, but he goes much further than that. He once used a pregnant woman in a wheelchair to smuggle explosives."

"Pregnancy and disability are both fairly easy to fake."

"Yes—so he didn't. He used a fanatical volunteer—of which there are no shortage, unfortunately—who was neither pregnant nor disabled. Both conditions were imposed, one through amputation."

Horatio stood and picked up the folder she'd

placed on the table. "There's another case you should be aware of." He told her about the mall shooting.

"What makes you think they're connected?" she asked.

"The weapon used was a gun disguised as a cell phone. And even though he killed his target in the middle of a crowd, nobody saw a thing. He also managed to evade almost every security camera in the place."

"What do you have on the victim?"

"Not much as yet, but we're working on it."

"Send me the file and I'll run it on my end." She hesitated, met his eyes.

Horatio held them for just a second, then smiled. "All right. I'll do that . . . Nadira."

The first thing Horatio did was call a meeting. Calleigh, Wolfe, and Delko arrived in his office all at once, looking slightly puzzled; Calleigh and Wolfe were in street clothes, while Delko wore a lab coat.

"What's going on, H?" asked Calleigh.

Horatio clasped his hands together on his desk. "I wanted all of you here," he said, "because several cases that we're working on may be related. They may also be a great deal more hazardous than they appear."

"You mean the junkyard killings?" said Wolfe.

"That, and the shooting at the mall. I've been in touch with someone from Homeland Security, and she informs me we may be dealing with an international terrorist with a very long and deadly track record . . ."

He filled them in on what he knew about the Hare.

"Great," said Delko. "Does this mean we're going to get our case yanked out from under us again?" The FBI had taken over the Pathan kidnapping investigation, and Delko hadn't forgotten—or forgiven.

"Just the opposite," said Horatio. "DHS wants to work with us—they're the ones who gave me the information on the Hare, and I think they'd prefer to stay in the background."

"For now, sure," Delko muttered. "We take the heat and they'll take the credit."

"For now," said Horatio, "I'm more concerned with the former than the latter. Any field investigation connected to these cases—and that includes the Pathan investigation—is to be conducted with the utmost caution. This guy is a master of booby traps, and if he thinks we're after him he won't hesitate to come after us."

"Horatio," Calleigh said, "do you think it was the Hare who planted that landmine? The one intended for you?"

"It's possible," he admitted. "So far, we haven't found a definitive link between Abdus Sattar Pathan and the Hare—but the circumstantial evidence is piling up. It could very well be that the event Pathan was trying to distract us from was the Hare's arrival in Miami."

"Or one of the subsequent deals he was involved in," said Wolfe. "We found security footage from the airport the day Sean Daltry flew in. He didn't have that briefcase with him when he got off the plane or when he left the terminal."

Horatio nodded. "Was there anything of interest in Daltry's hotel room?"

"Only a phone number," said Wolfe. "We've traced it to a man named Pierce Madigan. Calleigh and I were just on our way to pay him a visit."

"Be careful, okay?"

"We will," said Calleigh.

Delko stayed behind after Wolfe and Calleigh had left. "H? Just how dangerous do you think Abdus is?"

"It's hard to say, Eric. It depends on how deep his involvement goes—at best he's arrogant enough to think he can fool us. At worst, he may be responsible for terrorist acts."

Delko hesitated. "So it's probably not a good idea to be in his immediate vicinity."

"I wouldn't say so . . . Eric, what's going on?"

"I know someone who works on cruise ships. Come February, she's on the same one where the Brilliant Batin is performing."

"I see . . . well, I wouldn't worry about it too much right now, Eric. A month is a long time; I'm sure the case will have broken before then. Speaking of which—do you have a report on the explosives used at the junkyard yet?"

"Not yet—waiting for Trace to get back to me.

I've been trying to reconstruct the activator from fragments, but it's slow going."

"Then I'll let you get back to work."

After Delko left, Horatio sat and thought for a while. If there was one thing he hated, it was putting his team in harm's way. Crime scene investigation was, by definition, usually fairly safe; it took place after the dangerous part had already happened. That didn't mean there weren't hazards—CSIs had to deal with everything from burned-out buildings on the verge of collapse to the toxic leftovers of meth labs—but these were all dangers that could be dealt with through careful preparation and the proper tools. Horatio did everything he could to ensure his people employed both.

But could he protect them from the Hare?

Pierce Madigan was a senior partner at the investment firm of Sanchez, Madigan, and Cooper. Their offices, on the penthouse level of a skyscraper in Miami Beach, gave the immediate impression that if you had to ask what their services cost, you couldn't afford them. Wolfe and Calleigh stepped out of the elevator into a lobby that resembled the foyer of a luxury hotel more than a banking office: An immense skylight overhead flooded the space with natural light, while a pyramidal fountain made of glass burbled quietly in the center of the room. The receptionist's desk was an oval of marble and chrome with two sleek flatscreen monitors on top and a Latina woman who looked more like a supermodel behind it.

"Can I help you?" she asked as they walked up.

"We'd like to talk to Mister Madigan," said Wolfe. "And no, we don't have an appointment." He showed her his badge.

She gave them a bright smile. "I'm sorry, Mister Madigan isn't here right now. Can I give him a message for you?"

Calleigh smiled back. "No. I know that you're just doing your job, but are you aware that lying to a police officer about the whereabouts of a suspect is a crime?"

The woman blinked, and her smile faltered. "What?"

"I'm sure that what you meant to say is Mister Madigan isn't *available*," Calleigh continued. "Which is perfectly understandable; I'm sure he's a busy man. But he *will* make time to see us. After all, better to be interrupted for a few moments now than be presented with a warrant later—right?"

"I'll—I'll see if I can reach him," the woman said, reaching for the phone.

"Thank you," said Calleigh warmly.

"Uh, Mister Madigan, sorry to disturb you—yes, I know you said no calls—the police are here. They'd like to talk to you. What should I—all right." She put the phone down. "Go right in," she said. "First door on the right."

They walked past the desk, down a wide corridor, and up to an oak-paneled door. Wolfe hesitated before they went in.

"Nice job back there," he said, "but I don't think this guy is gonna be as easy to intimidate."

"Then we'll just have to charm him, won't we?"

She opened the door. Madigan's office was predictably big and ostentatious: The back wall was made of glass, looking out over the ocean; a living-room suite of designer furniture took up one corner of the room; a large, flatscreen television hung on one wall. A massive arrangement of fresh-cut tropical flowers in a crystal vase three feet high stood beside his desk like some kind of exotic alien pet.

Madigan himself stood beside his desk, his shoes and suit jacket off—apparently he'd been taking a nap on his expensive sofa when the receptionist called. He was a big man, with the kind of build old football players get when the muscle turns to flab; the suspenders that stretched over his bulging gut looked like a railroad track going over a hill. The sparse white hair of his combover was a little disheveled, and his jowly face bore a frown.

"Officers? What's the matter? Is my family all right?" were the first words out of his mouth. Wolfe felt a twinge of sympathy; the man's automatic reaction was concern for his family, not anger at having his routine interrupted.

"Your family is fine, sir," said Calleigh. "We're here to discuss another matter. Do you know a man named Sean Daltry?"

"Daltry . . . it's possible," he said. "I deal with a great many people, Officer . . ."

"Calleigh Duquesne. This is CSI Ryan Wolfe."

"As I was saying, Officer Duquesne, I deal with a great many people every day. Some of them I only talk to on the phone, others via email—"

"This would be over the phone, Mister Madigan." Calleigh's tone was still friendly, but curt.

"Ah. Can you give me some idea what this relates to? It might help jog my memory if I could add some context."

"Sean Daltry called you at home," said Calleigh. "Five days ago, at nine-twenty-two in the evening." She smiled, but now her eyes were hard. "Does *that* ring a bell?"

If it was supposed to rattle him, it didn't work; he simply looked thoughtful. "Nine-twenty-two . . . oh, yes, I remember. Some distant cousin of my wife's, in town for the holidays. Wanted to get together for a drink."

"Did you?" asked Wolfe.

"Sure. We had a pint down at a bar just around the corner the next day. I was too busy to stay longer—Christmas is always crazy, isn't it? So we just had a quick one and I was on my way."

"I see," said Calleigh. "What did you two talk about, if you don't mind me asking?"

"Not at all. However . . . it would be nice to know what this is all about."

"Please, sir," said Calleigh. "Answer the question."

"Well, I don't recall, exactly. Just some general pleasantries. I asked him how he was enjoying Miami, he inquired after my wife . . . nothing earth-shattering." He frowned. "Now—why do you want to know?"

"I'm sorry to tell you that Sean Daltry was murdered in a shopping mall yesterday," said Calleigh calmly. "Did you two discuss any specific family business other than your wife?"

"What? Oh, my God. How? By whom?"

"We're trying to find that out, sir. Please—did you discuss any family business?"

"No, no. You don't think this was done by a relative, do you? Am I under suspicion?"

"This is just a preliminary investigation," said Wolfe. "We're not—"

"We will need to know your whereabouts yesterday afternoon," said Calleigh.

"Yes, yes, of course. I was here, at the office. I saw several clients; my secretary will confirm that."

"We'll talk to her next," said Calleigh. "Was Sean involved in any sort of activity that might have put his life in danger?"

Madigan's stare turned stony. "I'm not sure I understand your meaning," he said. "He wasn't a criminal, if that's what you're implying."

"What about his associates? Did he have ties to anyone with a history of violence?"

"Why don't you just come out and say it, Miss Duquesne? You want to know if he was caught up in the Troubles. If he was in the IRA. After all, he was Irish and he was shot, so he must have been one of those mad bombers. Isn't that where you're going?"

"Calm down, Mister Madigan. I never mentioned the IRA, nor do I assume Mister Daltry's nationality has anything to do with his death. I'm just gathering information."

"Well, you've gathered enough from me. I'll have to ask you to leave now."

"We'll be in touch," said Calleigh.

Once they were back out in the hall, Wolfe gave Calleigh an incredulous look. "What happened to charming? You call *that* charming?"

Calleigh smiled apologetically. "You have to judge people on the fly sometimes. When I saw he wasn't quite awake, I thought hitting him hard and fast before he got his defenses up might produce better results. Sorry I didn't have time to give you a heads-up."

"Well, whatever works, I guess. Too bad we didn't get much."

"Didn't we? I never told him Daltry was shot . . ."

"H?" Delko said, walking into the lab. "I've finished analyzing the trace from the explosives used at the junkyard. Looks like the magazines of two forty-five-caliber automatics were filled with C-4 and detonated with a radio-controlled remote."

Horatio put down the magnifier he was using to examine the toothpick box. "So our killer is well-versed in deception . . ."

"What's this?" Delko asked.

Horatio told him. "And the prints I've found are a match to the ones Calleigh lifted from the magazine," said Horatio.

"Which puts us right back where we started—with evidence that contradicts itself."

Horatio's cell phone rang. "Caine. Yes? Is that so . . . thank you, Valera. Much appreciated."

Horatio shut his cell phone with a snap. "Not anymore, Eric. Results on the blood we found at the junkyard shooting just came back, and we have a match."

Horatio shucked out of his lab coat as he headed for the door. "It's Abdus Sattar Pathan's . . ."

5

HORATIO DIDN'T TAKE ANY CHANCES.

He called in a Special Response Team to back him and Delko up as they served the warrant. An SRT was a SWAT team tasked with high-risk situations, including hostage-takings, hijackings, and snipers. The Miami-Dade SRT was well-known as one of the best in the country; its members handled hundreds of calls every year and kept themselves in a constant state of readiness. They were trained to operate on the land or the water, in an urban alley or the depths of the Everglades.

"All right," Horatio said to the ten members of the unit. They were gathered in the street a block away from Abdus Sattar Pathan's house. "This guy is dangerous. Even though the house was cleared as a crime scene a few days ago, it's possible the subject was involved in a major weapons buy since then. There could be anything in there, including booby traps."

The lieutenant in charge of the unit was named Winston, a short, bulky man with sun-reddened skin and hard black eyes. "Anyone else on the premises?"

"Unknown," said Horatio. "He lives alone, but may belong to a larger terrorist cell."

"Terrorists? Gee, nobody said anything about terrorists," a broad-shouldered man with a bushy brown mustache remarked. "That's it. I'm gonna quit and go raise daisies."

There were a few chuckles from the other men.

"I'd advise you to take this seriously," said Delko. "This may be the same man who killed a federal agent last week with a landmine."

"We take everything seriously," Winston said. "Every second of every job. We didn't crack wise every now and then, we'd just plain crack. So forget the pep talk, okay? We know what we're doing."

"All right," said Delko. "Sorry."

"Let's go," said Horatio.

"So Madigan knows more than he's letting on," said Wolfe. He and Calleigh were in the AV lab, studying footage from the mall security cameras.

"Definitely," said Calleigh. She was seated, Wolfe peering over her shoulder. "I avoided mentioning any possible political motive for the killing, though I did choose my phrasing carefully."

"You did?"

"Sure. I said, 'Did he have ties to anyone?' instead of 'Did he know anyone?' and 'a history of violence' instead of 'a violent past.' The first phrase calls to mind 'ties to terrorism' and the word 'history' suggests a long-term organization."

Wolfe shook his head. "So when you said you were going to charm him, you meant you were going to take his brain and put it in a blender."

"Of course not. That would be science—what I did was pure art."

"Speaking of pure art—I can't get over how this guy avoids the camera."

"I know. It's sorta spooky. It's like he instinctively knows where the dead zones of coverage are and moves from one to another as quickly as he can."

"Like a rabbit bolting from one thicket to another . . ." Wolfe muttered.

"You know what this reminds me of?" Calleigh said. "The security tape of the convenience store attack that Pathan was charged with. It was a warm night, but the attacker made a point of covering his face with a scarf before approaching the till. Robbery wasn't the motive and the attack itself seemed spontaneous—but he still took that precaution beforehand."

"So either the attack was more premeditated than it seemed—"

"—or the attacker was just used to being paranoid."

"Well, you know what they say," said Wolfe. "Just because you're paranoid doesn't mean people aren't out to get you."

"And this guy seems to have a policy of getting them first."

Wolfe stretched and yawned. "Well, we still have to check out Daltry's car. Maybe it can tell us something."

"You go ahead. I want to see if I can trace that cell phone gun."

Two officers circled around back. Two covered the windows on one side of the house, two on the other. Two snipers positioned themselves behind the armored bulk of their vehicle, and two more were positioned in the front with a battering ram. Horatio and Delko approached the front door, one on either side.

"Abdus Pathan!" Horatio called out. "This is the Miami-Dade police! Open the door!"

No response.

"Take it down?" one of the officers holding the ram asked.

"Hold on a second," Horatio muttered. His bomb squad training had taken over, and he was checking for any obvious signs of a trigger. Of course, a professional like the Hare wouldn't leave anything obvious . . .

Horatio tried the door. It was unlocked.

He pushed it open no more than an inch.

Doorjamb clear. No wires, no pressure switches. He pulled a tool from his breast pocket, an angled mirror mounted on a telescoping rod, and snapped it open to full length. He carefully angled it through the crack and used it to see as much of the other side as he could.

Still nothing.

He pulled the rod back, snapped it shut, and put it back in his pocket. He drew his Glock, took a deep breath, and nodded at Eric.

Horatio pushed the door open and stepped inside.

The first cell phone gun, as near as Calleigh could determine, had been built in Croatia. It was more than just a shell around a gun; the keypad was actually wired to a small circuit board. Pressing any number from five through eight would fire one of four twenty-two-caliber rounds. Law enforcement agencies had been alerted to the existence of such guns over six years ago, and so far none had been reported in the U.S.

Guess this is the first, she thought.

She downloaded video that showed one in action. The gun broke into two pieces, the upper half with the screen and the lower half with the keypad. The bullets were stored in four side-by-side barrels in the upper half. The case itself was made of plastic, but was heavier than a normal cell phone. When the two halves were put together, twisting a catch at the bottom locked them in place and primed the gun for firing.

Calleigh studied the monitor with a troubled look on her face. She appreciated firearms; used properly, they were an efficient and powerful tool.

Used improperly, they were one of the most destructive forces on the planet.

Building a gun into a cell phone was definitely *not* a proper use.

The question now is—how did it get here?

She thought about it. Despite increased security precautions, not all airports followed the same guidelines. The cell phone gun, while made primarily of plastic, definitely had enough metal in it to set off a detector. Some airports required you to show any piece of electronic gear you were carrying actually worked, but some only checked laptops and let smaller items like cell phones slide.

Someone like the Hare wouldn't risk it. He'd rely on agents within the country to supply him with weapons, using a pre-existing network. Getting—or even building—something like a cell gun wouldn't be that difficult if you had the right contacts.

But Calleigh had a few contacts of her own.

The door swung open silently. The distant, high-pitched cry of a gull echoed in Horatio's ear like a warning.

He entered the house, Glock held rock-steady in front of him, sighting down the barrel. Delko was no more than a step away. Horatio moved slowly through the large living room, noting that it had been cleaned up since the last time he'd been here; the blood on the walls had been washed away, the splintered furniture removed.

He could see a seated figure through the doorway to the kitchen, its back to him.

"Place your hands on top of your head!" Horatio called out.

The figure turned slowly, the chair itself swiveling.

Abdus Sattar Pathan regarded Horatio with a slight smile on his face.

During her time in charge of the Miami-Dade ballistics lab, Calleigh Duquesne had gotten the chance to examine a wide variety of weapons ranging from Saturday night specials to homemade grenade launchers. Police access to firearm databases gave her plenty of information to work with when she was tracking a weapon, but unregistered and custom-made models usually weren't in the system—so for the more unconventional examples of firepower she had developed her own resources.

Specifically, she'd gotten to know Billy Lee Garenko.

She'd been introduced to him by his parole officer. Billy Lee had been caught jacklighting deer in the 'Glades, and as a condition of his release had been ordered to stay away from any sort of firearms. This was, to Billy Lee's way of thinking, like ordering Spider-Man to stay away from tall buildings. He had begged, pleaded, and cajoled his PO into striking a deal; Billy Lee could, with strict supervision, handle firearms at an approved gun range—but only if he would put his considerable knowledge at the disposal of the Miami-Dade police.

Billy Lee had agreed, with tears of joy in his eyes. If Calleigh's appreciation of firearms was filtered through the measured gaze of a professional, Billy Lee's vision had the wild-eyed euphoria of a fanatic. He didn't just love guns; he lived, breathed, ate, and slept guns. He bought them, he sold them, he traded them, and built them. On occasion, he even fired them.

Billy Lee lived out near Opa-Locka, on an overgrown patch of land he had decorated in his own peculiar way. At some point in his career he had bartered his way into ownership of five shipping containers, the big steel ones that were usually transported in the hold of a ship or strapped to railway cars or semi-trailers. He'd connected them with the kind of big, galvanized culverts used for ditch drainage, welding them together into a sort of oversize metal hamster run. There were no windows, but he kept the place ventilated and cool with jury-rigged equipment from a reefer truck. Calleigh found the place dark, claustrophobic, and cold—Billy Lee seemed to like it around the temperature of a meat cooler. However, she had to admit one thing; it was about as secure a place for Billy Lee's collection of firearms as she could imagine.

She pulled her Hummer into his rutted, muddy driveway and got out. She walked up to the front door—which consisted of an entire wall on hinges—and rapped on the metal. "Billy Lee!" she called out. "You home?"

A metal slot slid open and a pair of eyes peered out. "Who's there?"

"It's Calleigh."

"Calleigh Duquesne? Well, hot damn." The slot closed and she heard bolts being drawn. She stepped back just as the wall swung open and Billy Lee jumped out. Billy was short and stout, with a body that was gradually sliding from barrel- to pear-shaped. His skull was as bald as an old tire on top, but he'd compensated with an Amish-style beard—the kind where the front of the chin is kept bare, but the hair beneath the jawline is allowed to grow. Billy's beard sprouted from the bottom of his ears to halfway down his throat, a curly, reddish-yellow mane that made him look like an aging lion. He wore a pair of dirty, grease-stained jeans, army boots, and an old plaid shirt with the sleeves cut off.

He had a gun in his hands, of course, but Calleigh would have been surprised if he hadn't. "Hey, Billy," she said warmly. "New toy?"

He grinned back at her and held it out. "This little thang? Just a curiosity I been tinkerin' with."

She took the gun and examined it. It was about four feet long, with a polished wooden stock of some light blond wood and a thirty-inch nickel-plated smooth-bore barrel with a long tube slung beneath it. "Gas-powered?" she said.

"Yep. Farco air shotgun. Ain't that wood nice? Philippine hardwood—that's where she's from."

"What caliber?"

"Fifty-one. Takes shot or round balls, delivers 'bout a hundred foot-pounds once she's broke in. Handmade, o' course. You got to load it with a gas cylinder."

She handed it back. "Probably the quietest shotgun I've ever seen."

He chuckled. "Well, it don't got the range a regular one does, so you got to get closer, too."

"The reason I'm here, Billy Lee, is I'm trying to track down a gun myself—kind of an unusual piece. My regular channels aren't much use, so I thought I'd try you."

"Well, I'll surely try to help, if I can. What's the piece?"

"A gun designed to look like a cell phone."

His reaction was immediate. He blinked rapidly, then looked away. "Nope. Can't say I ever heard of one o' those."

"Maybe you've never seen one—but I find it hard to believe there's a gun you've never heard of, Billy Lee."

He shuffled away from her, back toward the dim coolness of his metal bunker. "Got a lot to do, Calleigh. Sorry I can't help you."

"Hold it, Billy Lee."

He stopped, but didn't look at her.

"All I want is a little information. Come on, it's just you and me talking guns, all right?"

"I can't tell you who might have such a thing, Calleigh. I got no idea."

She sighed. Billy Lee was a simple man, as eager as a child about certain things but as stubborn as a two-year-old about others. She knew that pushing him was more likely to provoke the second reaction than the first. "Okay, then—let's just keep this hypothetical. Say someone came into the country from somewhere else, and wanted to obtain a weapon like that. You think he'd try to make his own, or find somebody to buy one from?"

"Depends on who it was, I suppose." He reached up and scratched his chin with a grimy fingernail. "If you was from Yugoslavia, you might make your own. I guess."

So he knows where cell phone guns originated—not much of a surprise, really. "What if you were from somewhere else? Somewhere a little farther east?"

He frowned. "You mean like Japan?" Geography wasn't one of Billy Lee's strong points.

"No, I mean like the Middle East."

"No, no, I don't know anyone like that."

"Billy Lee," she said gently. "I can see that something's bothering you. You want to tell me about it?"

"No, Calleigh. I just want to be left alone, you know? Just let me go back to work, okay?" There was pleading in his voice and eyes.

"I can't do that, Billy Lee. A cell phone gun was used to assassinate someone in the middle of a crowd, and if we don't stop the killer other people may die. You don't want that, do you?"

"People do all kinds of bad things. It's not the gun's fault."

Calleigh had heard this sort of logic from Billy Lee before; in his mind, guns were completely separate from the actions of the people who used them. Firearms were an example of craft as opposed to hostile intent—he was more interested in guns than bullets.

Unlike Calleigh.

"Maybe not," she said, "but once a gun is used on an innocent person it's my job to bring in the shooter. The guy that has this gun has to be stopped, Billy Lee. Otherwise, he's going to hurt more people."

Billy Lee muttered something she couldn't quite hear. "What was that?"

"I said, I'm a person *too,* Calleigh."

"Of course you are, Billy Lee—"

"Then don't ask me any more questions." His hands were gripping the shotgun so tightly his knuckles were turning white. "I don't want to die," he said. "Please. I don't want to die . . ."

For Horatio, time seemed to have frozen. He seemed to hear, quite clearly, a single beat of his heart.

The only thing in Pathan's hands was a small demitasse cup of espresso. He was dressed casually. He raised the cup slowly to his mouth.

"Do *not* move," Horatio said.

Pathan paused—just long enough to indicate that he'd heard—then took a long sip from the cup anyway. When he was done, he set the cup down on the table next to him. Having several loaded guns pointed at him didn't seem to bother him in the slightest.

"Abdus Sattar Pathan," said Horatio, "you are under arrest. Get on the ground, facedown. Do it *now*."

Moving slowly, even gracefully, Pathan did so. Horatio moved in to cuff him. Even once he had Pathan in restraints, he didn't relax; this was a master of sleight of hand, after all.

"Target secure," one of the SRT officers said into a radio.

"Check the rest of the house," said Horatio.

Horatio had pulled Pathan to his feet. Now, the magician shook his head. "I wouldn't do that," he said.

Horatio grabbed his own radio. "Stop! Do not proceed!" He glared at Pathan. "What have you done, Abdus?"

"A man's home is his castle, Lieutenant Caine. Surely it's not unreasonable to protect that castle?"

Horatio met Pathan's eyes. After a second, Pathan looked away.

"Merely a jest, Lieutenant. After all, if I had truly left any unpleasant surprises for you or your officers . . . do you really think I'd *warn* you?"

It was a question Horatio had no answer to.

No amount of cajoling could convince Billy Lee to share what he knew. Even the specter of having his parole revoked didn't convince him; apparently, living without guns was still better than not living.

Calleigh drove back to the lab, hoping that Wolfe had had better luck.

"Sorry," said Wolfe. "The car's a rental, our vic liked to drink coffee while he was driving, and that's about it. Whatever was in that case, it didn't leave any trace behind."

"Well, I hit a dead end, too. My source seemed to know something about the cell phone gun, but he was too scared to talk."

"What do you say we go for lunch and brainstorm?"

"Sounds good to me."

They went to Auntie Bellum's, a little diner a block away from the crime lab. Wolfe ordered a corned beef sandwich and Calleigh decided on the jambalaya. After they'd ordered, both of them stared out the window for a moment, collecting their thoughts.

"All right," said Calleigh. "Let's go over what we have so far. Sean Daltry flies in from Ireland, presumably for a 'vacation.' While he's here, he contacts Pierce Madigan. Mister Madigan is less than forthcoming about his relationship with Daltry, other than to claim he's a distant relative on his wife's side."

"Right. At some point after his entry into the States, Daltry acquires some heavy-duty firepower and a metal case. While he's taking a stroll in a mall, a mysterious person—who may or may not be an international terrorist—stalks him, kills him, and relieves him of the case."

"After presumably killing nine men in a junkyard."

"And so far, we don't even know why." Wolfe leaned back against the leather seat of the booth and tapped his fingers on the table.

"Well, let's say Madigan and Daltry are involved with the IRA. We know the victims of the junkyard shootings had mob connections. What do those two organizations and a terrorist have in common?"

"They all kill people."

"Well, sure—but for different reasons. Two of the players are political, one is mainly a business organization. And the Irish Republican Army doesn't have a lot of overlap with Islamic extremists."

Wolfe shook his head. "So what's the common denominator?"

"It's got to be weapons. If Khasib Pathan is bankrolling the Hare, money isn't a problem. I think the Hare is in town building a stockpile—but that's not what worries me."

"Yeah. It's the fact that he's burning his bridges behind him."

Calleigh nodded soberly. "Underground organizations rely on each other for a certain amount of discretion. It's not exactly trust, just a system of alliances and favors—but you don't bite the hand that supplies you."

"Unless what you're planning is so big you can't risk word getting out."

"Or because the payoff is big enough to justify the cost."

Their food came, and both of them dug in—not so much out of hunger as for a chance to mull over the problem.

Calleigh set down her spoon. "We have to go after the weak link in the chain," she said.

Wolfe chewed and swallowed before answering. "Okay. Well, so far the Hare isn't leaving a lot of players alive. Who'd you have in mind?"

"Madigan. He has to know what was in that case. And if we can bring some pressure to bear—"

"—so will we," Wolfe finished. He tossed his napkin down and stood up. "You know, I'm not really as hungry as I thought."

"Me neither," said Calleigh. "Not for food, anyway . . ."

Delko patted down Pathan in the kitchen. He was extremely thorough, checking inside the man's mouth, in his hair, the seams of his clothes, and his shoes. He found nothing.

"Guess you think you're pretty slick," said Delko, emptying Pathan's pockets.

"I'm a professional—just like you."

"You're nothing like me."

Horatio was outside, talking to someone on his cell phone—his Homeland Security contact, Delko guessed. The SRT members were searching the house. "You know why I'm searching you here instead of outside? Because if anything detonates, I want to make sure you're nice and close to it."

"Perhaps that's what I want. You seem to think

I'm some sort of jihad-crazed suicide bomber—isn't that what they do? Destroy themselves along with their target?"

"We know what you are," said Delko. "See, we're a whole lot harder to fool than a cruise ship audience."

"Really." Pathan smiled. "Because I'm quite sure you don't know nearly as much as you claim."

Delko leaned in close to Pathan's ear. "I know one thing. Someone tried to kill Horatio—and that person should feel very, very lucky he didn't succeed. Because if he had, it would be the last victory he ever celebrated."

Pathan met Delko's hard gaze placidly. "Your loyalty is commendable. It's a shame it's so misplaced . . ."

"I could say the same about your self-confidence."

"We'll see."

The SRT team finished their sweep—they'd found nothing obvious. No booby traps, no weapons, no contraband.

"Why don't you just tell me what you're looking for?" Pathan asked. "Perhaps I can help."

"Thanks for the offer," said Delko. "But this place isn't clean until I say so—and I intend to look a whole lot harder."

Doctor Alexx Woods finished the autopsy on Sean Daltry, sewing the last stitch in the Y-shaped incision on his chest. She had done the same thing many, many times before, and she always felt an odd twinge of sadness and satisfaction. In one sense, she was finished; the body could now be released to a funeral home for embalming or cremation. But there was still work to be done—forms to be filled out, reports to be filed, toxin screens to look over. Sean Daltry had become not just a statistic, but a whole list of them—and to the people who looked at those numbers, that's all he would ever be. They wouldn't know about his friends, his lovers, his favorite foods; his humanity would be buried with him, leaving only a cold, digital ghost consigned to a cybernetic eternity.

Alexx sighed. She picked up the twenty-two-caliber bullet she'd pulled from the body and studied it. She was always amazed that something so small could destroy a life. She bagged it as evidence and finished up.

When she sat down in front of her computer to do some work, she noticed that bloodwork from the lab had come in. She flipped through a few sheets, then frowned. "This can't be right . . ."

She went back to the autopsy room, opened the drawer with Sean Daltry in it. She performed a very simple test—one so basic that it had never crossed her mind to do it.

Her eyes widened at the result. She grabbed for her cell phone.

6

Horatio regarded Abdus Sattar Pathan. The magician sat upright but relaxed, his hands in front of him on the interview table. Golden sunshine behind the hexagon grid of the window threw a honeycomb of light across his calm features. He seemed alert, poised, not at all worried.

"Well, Abdus," said Horatio. "Here we are again."

"Yes. People are going to start to talk."

Horatio smiled. "A joke? You don't seem to be taking this very seriously."

"Forgive me if I seem flippant. It's just that, after being mistaken for a robber, then kidnapped and almost killed . . . well, it's hard to believe things can get any worse."

"Things can always get worse, Abdus. I'd say being charged with nine counts of homicide, for instance, is considerably worse."

Pathan laughed once, a harsh bark with little

mirth in it. "Of course, of course. You've accused me of assault, kidnapping myself, and now murder. What next, Lieutenant? Am I guilty of blowing up an orphanage, too?"

"I'm not sure what you're capable of, Abdus. But I do know that your next trick will be staying out of prison."

"As I said to you the last time we talked, at the FBI office—tricks require preparation."

Horatio waited, but after this statement his prisoner fell silent.

"In that case, you'd better start preparing," said Horatio. "Beginning with a lawyer." Normally, suggesting a lawyer was the last thing Horatio would do—it was always harder to get a suspect to talk once he had legal representation. But in this case, Horatio hoped that the mysterious Francis Buccinelli would make an appearance—he was the one who had apparently helped Pathan fake his fingerprints the first time he was arrested.

"Oh, I have legal counsel on its way," said Pathan. "A most interesting gentleman—I do believe you'll find talking to him an illuminating experience."

"I'm looking forward to it . . ."

Nadira Quadiri was waiting in Horatio's office. She didn't waste any time; the second he walked in, she said, "You think Abdus Sattar Pathan is the Hare."

"I didn't say that, Nadira."

"But it's what the evidence says."

"What the evidence says is that Pathan was present at the junkyard shooting. Blood found there is a match to his. Beyond that, we have only hearsay."

"I'd like to sit in on the interrogation."

"I have no problem with that. It might take a while before that happens, though."

"Why is that?"

"Because Pathan wants his lawyer present—and we want his lawyer." He explained to her about Francis Buccinelli, including the fact that he'd used fake credentials.

She looked dubious. "I don't know, Horatio. Pathan's too smart to try to pull the same stunt twice. I have my doubts about whether this Buccinelli will show."

"If he does, he's facing criminal charges."

"And if he doesn't?"

"Then Mister Pathan will have to go it alone . . ."

"Any other developments I should know about?"

"We've traced the man shot in the mall, Sean Daltry, to someone named Pierce Madigan. I was wondering—"

"I'll liaise with your people. I can tell you this much, now—according to what we found, Sean Daltry was RIRA."

Horatio nodded. The Real Irish Republican Army was a radical faction of the IRA that had split off in 1997. "I see."

"Daltry was a hardcore member. We think he was being used as a go-between for some kind of deal—we just don't know for what."

"Whatever was in that case, no doubt . . ."

"I've looked at the footage from the mall, Horatio." She hesitated.

"And?"

"I don't know. If it is the Hare, these are the best shots of him we've ever obtained. Even so—"

"Even so, they're basically worthless."

She smiled ruefully. "I'm afraid so. Which says, to me, that it *is* the Hare—it would take great skill to evade that many cameras successfully."

"Even a rabbit can be run to ground eventually."

She sighed. "When it comes to the Hare, I've learned not to get too optimistic. He's disappeared on me enough times to earn his name tenfold."

Delko stuck his head in the door. "H? Pathan's lawyer is here." Delko looked grim. "And it's not exactly what we were expecting."

George Lorngren III was not just an attorney. He was a celebrity, and he moved in the same circles as many of his clients—famous recording artists, actors, models. He was as well-known for his appearances on Court TV as he was for the people he defended, and he didn't come cheap.

Horatio knew exactly what he was: a hired gun. A very, very good one.

Lorngren had a head full of thick, wavy gray hair, and a short gray goatee. He favored silk suits in pastel colors; his current outfit was pale green. He held a hand-tooled alligator-skin briefcase in one hand, and a piece of paper in the other.

Nadira stood beside Horatio but didn't introduce herself.

"Lieutenant Caine," Lorngren said pleasantly. "I believe you're holding a client of mine."

"Would that client be Abdus Sattar Pathan, Mister Lorngren?"

"That's correct."

"Your client is in interview room one, Mister Lorngren. If you'd like to accompany me—"

Lorngren shook his head. "I don't think that'll be necessary, Lieutenant."

Horatio cocked his head. "Oh? You don't want to be present during questioning?"

"No need. After all, I'm sure you don't want to waste time questioning an innocent man."

Horatio smiled despite himself. "I'm afraid I have to disagree with you, Counselor. Mister Pathan is being charged with multiple counts of homicide."

"Really? How strange. I would think that his alibi would have cleared all this up."

Horatio knew bad news when he heard it. "And what alibi would that be, Mister Lorngren?"

"At the time of the murders, Mister Pathan was onstage."

"Time of death in this case is only approximate—"

"He was also a hundred miles away from Miami, on a cruise ship. Staff and passengers will attest to frequent sightings and interactions with Mister Pathan in the twenty-four hours prior to, during, and after the killings." He handed the paper he held to Horatio.

"I should have known," Nadira muttered.

"If you haven't talked to your client yet," said Horatio, scanning the page, "how are you aware of all this, Mister Lorngren?"

"The relevant information was provided to me by my client's father, Khasib Pathan."

Horatio nodded. "I see . . . I suppose he'd be the one providing your paycheck, as well?"

"You can suppose whatever you'd like, Lieutenant. The person picking up the bill is entitled to confidentiality."

"Alibi notwithstanding, I still have a few questions for your client."

"Then let's get to it, Lieutenant."

Horatio led the way to the interview room. If Pathan was surprised to see Lorngren, he didn't show it. Lorngren took a chair next to Pathan, and Nadira sat next to Horatio across the table.

"Well, Abdus, it seems you're moving up in the world," said Horatio. "What happened to your old lawyer?"

"Mister Buccinelli? I understand he's left the country."

"Isn't that a shame . . . tell me, Abdus, how do you explain your blood being found at the scene of a multiple homicide?"

"I'm glad you asked, Lieutenant. You see, I spent a great deal of my time in captivity unconscious—I surmise that during that time, my captors extracted some of my blood."

"For what purpose?"

"To prove I was their prisoner, of course. After I escaped, they must have planted it at a crime scene to implicate me."

"In that case, the blood would be degraded—or have traces of preservative agents present," said Horatio. "We didn't find any evidence of that."

"Perhaps you made a mistake," said Lorngren. "I understand this isn't the first time you've done so in regard to my client."

Horatio fixed Lorngren with a cold stare. "You're misinformed, Counselor."

"I don't think I am," said Lorngren. "As a matter of fact, two such blunders in a row might be seen by a jury as more than just mistakes."

"Careful, Counselor."

"Caution is my watchword, Lieutenant. Now, since Mister Pathan has provided both an explanation of his circumstances and proof of his innocence, I assume he's free to go?"

"For now," said Horatio.

"I can't believe this," said Delko. He was staring in disgust at Abdus Sattar Pathan's back as he left with his lawyer. "We have the guy dead to rights."

"With the Hare, nothing's ever certain," Nadira said. She filled a paper cup from a watercooler in the hall and took a long, slow sip. She didn't seem angry or even frustrated; she'd hardly spoken a word since Pathan's interview.

"Eric Delko, this is Nadira Quadiri," said Horatio. "She's with Homeland Security."

"Pleased to meet you," Delko said. "Sorry it wasn't under better circumstances."

"Hello," Nadira said. "Horatio, I have to make some calls. If you'll excuse me?"

"Of course."

She walked quickly away. Delko glanced from her to Horatio and back. "So that's our contact with DHS, huh? How is she to work with?"

"So far, I think she's being straight with me. She's going to help Calleigh and Wolfe run down some background in the mall shooting—maybe we'll catch a break from that angle."

"We could use one. What's next?"

Horatio's cell rang. "Hang on a second, Eric . . . Lieutenant Caine."

"Horatio, it's Alexx. We've got a problem—a big one."

Horatio listened intently for a few seconds. "You're sure? Uh-huh. I'll get the warrant. Thanks, Alexx." He hung up. "Eric, we still have the car Sean Daltry was driving?"

"Yeah, it's down in the garage. Why?"

"I need you to get down there, now. And bring a radiation detector with you . . ."

"His blood had all the classic symptoms of hematopoietic syndrome," Alexx said. "Extremely low white blood cell count, decreased platelets and red blood cells. Numbers were so low it couldn't have been simple anemia. I tried pulling out a little of his hair, and it practically fell into my hand."

"Radiation poisoning," said Horatio. "You've confirmed?"

"Dosimeter registered two Grays' worth of IR. Might have killed him eventually, but he was in the postexposure phase; probably felt just fine. Any initial symptoms—fatigue, loss of appetite, nausea—he could have thought was just the flu. Another few days, though, and he would have gotten a lot worse—difficulty breathing, muscle weakness, opportunistic infections."

"Two Grays' isn't that high a dose."

"Not enough to worry about the body being dangerous, no."

"But whatever he came in contact with," said Horatio, "is another matter."

The first device Delko used to scan Sean Daltry's rental car was an updated version of the Geiger counter that had been in use for decades to detect radiation. In principle it was much the same: the operative component was a tube with a metal inner surface and a charged wire running through the center, filled with an inert gas like helium or argon. The presence of radiation would ionize the gas, triggering an electrical cascade between the wire and the inside of the tube; in order to properly measure the amount of radiation, Geiger counters used a small amount of an organic vapor such as ethanol or butane to regulate the flow of electricity, while the newer kind used a halogen like chlorine or bromine. Both types were effective in detecting alpha or beta radiation—which he didn't find.

Next, he tried the sodium iodide detector, in which radiation hitting a crystal would create a burst of light, which was then turned into an electrical pulse by a photomultiplier tube. SIDs were useful in detecting gamma radiation, which was much more dangerous than alpha or beta.

And that was exactly what Delko found—especially in the front, in the passenger seat.

Horatio got off the elevator and strode into the garage. "Eric? Talk to me."

"We got gamma radiation, H."

Horatio nodded. "Which finally gives us an idea of what was in that case."

"Can't say I like the list of possibilities."

"Nor do I, Eric. But it gives us another way to look—and, I suspect, as much assistance as we might need . . ."

Nadira found Wolfe and Calleigh in the Ballistics lab. "Hello," she said, and introduced herself. "Horatio said we should talk." She told them what she'd discovered about Sean Daltry, and in return Calleigh gave her a brief rundown of their encounter with Pierce Madigan.

"I'm sure he knows more than he's letting on," said Calleigh.

Nadira nodded. "I'll run him, see what I can find. Most likely he's some sort of middleman for RIRA funding."

"Great. Will you excuse me for a moment?" asked Calleigh. "I promised I'd run this down to Trace."

"Sure."

"So, Nadira," said Wolfe as Calleigh headed for the door, "you work in intelligence, huh? Guess that makes you sort of a Bond girl."

"I stopped being a girl some time ago, Mister Wolfe. And my name is nowhere ludicrous enough to appear in one of those films."

"Yeah, they were pretty ridiculous. Pussy Galore, Holly Goodhead . . . still, they usually wound up kicking—uh, kicking the bad guy. In the, you know."

"Ass?" she asked, raising one eyebrow.

He hesitated. "Yes. Which is what I kind of feel like right now."

"Don't fret, Mister Wolfe. The first thing you learn in superspy school—after how to make a proper martini, of course—is never to lose your composure. So I am completely oblivious to any double entendres you may inadvertently make."

"I take it back. You are far, *far* too cool to be a Bond girl. You're like *Jane* Bond."

She rewarded him with an amused look that was almost friendly. "Thank you, Mister Wolfe. And with all your expertise in matters forensic, I suppose you bear some resemblance to the infamous Q."

"Really? Q?"

"Well, perhaps not quite. But an L, at the very least."

"Uh, thanks."

It wasn't until after she'd left that Wolfe frowned and said, "Wait. Did she just call me a loser?"

The judge refused to grant Horatio a warrant.

"You've searched this man's place twice," Judge Josephine Kitta told him. "You've also brought charges against him twice, and both times the court has been forced to drop those charges. If I issue a third search warrant and you don't find anything, he will bring suit against the state—Mister Lorngren has made that abundantly clear. I cannot, in good faith, grant a warrant at this time."

Normally, that would leave Horatio stalled. But in this case, he had an ace up his sleeve—an ace called Nadira Quadiri.

Under section 213 of the PATRIOT Act, a law enforcement official investigating a suspected case of terrorism could enter a residence and search it without the consent or knowledge of the resident—as long as that resident was notified of said search within thirty days. The radiation Delko and Alexx had found was more than enough justification for a so-called sneak-and-peek; less than eight hours after SRT officers had descended on Pathan's house they returned, this time with radiation sniffers. Abdus wasn't there.

And neither was anything else.

"Nothing hot, H," Delko reported. Nadira just nodded, her expression distant; again, she didn't seem surprised.

Horatio leaned against his Hummer, arms crossed, staring at the setting sun through tinted lenses. "No. Whatever the Hare has, he isn't stupid enough to store it here."

"We'll find it," said Nadira. "We know what we're looking for, now."

"Maybe you do," said Horatio. "I'm still making guesses, and I'm getting tired of it."

"I can't divulge specifics, Horatio." Nadira's voice had hardened. "I'm sorry, but there's nothing I can tell you that would help us find what we're looking for."

"You knew all along, didn't you." Horatio's tone was flat.

"I'm just doing my job, Horatio. I report to superiors, just like you."

"I may report to the brass," said Horatio, "but I work for the public. And I can't protect them without accurate information, can I?"

"I've given you all I can." Nadira took out her own pair of sunglasses, slipped them on. "I'll be in touch if I hear anything new." She got into her car, an anonymous-looking dark-blue sedan, and drove off.

"Nice," Delko said, disgust in his voice. "So where does that leave us?"

"In better shape than you might think, Eric. Pathan can't make a move now without us knowing about it. His father's money won't protect him against something this big."

"Yeah, but we still don't know exactly what

we're dealing with, H. Radioactive isotopes? A dirty bomb? We just don't know."

"No. But I know someone who might . . ."

Horatio had known Emilio Augustino for many years. Despite that, he didn't know the man well; Emilio's personality, like his past, was as hard to gauge as the depth of swamp water. Sunshine might glint off a smooth and placid surface, but anything from hungry alligators to quicksand might be lurking underneath.

They met, as they often did, in Little Havana, at an outdoor café. When Horatio arrived, Emilio was already seated, sipping a thumble-sized paper cup of strong Cuban coffee and reading a newspaper. The paper, Horatio saw with little surprise, was Chinese.

"Afternoon, Emilio," said Horatio.

Emilio glanced up. Despite the bright sun, he wore no sunglasses, using a broad-brimmed straw hat to keep the sun out of his eyes instead. He wore a lightweight linen suit of white, with tan sandals. He smiled warmly at Horatio and motioned him to sit.

"Horatio, my friend," said Emilio. "What a coincidence. I was just thinking of you."

Horatio pulled up a chair. "It must be fate, then."

"Indeed. Who knows what it has in store for us, eh?"

"I was hoping you might have some ideas."

Emilio took a sip of his *café cubano*. "Perhaps." He

fell silent then, and studied Horatio for a moment before speaking again. "Perhaps there are some things it is better not to know."

Horatio frowned. While Emilio—who was rumored to be ex-KGB, ex-CIA, or possibly both—was always closemouthed about information, this was the first time Horatio had ever seen him suggest ignorance as an option. It was like hearing a vampire offer vegetarianism as a possible menu choice.

"You've heard something," said Horatio.

"I hear many things. But hearing something does not necessarily make it so; a scream in the night could be a murder or a macaw. Sometimes it is best to simply pay no heed."

"Not in this case, Emilio. Too many lives are at stake."

"Too many lives. For you, one is too many, Horatio." Emilio smiled and nodded at two tourist girls in their twenties dressed in shorts, sandals, and bikini tops. They smiled back as they walked past. "You understand that I—pathetic creature that I am—am not so sentimental."

"Sure." Suddenly, Horatio was fed up with Emilio and his studied posture of indifference. "Let's stop playing this game, shall we? I come to you for information, and you supply it for whatever reasons of your own. Maybe it amuses you. Maybe you're trying to atone for something. I don't know." Horatio hunched forward, staring at Emilio intently, and now the look on the man's face told him he'd touched a nerve. "Listen to me, Emilio. This isn't about catching a carjacker or a two-bit grifter. If I don't stop this guy, he's going to commit an atrocity—hundreds of people could die, maybe thousands. I don't have the luxury of sitting back and pretending it isn't my problem, and neither do you."

"Don't I?" Emilio's voice was cold, but it held more anger than Horatio had ever heard the man express before. "Refusing to care is not a luxury with me, Horatio. It is a necessity. It is what enables me to function. If I had not cultivated such a skill I would have been devoured by an army of ghosts long ago."

Horatio knew what he meant. Horatio had developed his own skills, his own methods of dealing with the restless corpses that roamed the halls of memory . . . and it was not a skill that could be taught. For all Horatio's intellect and experience, there were some things bred so deeply in the bone they couldn't be passed on with words. He suspected that Emilio, were he pressed, would admit much the same thing.

"I'm not talking about caring, Emilio. I'm talking about responsibility. Maybe you could walk away before, but not now. Like it or not, you're involved. Whatever happens, you'll always know that."

Emilio smiled. It wasn't pleasant; it was the look of a man who's just wiped his own blood off his lips with the back of his hand, and is glad to see it.

"A hit, a palpable hit," he said softly. "You are

right, my friend. This is not something I can dismiss, much as I wish I could. So. I will tell you what you need to know, and hope that is enough . . ."

Emilio's words confirmed Horatio's darkest suspicions. When he was done, Horatio simply nodded. There was little to say.

"What will you do?" Emilio asked.

"Whatever I can," said Horatio. He stood up. "Thank you."

"No, Horatio. Thank you." Emilio stood as well, tossing his newspaper down on the table. "You want to know why I provide you with information? Physics."

"Physics?"

"Yes. For every action there is an equal and opposite reaction. Opposites attract. Nature abhors a vacuum—and that is what I have within me. A vacuum, a void. Is it so strange that a blind man would seek to help one who sees too much? You are a man of conscience, Horatio, and I am a man without one. Absolution or atonement hold no attraction for me."

"Then what *do* you want, Emilio?"

The man shrugged. "Balance, I suppose. A little more order in a chaotic world. Is that such a terrible reason to offer my assistance?"

"I've heard worse."

"So have I, my friend. Far, far worse . . ."

And then, the unthinkable happened.

Nothing at all.

Days crawled by, metamorphosing slowly into weeks. Other cases came up while the Pathan investigation stalled. Nadira Quadiri got in touch to confirm that Pierce Madigan was indeed a financial backer of the RIRA and requested that Horatio's team stay away from him while she was following up a possible international connection. Other than that, Horatio didn't hear from her.

Horatio didn't tell his team what he'd learned from Emilio. He understood why Nadira hadn't told him.

Delko saw more and more of Marie. He showed up to work more than once yawning and bleary-eyed, but in an extremely good mood anyway. Calleigh diagnosed him as suffering from "sexhaustion," and actually made him blush.

Abdus Sattar Pathan returned to his normal routine, performing aboard cruise ships. When not working, he stayed at home and practiced his craft.

There was no trace of the man who called himself Francis Buccinelli. Horatio suspected he was rotting in a swampy grave—or perhaps he'd left the country as the Brilliant Batin had claimed.

Khasib Pathan left for Saudi Arabia on business. He had no direct contact with his son, or at least none that the Homeland Security operatives who were monitoring him could determine.

And the Hare did what he'd always done when the hunters got too close; he disappeared.

7

CALLEIGH DUQUESNE DIDN'T FORGET.

She could be sweet, she could be charming, but the tenacity of a bloodhound flowed through her veins. There were only two kinds of cases as far as Calleigh was concerned: the ones she was working on, and the ones she had solved.

Abdus Sattar Pathan bothered her. He bothered her the way a twenty-two casing in a pile of spent semiauto rounds did—he just didn't *fit.* His background, his profession, his lifestyle, his faith; so much was at odds with the rest. She couldn't quite put it together, so she was doing what she often did when she needed to think; she was blowing holes in targets on the firing range.

Target. Breathe out. Squeeze. The pulse of the pistol in her hand, the muffled reports thudding through the padded headset. Nothing focused her like the zen of a bullet; in the instant of release she was both calm and centered.

Target. Breathe out. Squeeze.

The Brilliant Batin. Muslim magician, a contradiction in terms—Muslims are forbidden from attending magic shows, let alone performing them. Didn't go into the family business, like the other sons. Gave up money for freedom?

Calleigh knew what it was like to come from a family with problems; both her parents had been alcoholics. But even so, she'd followed in her father's footsteps to a certain degree, winding up with a badge instead of a lawyer's shingle.

So what made the Brilliant Batin different from his brothers and sisters? What was the deciding factor? Magic? But . . .

She stopped, hit the button to bring the target in and check her shots. She squinted at the body outline critically; a few of her head shots were a little closer to the edge than she liked. She tore it off, clipped a new one in place and sent it out.

Target. Breathe out. Squeeze.

It was the magic, somehow, that was bothering her. Sure, she could envision a scenario where a young Abdus watched his first magic show, maybe an actual magician at someone's birthday party, maybe on television, and was enthralled; could imagine him ordering his own magic set, practicing in secret, not letting his parents know what he was doing . . .

But that just didn't work. Abdus hadn't grown

up in an environment where he'd be exposed to such things. He'd grown up as royalty, in the midst of what was still a very conservative culture. There would have been no birthday parties with magicians, no decadent Western television. How could he have been exposed to such a thing—let alone developed the kind of obsessive interest that led to choosing it as a career—in such an environment?

Target. Breathe out—

And then, she saw the piece of the puzzle that had been eluding her.

She smiled, and squeezed off one final shot.

Right in the heart.

Ryan Wolfe found himself tapping his fingers more and more often.

It was a nervous tic he thought he'd lost long ago, but now it crept up on him at unexpected moments: when he was driving, when he was waiting for a file to load, even in bed when he was going to sleep. What all these activities had in common was that when his attention wandered, it always wandered to the same place.

Someone had tried to kill Horatio . . . and that person was still out there.

Like Calleigh, Wolfe worked on the case whenever he could—despite the fact that the trail had turned as cold as a corpse. He pored over the slim folder that Nadira Quadiri had provided and did his own research as well.

The file on the Hare wasn't large, but what it

contained was chilling. The matter-of-fact accounts of assassination and destruction were accompanied by photos that told their stories in even starker, more brutal detail. The blackened wreckage of a school bus, only the chassis still recognizable; the rest was a torn thicket of jagged black metal. Human forms strewn about in that horrible, limb-twisted way that robbed a body of its dignity as well as its life.

Other than a litany of death, the file told him little of the Hare himself. He was obviously skilled with explosives, and was apparently an excellent sniper as well; the hills of Afghanistan were littered with his victims. He was adept at disguise, fluent in English, and could apparently blend into an urban environment just as easily as he could vanish into a cave-riddled mountainside. He killed from afar when he could, but he was just as deadly at close range; he had cut more than one throat in his long career.

If the Hare was behind the attempt on Horatio's life, it was the first time his target had ever survived. Somehow, Wolfe didn't think the Hare would let that stand.

Which meant that Wolfe had to find a way to stop him.

Eric Delko thought he might be falling in love.

It wasn't like it had never happened before, but this time was different; for one thing, he wasn't just focusing on how he felt—he was thinking about other things, longer-range things. Being with Marie was making him evaluate his own life, and what he wanted out of it.

Not all of his thoughts were good ones. Miami was a summer city, a place of golden light and warm nights, and sometimes it seemed to Delko that the sweetest perfume was the mingling of a midnight breeze off the ocean with the tang of hot asphalt as the streets slowly cooled. It was a city smell, *his* city, and he loved its rich complexity and many diversions.

But now, he wondered if summer was coming to a close.

It was a bittersweet thought, colored all the more by the unsolved Pathan case and the knowledge that soon Marie and the Brilliant Batin would both be on the same boat in the middle of a vast, uncaring sea. He worried about her and worried about why he was worrying, and on top of it all was the knowledge that the Hare had already tried once before to kill someone he cared about.

And might again . . .

The piece that didn't fit was Abdus Sattar Pathan's mother.

Bridgette Pathan was the only one of Khasib Pathan's wives who wasn't Saudi. She was Swedish; her maiden name was Annik. What, Calleigh wondered, had brought her and Khasib, a wealthy oil mogul, together?

She decided to find out.

Bridgette Annik, it turned out, was not a common name. The Internet told Calleigh the woman had been born in Stockholm, had gone to university at Stuttgart, and had once published a book of poems. She was an attractive woman, but Calleigh could find no areas of overlap between her and a member of the Saudi royal family. Had Khasib met her while traveling? Had she traveled to the Middle East and encountered him?

The problem was, she needed the kind of information that only international agencies had access to. So she did what any good investigator did: she reached out to someone with better contacts than she had.

She met Nadira Quadiri in the restaurant of the hotel where Quadiri was staying at. The decor seemed to be a battle between raw gray concrete and lush tropical plants, the overall effect like a rainforest trying to overgrow a prison. Calleigh wasn't sure who was winning.

Nadira sat in a booth in the far corner, sipping a cup of chai tea. Calleigh slid in opposite her.

"Thank you for agreeing to meet with me," said Calleigh. "I wasn't even sure if you were still in town—haven't seen you around lately."

"I'm still here." Nadira was dressed in a loose black T-shirt and khaki shorts, her brown feet in sandals; though her attire was more casual than the last time Calleigh had seen her, her demeanor was just as businesslike. "What would you like to talk about?"

"Bridgette Pathan."

"Abdus's mother?"

"Yes. You have resources we don't—I was wondering if you could use them to get me some background on her. Specifically, how she met and wound up marrying Khasib."

"Can I ask where you're going with this?"

"Honestly, I'm not sure." Calleigh hesitated. "I'm working from the basis of first principles, I guess. Abdus must have gotten his interest in magic somewhere, and his mother seems the likely place to start."

"His magic." Nadira's voice was skeptical.

"I know, in a case like this the fact that one of the suspects is a magician might seem trivial. But Horatio thinks it's important, and I trust his instincts."

"I don't mean to slight your superior—but sometimes, loyalty must be tempered with perspective." Her tone was gentle, her eyebrows raised.

"I don't follow."

"I can tell that Horatio is very good at what he does—but that doesn't mean you don't have instincts of your own."

Calleigh frowned. "I'm sorry, Nadira, but I think you've got the wrong idea. Horatio isn't the kind of leader who expects blind obedience; he leads by example. I'm following this up because I think it's a direction that needs to be explored."

Nadira's smile was apologetic. "I'm the one who should ask forgiveness. But in my line of work—and yours, as well—we have to deal with strong male figures every day. Having come from a culture that expects a certain amount of subservience from their women, I suppose sometimes I overreact."

"I understand. Where I come from, women aren't exactly unfamiliar with that sort of culture."

"Of course. And like myself, you have adapted."

"Well, you do what you have to . . . what I'm wondering at the moment is what sort of adapting Bridgette Pathan had to do. From Stockholm to Saudi Arabia is one heck of a leap."

"Yes. Perhaps you're right—I'll look into it." Nadira shook her head, and suddenly she looked exhausted. "Right now, any new insights are welcome."

"Sounds like you're bogged down."

"It's always this way with the Hare. He vanishes at will, like smoke. Maybe he is a magician, after all."

"No such thing, Nadira. No matter how smooth their patter is, no matter what kind of tricks they have up their sleeve, they're still subject to the same laws we are."

"Sadly, the Hare has little respect for the law of any nation."

"Oh, I wasn't talking about those kinds of laws," said Calleigh, getting to her feet. "I meant the laws of nature. Those apply to everyone—and even the Hare can't break them."

* * *

"He *can't* be in two places at the same time," Wolfe muttered to himself. "It's just not possible."

He stared intently at the monitor. On one side of the screen he'd put up the dates and sites of attacks the Hare was believed to have committed; on the other, a detailed list of every place the Brilliant Batin had performed, and when he'd appeared. To this he'd added credit card receipts and other bills that placed Pathan at a specific location on a specific date.

Horatio walked into the computer lab. "Mister Wolfe? It looks like you've compiled quite the stack of data."

Wolfe sighed. "Yeah. Too bad it doesn't make sense . . . none of the dates line up, H. Look—when the Hare was masterminding a bombing in Lebanon, the Brilliant Batin was on a cruise ship in the Caribbean. When the Hare was ambushing a convoy in Kabul, Batin was performing in Palm Beach. There's no way they could be the same person, not if half the intel in this file is right."

Horatio studied the screen, his eyes narrowing. "Very good, Mister Wolfe."

"Good? I haven't solved a thing."

"Thomas Edison once said, after seven hundred unsuccessful experiments, that he hadn't failed at all. He'd succeeded in proving that seven hundred methods didn't work."

"Yeah, well, I feel like I'm on method number six hundred and ninety-nine."

"Then you're close to a breakthrough, aren't you?"

Wolfe glanced at his boss, smiled, and shook his head. "Horatio, doesn't this make you a little, I don't know . . ."

"Crazy?" Horatio smiled back. "We're all a little crazy, Mister Wolfe. I find that channeling that energy is infinitely more productive than complaining about it."

"I don't mean to sound negative. But this guy Pathan—he really gets under my skin, you know? I mean, he's *laughing* at us."

"And that's a good thing, Mister Wolfe. When two opponents meet, the one that takes the battle seriously is the one that survives."

Wolfe's fingers started drumming beside the mouse pad.

Frank Tripp decided it was time to play hardball.

Despite the respect he had for Horatio and his team, he knew that sometimes the only way to break a case was to pound on it until something—or someone—cracked. One of Tripp's favorite authors was John D. MacDonald, particularly his Travis McGee novels; McGee was a Florida "salvage specialist," whose preferred MO was to find out who was dirty, then make as much trouble for them as he could. This approach held a certain amount of appeal, and Tripp had found it effective on more than one occasion—but it was the sort of thing he saved as a last resort. Usually, the crime lab's more sophisticated techniques provided ample evidence for a conviction long before cruder methods had to be employed.

Besides, no matter how appealing the fantasy might be, Tripp wasn't an independent adventurer living on a houseboat and sipping Boodles gin with bikini-clad lovelies; he was a public servant, with all the responsibilities and restrictions that entailed. Of course, he was also from Texas, which meant that a certain amount of hell-raising was just in his blood . . . and every now and then, he let it out.

First on Tripp's list was Pierce Madigan. Men with money could be hard to intimidate, at least with the direct approach—but Tripp could be a lot more subtle when he had to be. And anyone could be pressured, if you were willing to do a little research beforehand. Money often revealed as many weaknesses as it protected.

Unfortunately, Tripp didn't get the chance. Pierce Madigan had vanished.

His office hadn't heard from him in days. His family didn't know where he was. His credit cards hadn't been used, nor had any large amounts been withdrawn from his bank account. He hadn't purchased any airline, bus, or train tickets. His car was parked in his regular spot in the office lot.

Strike one, he thought. He wondered how long it would take for Madigan's body to surface, or if it ever would.

* * *

Tripp was about to tuck into an extra-large helping of garlic prawns and wild rice when a young, extremely attractive woman with dusky skin sat down in the chair opposite him. Tripp frowned, then said, "Quadiri, right?"

"Yes. I believe Horatio Caine introduced us a few weeks ago."

"Right. Homeland Security. What can I do for you?"

"I understand you've been looking for Pierce Madigan."

"That's right. Why, you have a lead on him?"

"Actually, we have him."

Tripp paused. "You mean he's in custody?"

"He's being detained, yes."

"Whereabouts? I'd like to have a word with him."

"I'm afraid that won't be possible. As an Irish national, he's being held under the terms of the PATRIOT Act as an enemy combatant."

"You're kidding."

"No. We have reason to believe he aided and abetted a known international terrorist. We are questioning him, but he hasn't been formally charged."

"Right. He giving you anything useful?"

"I can't discuss that at the moment."

Tripp nodded. "Okay. So, why exactly are we having this conversation?"

"I just didn't want you wasting your time." Quadiri's look was steady and cool.

"Thanks," said Tripp. "Thanks a whole bunch."

* * *

Next on Tripp's list was Billy Lee Garenko. He knew Calleigh had talked to Billy Lee, and he knew Billy Lee had been too frightened to give her anything; that was bad news, because if Calleigh had found Billy Lee too tough a nut to crack then Tripp probably wouldn't do any better. Calleigh could be downright scary when she wanted.

But you couldn't win if you didn't play, so Tripp figured it was time to step up. If Garenko couldn't be persuaded by having his parole revoked, maybe he could be finessed. Of course, if he was going to go that route, he'd prefer to have the help of an expert . . .

"It's worth a try," Horatio said. He leaned back in his office chair. "But I really think it's Calleigh's call."

"Already asked her," said Tripp. "She didn't think we could budge him either, but wouldn't hold the attempt against us."

"Good enough for me . . ."

They took a department Hummer, Horatio driving. "How do you want to play this, Frank?"

"Been giving that some thought. Could be we'll catch more flies with honey than vinegar."

"Nice cop, nicer cop?"

"Something like that. Appeal to his better nature, maybe. A lot of these good old boys, they'll show a whole different side if you can put a patriotic spin on it. Even wise guys think of themselves as American—hell, when Little Pooch Berretano gave me that tip he did everything but sing the Star-Spangled Banner."

"True enough. Didn't Bugsy Siegel offer to put out a contract on Castro once?"

"So they say. Anyway, I figure if we play up the terrorism angle maybe we can get some results."

"In that case," said Horatio, "let's play . . ."

But when they got there, they found the game had changed.

Black smoke was visible from a mile away, curling into the air in a dark, greasy cloud. Horatio knew with a sickening certainty that it was more than just a trash fire.

The Hummer crunched to a stop at the end of the dirt track Billy Lee called a driveway. Billy Lee's residence—what was left of it—looked like it had been overrun by an army. Jagged-edged holes gaped in almost every wall, and smoke poured out of most of them.

Billy Lee Garenko lay just outside the open front door, a large pool of blood around his body. Horatio approached cautiously, gun drawn, but it was obvious the man was dead. Tripp backed him up, scanning the surrounding woods for any sign.

"Looks like a single shot to the chest," said Horatio.

"Only one? Seems like a war went on here."

"Looks can be deceiving, Frank. Those bullet holes are exits, not entrances—you can tell by the direction the metal's buckled."

"So the firefight was inside?"

"In a manner of speaking." Horatio pointed to a heap of charred wood that ran in a line down the length of the nearest wall. "Someone stacked fuel along the walls, doused them with an accelerant, then found cover in the woods. Started the fire with a time-delay or maybe an incendiary round. Then all he had to do was wait until Garenko ran outside."

"So all the shooting was Garenko, trying to nail his killer first by firing in every direction through the walls?"

"No, Frank. Garenko didn't get off a shot. The collateral damage was all caused by ammo cooking off inside—Garenko was a gun fanatic, remember? He must have had thousands of rounds stored."

"All that weaponry," said Tripp, "and it didn't do him a damn bit of good."

"Not against being roasted alive. All the shooter had to do was wait until he bolted, then pick him off."

"Sure—but Garenko was bound to stick his head out sooner or later anyway. Why the barbecue? Why not just hole up and wait for a good shot?"

Horatio straightened up and put his hands on his hips. "Either the shooter was in a hurry, or Garenko was scared enough to be extra-cautious. Either way, it didn't make much difference in the end."

"Think he's still out there?"

"No, Frank. If this was who I think it was, he's far too professional to stick around."

"You think it was this Hare character."

"I do. He's cleaning up loose ends."

Tripp didn't mention the obvious; that Horatio was one of those loose ends . . .

"Through and through," Alexx said, inspecting the exit wound on the back. She let the body settle gently to the ground. "Looks like some smoke inhalation, too."

"He knew what was waiting for him, Alexx," said Horatio. Calleigh and Delko were just gloving up in preparation to processing the scene; Tripp had already left.

Calleigh gazed down at the body. "Poor guy," she murmured. "All he wanted to do was tinker with his guns. I doubt he ever shot a living thing he didn't wind up eating."

"Not going to be easy finding the slug that killed him, either," said Delko. "Not with all the ammo that cooked off."

"It might be easier than you think," said Calleigh. "After all, it was the only bullet traveling toward the vic instead of away."

"Well, I'll leave that to your expertise," said Delko. "I'm going to scout the woods, see if I find the spot the shooter was firing from. That bluff over there looks like a good spot to start."

"Eric," said Horatio. "Be careful."

"Always, H."

* * *

Calleigh investigated the outside of Billy Lee Garenko's jury-rigged home first. She found what she was looking for on the far side of the structure: a back door. A circular exit had been cut into the metal and a metal hatch bolted on, then disguised with an old metal sign leaned against it. The sign had been dragged away and the hatch jammed shut with an old, rusty crowbar.

"I knew you were smart enough to have an escape route," Calleigh murmured. "Too bad the Hare was smarter."

She took pictures, then examined the site more closely. No prints on the sign, hatch, or crowbar. No footprints. She found an empty gas can, which told her where the accelerant came from.

She moved inside. The fire was out, but the place stank of gunpowder smoke and hot metal. Exploded boxes of ammo lay strewn about like the hatched eggs of some lethal monster.

Something Alexx had said nagged at her. *Smoke inhalation*. If Billy Lee had stayed inside long enough to suffer from smoke inhalation, he knew who was waiting for him outside. And maybe he'd tried to leave behind a message . . .

But where? Normally, Calleigh would check for something like a safe—but Billy Lee had turned the whole *house* into a safe. Plus, he wouldn't have had much time.

Calleigh's gaze fell on the stove.

"A little counterintuitive, maybe," she murmured, "but if you can't stand the fire . . ."

She pulled the oven door open. A single sheet of paper lay inside, with something scrawled on it.

". . . get creative in the kitchen."

The small bluff that Delko had spotted was perfect for a sniper; it offered an almost unobstructed view of the front of the building, with only a few thin saplings in the way. It had some low scrub at its crest, just enough to provide cover for someone lying prone.

Delko checked out the area carefully. No shell casings, but he did find a boot print: it looked like it might match the boot print found under the window of Talwinder Jhohal's house. He took a picture of it, then noted that the grass behind the scrub was pressed down, as if someone had laid a blanket or something down. He examined the area closely for fibers, but found nothing.

Could have been a plastic sheet. He took photos, then a few samples of the grass. When he was done, he crouched in the position in which the shooter must have lain. There was an almost perfect gap in the shrubbery that gave him a clear view of the building.

Almost too perfect. Delko studied the edges of the gap—sure enough, a few leaves and branches had been clipped off with some sort of implement. He took more photos and samples, including the clipped-off leaves he found at the base of the bush.

* * *

Horatio's cell rang while he was still a few miles outside Miami. "Horatio Caine," he said.

"Horatio? It's Nadira."

"Ms. Quadiri. What can I do for you?"

"You can thank me."

"Oh? What for?"

"Figuring out the Hare's secret."

Horatio paused. "If you're referring to the weapon that was smuggled into Miami, I already know."

"You have good sources, then." It was her turn to pause, and when she spoke again there was an unmistakable note of regret in her voice. "Have you told anyone else?"

"What do you think?"

"I think . . . I think that you would find making a choice between your duty as an officer and your responsibility to those you care about extremely difficult."

"And you wouldn't?"

"Compassion is not always a police officer's friend, Horatio."

"No, it isn't. But it should always be his—or her—companion."

"Well put—but you still haven't answered my question."

"Perhaps I didn't understand it. Let's see if I can rephrase it for more clarity . . . did I, Horatio Caine, deliberately conceal my knowledge of a potential terrorist attack on the city where my friends, coworkers, and family live? Did I fail to warn them of an imminent threat to their safety, even though it was within my power to do so?"

He waited, but she said nothing.

"Yes," said Horatio. "That's exactly what I did."

She sighed. "Do you want me to apologize? To tell you how hard it is for me to keep things like that secret? Because if you want to play the martyr and cast me as the villain, that's fine. But at the end of the day, you know we both want the same thing—and I think that objective is now within our grasp."

"Tell me," said Horatio.

She did.

"That certainly explains a lot," said Horatio. "We've been hunting the wrong man."

"Not anymore. Perhaps we can even catch him before he kills again."

"Too late for that, I'm afraid." He told her about Billy Lee Garenko.

"Wait—you say he used a sniper rifle? Where did this Garenko live? Was it urban or more remote?"

"Out in the middle of nowhere. Why?"

"Horatio, where are you now?" Her voice was suddenly urgent.

"On the outskirts of town, driving in. Why?"

"The last time the Hare performed an assassination in this fashion, the first killing was merely bait. He then shot and killed four more men who came to investigate."

Horatio slammed on the brakes.

Calleigh. Delko. Alexx.

But as he turned the Hummer around with a squeal of tires, he realized that a black Range Rover behind him had also stopped.

The Hare, it seemed, was tired of being chased . . .

8

HORATIO KNEW IT HAD TO BE HIM.

"Nadira, a black Range Rover just pulled up, about a hundred yards behind me. I think it's our friend."

"Horatio—*skzzzzzxxx.*" Nadira's words were cut off by a burst of static.

Wide-range radio frequency jammer. Horatio was familiar with them—the bomb squad used them to block remote-activated explosive devices.

But they worked just fine on cell phones, too.

Horatio had pulled a U-turn on the road, and now he was facing the Range Rover on the narrow shoulder. Other than their two vehicles, the road was deserted. A hundred yards of distance was enough to draw a shimmery curtain of heat between himself and the other vehicle.

"Okay, pal," said Horatio, "if that's how you want it . . ." He floored the accelerator. The Hummer roared forward, leaving black strips behind its wheels.

Horatio's plan was simple. At a hundred yards, the Hare could use a sniper rifle to blow him away without ever coming within reach of Horatio's Glock. But it would take time for him to set up, and hopefully Horatio could get close enough to negate the Hare's advantage before the killer could put it to use.

If the Hare had been named only for his elusiveness, the plan might have worked—but he had his namesake's speed, as well.

Horatio was ninety yards away when the Range Rover's door swung open. A man wearing a black scarf wrapped around his face and a hooded jacket jumped out.

Eighty yards. The man pulled a rifle with a telescopic sight out of the front seat.

Seventy yards. The hooded figure used the open window of the open door as a rest and sighted through the scope at the Hummer.

Sixty. Horatio yanked the wheel back and forth, swerving across the blacktop and making the Hummer a harder target to hit.

Fifty. The Hare took out the Hummer's right front tire with his first shot. The blowout came at exactly the wrong moment; the front edge of the rim dug in just as the front end was starting to swing into another swerve. The Hummer flipped and rolled, landing on its roof and screeching along the pavement in a shower of sparks. It traveled another twenty yards before grinding to a halt.

Thirty yards away, the Hare surveyed his handiwork through the rifle's scope. He saw no movement.

Calleigh's phone rang. "CSI Duquesne."

"Calleigh, this is Nadira Quadiri. Listen carefully and don't interrupt. The Hare has set a trap for Horatio. He's on a highway just outside Miami, and his phone is not working. Do you know where he would be?"

"Yes."

"Get there as fast as you can."

Calleigh was already moving. "We're gone," she said. "Eric! Drop what you're doing and get over here! *The Hare's after Horatio!*"

Horatio found himself hanging upside down from his seat belt. He undid it, dropped down, and scrambled out the open passenger-side window. He knew his best chance was to stay behind cover; while he could certainly return fire, a sniper rifle was vastly more accurate than a Glock at thirty yards.

He made it outside without hearing a shot; the bulk of the Hummer was between him and the shooter. The vehicle was right on the edge of the road, beside a wide, grassy ditch—beyond that was a stand of palmetto trees and some bushes. The bushes might hide him, but they wouldn't provide much protection.

The crack of a rifle and the *spang!* of the bullet

ricocheting off metal were almost simultaneous. Horatio had his own gun out, but knew the shot was meant to draw his fire; that way, the Hare could pinpoint his position.

Horatio didn't take the bait. Much as he wanted to take down the Hare, stepping out and blazing away wasn't the smart choice. If he could just wait the Hare out, another driver would see the accident and possibly report it. Horatio hoped that the next motorist wasn't *too* good a Samaritan, though; the last thing he needed was another target for the Hare to shoot at. If someone actually pulled over to help, Horatio had no doubt the Hare would kill them out of simple necessity.

It all depended on who drove by first.

"You know what route H was taking?" Delko asked, pulling out his cell phone. Calleigh was driving, ramming the big Hummer down the dirt track.

"There's two possibles, but I'm betting he took Northwest Fourteenth to Krome, " she said tersely. "Who are you calling?"

"Wolfe. He said he had an errand to run in Opa-Locka West today. If so, he might be able to get there before us—Wolfe? It's Delko. Where are you? Okay, here's the situation . . ." Delko ran it down quickly.

"So?" Calleigh asked after he hung up.

"We're in luck. He's in Medley—he can be there in a few minutes."

* * *

Horatio considered his options.

He could sprint for the trees. He could see heavier undergrowth beyond them, and it might be possible to either lose the Hare or set up an ambush of his own.

He rejected that one almost immediately. The Hare was a skilled hunter and tracker with plenty of experience—plus, the trees were simply too far away. Horatio wouldn't make it halfway before being shot.

Option number two: take the battle to him. The Hummer blocked the Hare's view of Horatio; he might be able to circle around to the other side and get off a shot from there.

He looked around carefully first, evaluating his immediate environment, seeing if there was anything within reach he was overlooking. A flicker of light caught his eye; he realized that the driver's-side mirror—though cracked, bent, and upside down—was now angled to give him an almost perfect view of the Range Rover.

Score one for serendipity, he thought.

The hooded man was still crouched behind his open driver's-side door, the rifle resting on the inside of the window frame. He was clearly waiting for his target to show himself, but he'd be just as aware as Horatio of the time factor. He wouldn't want to wait long.

Nor did he.

The next few shots *thunked* solidly into the Hummer's frame, but nowhere near Horatio. The shots were followed by an even more ominous sound: the gurgle of draining liquid.

He's holed the gas tank. Horatio could hear the fuel splashing onto the hot asphalt, could smell the heady fumes. *All he has to do now is ignite it . . .*

Wolfe had been running down a possible lead on Francis Buccinelli. It turned out to be a dead-end—Frankie Buckets, as he was called, was actually Francis Bukowski, and about as Italian as chow mein.

And then he got Delko's call.

He was in his Hummer and speeding through traffic within seconds. A distant part of his brain noted that he was close to panic, and he forced himself to calm down. He couldn't do Horatio any good if he ran the Hummer off the road before he got there.

His fingers rapped out a nervous tattoo on the steering wheel. Without even being aware of it, he started to count things: five traffic lights, two shopping carts, three palm trees.

Horatio would be all right. He had to be.

It was much harder to make a vehicle explode in real life than in the movies or on television—where a car hurtling off a cliff was practically guaranteed to blow up in midair—but one sure way was to set it on fire. The Hare accomplished this by ricocheting a few slugs off the road, throwing sparks at the growing puddle of gasoline from the ruptured fuel tank. It took him a few tries, during which Horatio prepared himself for the inevitable.

When the fire finally caught with a whoosh of flame, Horatio knew he had only moments to act. Staying put meant being caught in the inevitable fireball; leaving cover meant putting himself in the crosshairs of a sniper rifle.

There was only one viable alternative. Horatio aimed his Glock dead ahead and took one step backward, keeping the overturned Hummer between himself and the Hare. He took another step, then another, knowing that every foot he traveled shrank his cover.

The Hare would know it, too; he might even leave his own position, angling to one side or the other in the hope of catching Horatio in the open. Horatio didn't know which direction the Hare would pick, but it didn't really matter. They would see each other in the same instant, and both of them would be unprotected.

A gunfight. Rifle versus pistol, with both weapons already drawn.

The problem, of course, was that Horatio's Glock was designed primarily to be effective at close range; with every step he took backward, he gave the Hare a little bit more of an advantage. It came down to a brutally simple equation—the distance from the vehicle Horatio had to be when it finally blew up, versus how close he had to stay to have a fighting chance against the Hare.

The decision was taken out of his hands as the

Hummer exploded. A shock wave of heat and concussive force hammered him backward, and then everything went black.

Wolfe heard the deep-throated boom a few seconds before he rounded the curve and saw the blazing vehicle.

And then he saw Horatio.

His boss was lying on his back about twenty feet from the overturned Hummer. There was another vehicle, a black Range Rover, parked about thirty yards past that, but the oily smoke from the burning wreck obscured his view.

Wolfe slammed to a stop between Horatio and the flames. He scooted over and leaped out the passenger-side door, keeping low, trying to minimize his profile.

Horatio was moving, sitting up groggily and supporting himself with one arm. His Glock was in his other hand, pointed toward Wolfe's Hummer. Despite his having just regained consciousness, the gun was rock-steady in his hand.

"H, you okay?" Wolfe had his own weapon drawn, but his first priority was making sure Horatio was all right.

"Mister Wolfe?"

"Right here, H."

"I could have sworn that vehicle just blew up," Horatio muttered.

"It's mine, H. Yours is in worse shape."

"Ah. You show . . . excellent timing, Mister

Wolfe." Horatio got to his feet with Wolfe's help, his gun never wavering. "Stay low. We've got a sniper with a scoped rifle, and he's an extremely good shot."

They crouched behind the front tire of Wolfe's vehicle. "The Hare?" Wolfe asked.

"I believe so."

The wail of sirens rose in the distance, an angry chorus drawing closer. "Reinforcements are on the way, H. We're gonna nail this guy."

"Remember what he's famous for, Mister Wolfe. I'm not going to give him the chance to escape . . . You go left, I'll go right. I'll draw his fire; while he's concentrating on me, do your best to take him out."

"Got it."

Wolfe waited until Horatio had crept to the far side of the Hummer, then moved at his signal. He skirted the edge of the flames, ready to fire.

Horatio had no intention of letting the Hare get the drop on him. He darted from cover with his gun blazing, aiming for the open driver's-side door and targeting from memory.

His aim was true. His shots *thunked* into the still-open door, with a sound he automatically knew was wrong. He saw why instantly: a bulletproof vest had been draped over the door, transforming cover into armor.

The second thing he noticed was that the weapon the Hare was now aiming through the open window wasn't a sniper rifle. Its muzzle was big enough to stick a fist into, and it had a thinner barrel mounted alongside the thick one. The whole structure rested on his shoulder, rather than against it.

The smaller muzzle spoke first, spitting a bullet that shattered the windshield of the Hummer. *Spotting round,* Horatio had time to think, and then the larger muzzle fired with a noise like a giant's cough. As the missile streaked toward them, Horatio yelled, "Wolfe! *Get clear!*"

This time, the blackness was much more abrupt.

When Calleigh spotted the smoke from the first explosion, Delko hoped there were no other cars on the road between her and Horatio; he was convinced she'd just drive over them.

The second explosion sounded different from the first. "What do you think?" Delko asked.

"I don't know. Horatio's the explosives expert, not me—but the last one sounded a lot more powerful than the first."

It took no more than three minutes to cover the remaining distance, but to Delko it felt like hours. The scene when they arrived confirmed his worst fears: two overturned burning Hummers, two bodies lying in the road. Four radio cars, sirens screaming, pulled up a moment later.

Calleigh and Delko were already sprinting toward the figures sprawled on the pavement. Delko reached the nearest one first; it was Wolfe, lying on his back with blood running down his face. Delko checked Wolfe's pulse, found it weak but present.

"He's still breathing," said Delko. "How's H?"

"Still . . . among the living," said a familiar low voice.

"Just lie still, Horatio," said Calleigh. "Paramedics are on their way." She fixed a steely eye on one of the officers who'd just scrambled out of his car and snapped, "You! Get a first-responder emergency team down here, *now*!"

"How's Wolfe?" croaked Horatio.

"Unconscious but alive," said Delko. "Nasty head wound, though."

"Range Rover," said Horatio. "Black."

"He's gone, Horatio. You and Wolfe were the only ones here when we arrived," said Calleigh.

Horatio recited a string of numbers and letters, Calleigh nodding and repeating them back to show she understood. She waved another officer over and told him to get an immediate BOLO out for a black Range Rover with the license tag Horatio had given her.

"We'll get him, Horatio," said Calleigh. "Don't worry."

"Yes . . . ma'am," whispered Horatio.

"Horatio? *Horatio!*"

Horatio opened his eyes and saw that he was in a hospital bed. He was still fully clothed, though his suit was scorched and torn. A ruddy-faced doctor with a large nose was peering at him in the same manner Horatio reserved for studying evidence.

"How many fingers?" the doctor asked, holding up a splayed hand.

"Four," said Horatio. "And one thumb."

The doctor peered into his eyes, checked his reflexes, and asked him a few more questions before pronouncing him the victim of a mild concussion. "It looks far worse than it is," the doctor said. "I think your suit is a goner, though."

"I have others," said Horatio. "Ryan Wolfe—he would have been brought here with me. How's his condition?"

The doctor hesitated. "I'm afraid Mister Wolfe's condition is more serious; at present he's in a comatose state. We'll know more after we run some tests—"

"Take me to him," said Horatio. He swung his legs over the side of the bed.

Calleigh walked through the door at the same moment the doctor said, "Just hold on a minute, Mister Caine—we'd like you to stay overnight, just in case there are any complications—"

"It's *Lieutenant* Caine," Horatio said. "And while I appreciate your dedication to my health, I have responsibilities of my own." He straightened the cuffs on his shirt, ignoring the large singe mark on the left one. "So you're going to take me to see my CSI, after which I will leave you to do your job . . . and you'll let me leave to do mine." Horatio met the doctor's eyes. "All right?"

The doctor met his eyes without blinking, then sighed. "Okay, have it your way. Just make sure you come back if you have any dizziness, ringing in your ears, or nausea. Let me locate your friend, first; he may have been taken up to X-ray."

"I'd appreciate it."

Calleigh had watched this entire exchange without saying a word, her arms crossed, a slight smile on her face. She walked up to Horatio as the doctor left and said, "Well, I see it takes more than a surface-to-surface missile to put a dent in the famous Caine composure."

"What I seem to be composed *of,* at the moment," Horatio said, touching his forehead with two fingers and wincing, "is rusty wire and broken glass . . ."

"Maybe you should listen to the doctor, H. That was one hell of a—"

"The Hare, Calleigh. He got away. Didn't he?"

"I'm afraid so, H. We locked down the area, but somehow he slipped through."

"Delko's working the scene?"

"Yeah. I have to head back and give him a hand, actually—there's a lot to process. Just had to make sure you were okay, first."

"I'll be fine. I'm going to look in on Mister Wolfe, and then I'll join you."

"He'll be all right, Horatio. He's like you—too stubborn to die." She paused, then said, "We found something interesting at the Garenko scene, but I don't know what it means yet. Billy Lee left a note inside his stove, but he must have scrawled it at the last second, probably in a room full of smoke; all it says is, 'Daldev.' "

Horatio nodded. "Good work. You'd better get back before Eric feels unappreciated."

After Calleigh left, Horatio went to the bathroom and cleaned up as best he could. One of his eyebrows had been singed, there were abrasions on the side of his neck, and bits of dirt and what looked like charred plastic were stuck in his hair.

He was more shook up than he cared to admit. He hadn't even told Calleigh what Nadira had told him—somehow, it had slipped his mind. Maybe he was a little more concussed than he'd thought.

He stared at himself in the mirror for a long moment, then took a deep, shaky breath and nodded. "Okay," he said. "Okay . . ."

By the time Calleigh got back to the two ruined Hummers, Delko had finished with the Garenko site and was about to start processing the vehicle wreckage. She'd already updated him on Horatio's and Wolfe's conditions via cell phone; Delko was relieved that H was all right but worried about Wolfe. Despite the occasional friction between them, Delko trusted Wolfe with his life; he knew Wolfe felt the same way about him. Delko had been the one to drive Wolfe to the hospital when a suspect had fired a nail gun into his eye, and the emotions Delko felt at the moment were far too familiar.

"What a mess," said Calleigh.

"Yeah. Two CSIs in the hospital, two Hummers in the junkyard. This guy's a one-man army."

"Army is right," said Calleigh, crouching and inspecting the debris. "The weapon that did this is definitely military. A SMAW would be my guess."

"SMAW?"

"Shoulder-mounted Multipurpose Assault Weapon—a rocket launcher."

"Packs one hell of a punch."

"It should. They're primarily used for taking out tanks."

"Not exactly a commonplace item—where do you think he got it?"

"I"ll bet Miami Marko could have told us—if he wasn't occupying one of Alexx's drawers at the moment."

Delko nodded. "The junkyard shootings. Marko got hold of some heavy-duty ordinance and sold it to the Hare. Only . . ."

"—he wasn't expecting negotiations to be quite so . . . cutthroat," Calleigh finished.

"If the Hare killed Miami Marko over a major weapons buy, he has to be gearing up for something big."

"Well, whatever it is, we're not going to find out anything by standing here talking. Let's get to work."

Ryan Wolfe was not okay.

His one eye—not the one that had been previously injured by a nail gun, at least that was something—was swollen shut. Ugly red scratches crisscrossed his chin, and his lips were split and crusted over with dried blood in several places. There was an IV drip in his arm and an oxygen tube in his nose.

Horatio stared down at him with eyes that were far from calm. "Mister Wolfe," he began, but his voice cracked and he had to stop.

"Ryan," he said. "I'm . . . I'm sorry. You shouldn't have been there." He reached down and put his hand on Wolfe's shoulder. "But you were. You were there because you're a good cop. And one hell of a CSI. Okay?"

There was no reply from Wolfe other than his slow, raspy breathing.

"Don't give up, Mister Wolfe," said Horatio softly. "That's an order."

Once the scene was processed, Calleigh and Delko headed back to the lab. She concentrated on the rocket attack, while Delko took a closer look at the Garenko evidence. They'd discussed Billy Lee's final message, but neither of them had puzzled it out.

"I was right about the rocket launcher," said Calleigh. She was studying a schematic on a monitor and comparing it to a recovered fragment in front of her. "Even got a partial serial number."

Delko looked up from the comparison microscope. "Yeah? You've got a positive ID?"

"I do. It's a SMAW Mark one fifty-three, firing a high-explosive antiarmor rocket. Or to put it another way, the world's biggest nine-millimeter gun."

Delko frowned. "Nine mill? You've got to be kidding."

She gave him a tired smile. "I am, actually. The launcher has a built-in nine-millimeter rifle for spotting purposes—the ammo is stored right in the cap of the rocket, and the gun is calibrated to the rocket itself. You fire the rifle first, and whatever the bullet hits tells you exactly where the rocket's going to go."

"You find any nine-mill rounds at the scene?"

"No, but they'd be easy to miss in an explosion like that—especially if he only squeezed off one or two. If he's good, that's all he'd need."

"Good isn't exactly the word I'd use," said Delko. "Think you can figure out where the launcher came from?"

"It's probably one of ours—the one fifty-three was fielded in 1984 as a Marine Corps weapon. During Desert Storm, the manufacturer delivered a hundred and fifty launchers and five thousand rockets to the U.S. Army. I'll see if I can trace this one back . . . how are you doing?"

"The boot print I found matches the one at the Jhohal house, plus I've got tool marks on the edge of these branches. The Hare must have clipped them off to give himself a better view of the Garenko place while he was surveilling it. Most military types have a favorite knife or utility tool they always carry with them—if we can actually catch this guy, he may still have it."

"Not if, " said Calleigh. "*When.*"

Horatio arranged for Nadira Quadiri to talk to his staff. They used the conference room at the lab, and Frank Tripp sat in as well. It was time for everyone to be brought up to speed; he'd worry about the consequences later.

Nadira stood at the head of the table, Horatio standing beside her. She started by asking how Wolfe was doing.

"There's been no change," said Horatio. "But the doctors are hopeful."

"I don't mean to make light of an obvious tragedy," said Nadira. "But both of you are extremely lucky to be alive. You may be the only two men in the world to have survived the Hare's wrath."

"He wants wrath?" Delko said in a cold voice. "We'll show him *wrath.*"

"You got that right," said Tripp. "Hell, we know where this dirtwad lives—are you telling me we can't find *something* to bust him for?"

"That's just it, Frank," said Horatio. "Going after Abdus Pathan is exactly what the Hare wants us to do. In a way, it's Abdus's sole reason for living."

"Ms. Duquesne must be given the credit for seeing the solution," Nadira said. "She was the one who directed my attention to Abdus Pathan's mother."

"Bridgette Pathan?" said Calleigh. "I knew she didn't fit, but I couldn't figure out how."

"Bridgette Annik was a young college student when she was approached by Khasib Pathan," said Nadira. "He wooed her with expensive gifts, flamboyant gestures, and his own not inconsiderable charm. They were married within a year."

"So he adds another woman to his harem," said Delko. "What difference does it make whether she's Swedish or Arabic?"

"The difference," said Horatio, "is not in her nationality, but her DNA. Bridgette Annik belongs to one of twenty documented bloodlines with a particular genetic predisposition."

"Toward what?" asked Calleigh.

"Twins," said Horatio.

9

"YOU'VE GOTTA BE KIDDING ME," said Tripp. "An evil twin? What is this, a bad soap opera?"

"It is deadly serious," said Nadira. "With far worse consequences than might be immediately obvious. Conception took place in the seventies, at the time that effective fertility treatments were beginning to be developed. A man with Khasib's wealth and connections would certainly have been able to arrange access to early versions of the treatments."

"Fertility treatments," said Delko. "Don't those often cause multiple births?"

"They do," said Calleigh. "But they do so by causing more than one egg to be fertilized, leading to fraternal twins rather than identical."

"True," said Nadira. "But the actual cause of monozygotic—identical—twins remains a mystery. It is a trait that can be passed along, but the exact triggering mechanism is still unknown. And the effect that fertility drugs would have on someone with a predisposition for twins has never been studied."

"Hold on," said Tripp. "Are you trying to say that Khasib went to all this trouble just to produce a matched set of kids?"

"That's exactly what we're saying, Frank," said Horatio. "Khasib and Abdus have been working together all along—in fact, Khasib must have been orchestrating this operation for decades. And the thing is, we don't know how many children Bridgette actually gave birth to."

"The hospital records are missing," said Nadira. "The attending physician, the medical documents—all gone. All that is left is a single birth certificate, that of Abdus Sattar Pathan. But there must have been others. Perhaps one, perhaps three or four."

"A litter," said Tripp. "Just like a real rabbit. Goddamn."

"No," said Nadira, putting her hands on the front of the table and leaning forward. "Not a litter. An army. One raised in the most dangerous parts of the world—Lebanon, Palestine, Afghanistan. Soldiers trained from the moment they were born, trained to hunt and kill and disappear."

"Trained to hate," said Calleigh softly.

"Except for Abdus," said Horatio. "The Islamic meaning of his name is "slave to the one who conceals faults." Concealing faults is, in fact, what Abdus was created *for*."

Delko shook his head in disbelief. "He's a living alibi."

"He's more than that," said Horatio. "He's a sleeper agent. Brought up in the West to understand our ways, gather information, position himself strategically. He's also the perfect decoy; if the Hare gets in trouble, Abdus takes the blame. He uses his own skills to make sure the physical evidence is contradictory, which means we can't get a conviction."

"So Abdus never was the Hare," said Calleigh. "We've been chasing an illusion."

"Greyhounds," growled Tripp. "Running after a fake mechanical rabbit we can't catch."

"The difference being," said Horatio, "that we're no longer running on Pathan's track."

When Ryan Wolfe took a nail to the eye, it had affected his sight. Worried that his vision might become permanently impaired, he had gone for medical advice to Doctor Alexx Woods. She had treated him as best she could, but advised him to see a specialist; worried that an official diagnosis would jeopardize his job, he had put off doing so as long as possible—even though he developed an infection, orbital cellulitis, that could have made his condition far worse.

Alexx had chastised him, but not too harshly. She understood how important what he did was to him, understood what it was like to weigh the consequences of your actions against what you knew to be right. In the end, Wolfe had done the right thing.

Alexx had been in a similar situation, only it wasn't her own health she was risking, it was the health of others. In the end she had made her own choice, reporting the incompetence of a medical colleague that was endangering patients—a choice that had ultimately cost Alexx her job.

But not her career. She had discovered a new path, working with Horatio and his CSIs to find justice for the dead, and though it led through some dark areas, it was a path she was glad she was on. The darker the place, she believed, the more it needed someone to shine a light on it.

Where Alexx stood now, at the foot of Wolfe's bed, was very dark indeed.

"*Damn* it, Wolfe," she whispered.

Alexx occasionally suffered from nightmares. They varied in specifics, but never in content. They weren't of the disconnected, surreal type, where images and events bled together and leaped around, but the kind where every detail was vivid and completely ordinary. The dreams always began with her at work in the autopsy lab: she could smell the disinfectant, hear the squeaky left wheel in that one trolley, feel the comfortable, familiar weight of an instrument in her hand. Nothing was wrong, nothing was out of place.

And then one of her assistants would wheel in the body of someone she loved.

Sometimes it was Calleigh, sometimes Delko,

sometimes Horatio. CSI Tim Speedle had made the occasional appearance, until he had been shot and killed in the line of duty; Alexx had been the one who performed the autopsy. After that, he'd never shown up again—apparently her subconscious only cast the living.

Her reaction to seeing one of her friends on her table was never one of shock or horror or grief; it was always anger. She would still talk to the corpse, but it would receive barely restrained fury instead of her usual sympathy. She would berate it for dying, accuse it of having been careless or irresponsible or worse.

And then Calleigh or Eric or Horatio would open his or her eyes and try to explain.

She wouldn't listen. Instead, she'd grow even angrier, meeting reasoned words with sarcasm and impatience. The dreams always ended with her leaving the room in disgust, looking for someone official she could complain to about this serious breach of protocol. She never found anyone. She would awaken still angry, then feel an immediate rush of guilt.

Now, looking at Ryan's unmoving body propped up in the hospital bed, she didn't know what she felt.

"I don't know if you can hear me or not," she said briskly. "But there have been numerous cases where patients in a coma woke up knowing things they shouldn't; there's even an apocryphal story about an English tourist who falls into a coma while traveling in France and wakes up speaking perfect French—even though he didn't know a word beforehand. So, Mister Wolfe, I'm going to assume some of this is getting through."

She paused, took a deep breath, then continued. "First of all, you aren't dead. I feel a little strange saying that, but I don't want any misunderstandings. I'm not talking to you because you're on my table. I mean, you *aren't* on my table. You're in a hospital room, and I'm here strictly as a friend. I don't mean you can't depend on me for assistance—of *course* you can—just that you don't *need* my services at the moment. I mean, you're not *going* to need them. At all."

She broke off and muttered "*Damn* it," to herself.

"Look, if I seem a bit . . . formal, it's because I don't want you getting the wrong idea. I need you to know that I'm here and I'm worried about you, but I don't want your subconscious translating my compassion into an assumption that—well, that you're a corpse."

"I'm a corpse?" whispered Wolfe.

"*Ryan?* Ryan, oh, baby, how are you?" she blurted.

"You're the doctor," he croaked. "You tell me."

"You're okay, sweetie, you're okay. You suffered a concussion and you were comatose for almost a day, but otherwise you're fine."

"Horatio. How's—"

"He's fine, too, honey. On his feet and still working the case. Which you," she said firmly, "are *not*.

You try getting out of that bed and I'll have them put you in a body cast."

"Think I liked you better," whispered Wolfe, "when I was a corpse . . ."

"The fingerprints," said Delko. "The ones we couldn't match to the convenience store robbery, even though we had surveillance video of when they were laid down."

"It was the Hare, all along," said Calleigh. "He was the one who attacked the clerk."

"Yes," said Nadira. "To one indoctrinated his entire life to despise Western culture and Western beliefs, the sight of a nude Arabic woman in a Western magazine must have seemed a gross insult, a violation of everything he believes he's fighting for."

"So he attacks Jhohal," said Tripp, "only the guy proves a little tougher than the Hare's expecting, and they both wind up unconscious."

"Of course," said Delko. "The Hare wakes up in the hospital, handcuffed to a bed. He manages to drag the bed over to the cabinet, finds a cell phone, and calls his brother. That's why I found Pathan's number on the phone of the guy in a coma."

"Right," said Horatio. "Pathan gets the story and tells the Hare to not let the arresting officers take his fingerprints—not until Pathan gets there himself. Enter Francis Buccinelli, the disappearing lawyer."

"The Brilliant Batin, in a supporting role," said

Calleigh. "He disguises himself, uses fake ID to get in to see the Hare, then invokes client-attorney privilege to get some privacy."

"At which point," said Horatio, "the two switch clothes, the Hare dons the disguise, and the magician becomes the prisoner."

"And the Hare walks out the front door," said Tripp. "All right, I can see how that could be done. But if they're identical twins, then why don't Pathan's prints match the ones found at the crime scene? Shouldn't they be the same?"

"Actually," said Calleigh, "they shouldn't. What most people don't realize is that—though their DNA is the same—even identical twins have different fingerprints. We were so convinced that Pathan used some kind of sleight of hand to fake the prints that we didn't believe our own evidence—which told us that the person who left the prints on the magazine was not the same person who was fingerprinted while in custody. And he wasn't."

"Okay, we know how he did it," said Delko. "We still don't know *why*."

Nadira and Horatio shared a glance. "That's one of the reasons I called you here," said Horatio. "You know we discovered evidence of radioactive materials in Sean Daltry's car. Those materials were the reason he was killed . . . and, through sources of my own, I've discovered the nature of those materials. I haven't shared that information with you, and I apologize for that—"

"It's not Horatio's fault," interrupted Nadira. "I

asked him to keep that information to himself because the risk of starting a citywide—even a national—panic was simply too high."

"Are we talking nuclear terrorism, here?" asked Tripp.

"That is precisely what we are talking about, Detective," said Nadira. "We have been questioning Pierce Madigan for the last few days. He was reluctant to cooperate, but eventually saw reason. What he told us confirmed a scenario we have dreaded for some time . . ."

The Hare surveyed the weapons laid out on the table before him. His true name was Ashab al Din, which meant Lion of the Faith—but no one had called him that for a very, very long time; even his father, whom he spoke with exactly once a year, referred to him as Al-Arnab—the Hare.

In truth, most of those people who knew the name he'd been born with were dead; the doctor who delivered him, the men who trained him, his own mother. Of his siblings, only those who shared his birth were aware of his existence, and of those only Abdus had escaped the grave. The others had met their end by landmine or mortar shell or machine gun, none of them strong enough or smart enough or lucky enough to survive the brutal landscapes of their youth.

But the Hare had.

He had fed on the carnage, warmed himself with the flames, learned to speak the language of blades and bullets and bombs. He had understood, very early on, that he was blessed by Allah to be given a pure, true purpose; unlike most men, who walked through their lives as aimlessly as leaves blown by the wind, he was immune to doubt or hesitation.

And now he would accomplish his greatest, most important mission. Here, he would strike a blow for Allah that would show everyone—infidels and believers alike—that America, the Great Satan, would never crush the spirit of Islam.

In September of 2000, Nadira told them, a former presidential security advisor for the Soviet Union named Aleksandr Lebed made a shocking declaration: Before the collapse of the USSR, the KGB had not only designed but built something called an ADM, which stood for Atomic Demolition Munition. It was a suitcase-sized nuclear bomb with a yield of one megaton—and the Soviet Union's secret police division had, in fact, manufactured a large number of them in the 1970s.

But that, while disturbing, wasn't the worst part. According to the Russian ex-official, over one hundred of the ADMs went missing after the Berlin Wall fell.

"This much is public knowledge," said Nadira. "What is not is the concerted efforts of intelligence agencies across the globe to track, locate, and eliminate these devices. So far, these efforts have proven successful; no one wants these weapons to be available, let alone used. You would be amazed at some of the groups that have agreed to work together on this matter."

"That's what the Hare has?" asked Delko. "A suitcase-sized nuclear device?"

"Yes," said Horatio.

There was a moment of quiet as everybody in the room digested the information.

"Good Lord," said Calleigh softly.

"Wait a minute," said Tripp. "I thought you said people were cooperating on this. Why the hell would the IRA sell a nuke to an anti-American terrorist? There's plenty of Irish ex-pat supporters in the States, 'specially on the East Coast—I can't believe even those hotheads would put someplace like Boston or the Big Apple at risk."

"First of all," Nadira said, "it's not the IRA per se; it's a radical faction that calls itself the Real Irish Republican Army."

"Real original," muttered Delko.

"Second, after intensive questioning Pierce Madigan revealed that one of the conditions of the deal was that the device not be used on American soil."

"Sure," said Tripp. "You can always trust the word of a homicidal maniac, right?"

"Actually, Frank," said Horatio, "Nadira believes that Madigan was given information about the intended target—information that apparently convinced him to take the Hare at his word."

"So," said Calleigh, "if Madigan is talking, why

hasn't he given up the location of the target? Is he trying to strike a deal?"

"Not exactly . . ." said Horatio.

The Hare checked the weapons one more time, field-stripping the rifles one by one, making sure that every piece of equipment was in perfect working order. Preparation was always the key to a smooth operation, though adaptability in the field was even more important. No matter how swift the animal, one that ran only in a straight line sooner or later fell victim to a predator's fangs.

As he worked, his thoughts turned to Abdus. They had met only twice, but it had left a deep, lasting impression on Husam. The physical resemblance was remarkable, of course; Abdus had even painstakingly duplicated his scars, of which there were many. He touched the bandage on his calf, where he had cut himself on a jagged piece of scrap at the junkyard; even the famed Hare could suffer an unforseen accident.

But it had been the kindred spirit behind Abdus's eyes he had recognized most strongly, the bright, clear flame of belief. Although fear was an emotion he had ruthlessly expunged from his soul, the Hare had still dreaded that first meeting; to come face-to-face with another version of himself, one who had wallowed in Western indulgence for as long as the Hare had burned in the fires of faith. He had feared it would be like looking in some distorted, broken mirror, a demon with his own face peering back.

The reality had shamed him. The man who

looked back at him with his own eyes was no corrupted, weak imitation; his resolve was as unwavering as the Hare's own. In truth, Abdus had trod the more dangerous path—to keep one's faith in the midst of temptation, to remain resolute while evil tried to seduce you every day, seemed infinitely harder than waging war. Even more astonishing was the fact that Abdus had managed to not only maintain his faith, but do so while concealing it from all those around him.

They had spoken quietly, intently, their father in the next room. It was the first time, Husam realized later, that he had not felt alone since he could remember. It was as if they were two halves of a whole, coming together for the first time to form something complete.

The last rifle finished, the Hare studied the prize he had come so far to claim, had killed so many to obtain. It was an undistinguished metal case, the sides battered aluminum, flecks of red paint still visible where the Cyrillic lettering had been scraped away. Inside, two halves of a whole also waited to be brought together, a sphere of plutonium divided in two and backed by conventional explosives. When the explosives detonated, the halves would slam together, experiencing their own ecstatic reunion; a consummation that would reverberate around the world . . .

"Pierce Madigan went into cardiac arrest earlier today," said Nadira. "The agents conducting the interview were not aware he had a heart condition. He did not survive."

"So he died during questioning," said Delko. "Nice to know you DHS types are quick learners."

"What are you implying, Mister Delko?" Nadira asked, her tone neutral.

"I'm implying," said Delko, leaning forward, "that it used to only be the *other* guys who used torture as an interrogation technique. But ever since nine-eleven, Uncle Sam thinks it's okay to throw people into an offshore concentration camp without so much as a phone call, let alone legal representation—"

"Guantanamo Bay is not a concentration camp," snapped Nadira. "It's a containment facility for enemy combatants—"

"Hold it," said Horatio. He didn't raise his voice, but the edge in it cut through the argument like a sword. "Both of you. We're not here to argue politics, we're here to prevent a tragedy. Let's not lose sight of that."

The strained silence was broken by Delko's grudging, "Yeah, yeah, I'm sorry."

"Apology accepted," said Nadira. "As I was saying, Madigan died before he could tell us how the bomb was going to be used. While we could take Abdus Pathan in for questioning, it's highly unlikely he would talk."

Horatio shook his head. "Oh, I'm sure the Brilliant Batin would have all sorts of things to say. He no doubt has an elaborate cover story composed of half-truths and red herrings all prepared . . ."

Calleigh sighed. "So all we really know is that the Hare has the device and is prepared to use it. Madigan was convinced it wouldn't be employed in the U.S., but he might have been fooled by a professional deceiver."

"We also know," said Horatio, "that the Hare stocked up on some heavy-duty armaments in addition. That suggests that his target is well-defended."

"Or very public," said Tripp. "Weapons could be needed to buy him some time while he gets set up."

"If we knew exactly what was in that shipment," said Calleigh, "we might be able to extrapolate a target."

"I tried that angle," said Tripp. "No luck. The only people who knew are pushing up crabgrass."

"Maybe not," said Calleigh. "I found part of a serial number on a fragment of the rocket the Hare used on the Hummer. I've been able to ID the model, but I can't get into the military databases to find out where it's from."

"I can help with that," said Nadira.

"I was hoping you would," said Calleigh. "Plus, it's been a few weeks since the original deal—and the first thing I do when I get a new gun is try it out."

"Good idea," said Delko. "We should check for reports of automatic gunfire or explosions. While he's almost certainly using a remote spot for any dry runs, he's not a local—he might slip up."

"I don't think it's the dry runs we have to worry

about," said Horatio. "In fact, there's only one target I can think of that fits the established criteria of the target—and it's not dry at all."

Delko and Calleigh got it at the same time. "A very public target," said Delko. "One you'd need a lot of guns to take and hold."

"Full of American citizens but not on American soil," said Calleigh.

"And an environment one of our suspects knows intimately," said Horatio. "A cruise ship."

10

"ERIC?" Horatio said as everybody filed out of the room. "Can I have a minute?" Delko hung back as Calleigh closed the door behind her.

"What," said Horatio, "was that all about?"

Delko glowered, but didn't meet Horatio's eyes. "I said I was sorry, all right?"

"Eric, if you have a problem with Ms. Quadiri, I need to know about it."

"It's not her, H."

"Then what?"

Delko looked up, his eyes still angry. "Gitmo."

Understanding filled Horatio's eyes. "Ah. Camp Delta at Guantanamo Bay."

"Yeah. I'm as American as you are, H—but that doesn't mean I've forgotten my heritage. *Cubanos* are a proud people, and what my own government's done to the place I came from—it just makes my blood boil."

"I take it you're not objecting to the U.S. presence there so much as what they're doing."

"Exactly. I believe in the law, H. And holding prisoners without a lawyer, without charging them, subjecting them to psychological torture that even the UN has condemned—it's just not right."

"Many people agree with you," said Horatio. "It's even beginning to look like the camp will be shut down."

"Not soon enough. It makes me ashamed, you know? Like I'm being forced to do something obscene."

Horatio regarded his CSI with raised eyebrows. "I understand how you feel. My advice? Channel that feeling toward our target—not our allies."

Delko nodded. "Okay. I will, I promise."

"Good. Now, let's find out where the Brilliant Batin is appearing next."

"I can tell you that right now," said Delko. "The same ship my girlfriend's working on."

The *Heart's Voyage* was only a few years old, a massive ship just over 950 feet long with a beam of 123 feet and a gross tonnage of 112,000 tons. Her top speed was twenty-three knots, she could accommodate almost twenty-seven hundred passengers, and it took a crew of eleven hundred to service her lounges, restaurants, theaters, gyms, laundries, kitchens, and engines.

Horatio intended to search it all.

The pretext for the search was disease. Ever since

a number of cruise ship passengers had come down with an intestinal infection called the Norwalk virus—one that caused nausea, vomiting, and stomach cramps—in the early twenty-first century, the Center for Disease Control had been authorized to make two unannounced shipwide inspections per year on any oceangoing vessel capable of transporting more than thirteen passengers at a time. While the cruise ship line wouldn't be happy about the negative publicity, the cover story would cause far less panic than the possibility the ship might be carrying a one-kiloton nuclear stowaway.

The divers would be harder to explain. Horatio had a police boat dock a few berths away, with a Diving School sign prominently displayed; if asked, they were conducting a training exercise for police divers.

But this, Horatio thought, *is no drill.*

Delko was in charge of the external search, while Calleigh, Horatio, and Nadira would coordinate search teams inside. Nadira and Horatio had pulled together an impromptu task force, putting almost a hundred Miami PD, crime lab staff, and FBI agents side by side for the search. Everyone was in plainclothes, except for a few decoys in bright yellow CDC jumpsuits.

The ship was taking on supplies for its next cruise, meaning there were no passengers aboard yet and only a skeleton crew. Horatio hoped the term wouldn't prove more than metaphorical.

For the external search, Delko and three other

divers examined the hull closely below the waterline. They studied the maneuvering props inset into the keel, making sure no foreign objects had been placed in the waterways; they checked the intake and outtake for the main props, the bilgewater outflow, and the anchor housing. Horatio himself believed it unlikely the bomb would be placed externally—but if there was one thing the Brilliant Batin had proven so far, it was that he was far from predictable.

The interior search was far more complex. The *Heart's Voyage* boasted thirteen passenger decks, including nineteen bars and lounges, three swimming pools, four restaurants, a fourteen-thousand-square-foot fitness center and spa, two Internet cafés, a video arcade, several clothing boutiques, a full-scale concert hall, and a casino; in addition there were the crew quarters, the engine room, the bridge, the lifeboats and cargo hold, plus all the internal equipment and maintenance space.

They cleared out all ship personnel first, then began their search. They went deck by deck, starting at the top and working their way down. Horatio wanted the outside areas done first and as quickly as possible; the less attention the searchers drew, the better.

Unfortunately, the layout of the ship worked against them. People on cruises wanted a view, so there were many glass walls and open-air decks and even balconies.

Horatio had heard it said that in the event of an

atomic war, a microcosm of Western civilization could be preserved intact aboard a cruise ship. *But what happens,* he wondered, *when a nuclear holocaust starts on one?*

Every searcher was issued a PRD, a Personal Radiation Detector. It was a relatively simple, small device, not much larger than a cell phone, and had been designed to be used with a minimum of training or dexterity—including the possibility of the user wearing the bulky gloves of an antiradiation suit.

The unit worked by acquiring a reading of the local gamma-ray spectrum, measuring the gamma dose rate and looking for neutron radiation. If it found something out of the ordinary an alarm sounded, and it compared the reading with its own internal library of radionuclides to get an ID.

Calleigh knew exactly what that alarm sounded like. It was a sound she dreaded hearing, but she listened intently for it just the same—not just from her own unit, but from those of the dozens of other officers now searching the ship. She headed a search team that was currently going through the backstage spaces of the concert hall, reasoning that the areas Batin would be most likely to use would be the ones he was most familiar with.

The Brilliant Batin's equipment had already been delivered; Calleigh had torn apart every available space large enough to hide what they were looking for and scanned every square inch.

She'd found numerous concealed compartments, of course, but nothing in any of them—not even a stray gamma ray. Batin was too clever to do anything so obvious, but he'd had access to the ship the previous week, performing two shows a night as it sailed from Miami to Nassau and back—he could very well have smuggled the bomb aboard then.

As she worked, Calleigh thought about Billy Lee's final, desperate note and what it possibly meant. "Daldev." Was it the name of a person, a boat, a place? She didn't know, but what she *did* know was that the message had been left for her. She and Billy Lee hadn't exactly been friends, but—despite their vastly different backgrounds—their relationship was closer to that of peers than that of a cop and a criminal. Calleigh had a great deal of respect for Billy Lee's craftmanship, but she admired his attitude, too; he didn't love guns because they were weapons, he loved them because they were tools. To him, a well-made gun was no different than a well-made hammer or pair of scissors.

She had no doubt that he'd built the cell phone gun, probably more as a challenge than from any monetary motive. She wondered why the Hare hadn't killed him immediately, the way he'd done Miami Marko and his crew. It didn't make any sense . . .

Unless the Hare had asked him to build more than one thing for him.

She stopped in the middle of running her PRD over the surface of a foam-lined moving crate. Is that what "Daldev" was? A weapon? If so, what did the Hare need it for?

She sighed, and went back to checking the crate. Billy Lee, she knew, also held her in high regard; she'd told him about a few old cases involving unusual guns—including a Russian-made one designed to fire underwater—and how she'd helped solve them, and he'd been fascinated. "That's just wild," he'd said, grinning and shaking his head. "How you can take just the little bittiest thing and make it spin all sorts of stories. I betcha you could put my dandruff under a microscope and get it to tell you the time."

Sorry, Billy Lee, she thought to herself. *Guess I'm not quite the genius you thought I was.*

She kept working.

Frank Tripp stared at the man on the other side of the table like a pit bull studying a cat through a chain-link fence. Abdus Sattar Pathan looked back with a slight smile on his face; the fact that he was handcuffed to the table didn't seem to bother him at all.

"I don't understand why I'm in custody," Pathan said in a conversational tone. "What am I being charged with?"

"You haven't been charged," said Tripp. "Yet."

"Then why am I being treated as a prisoner?"

"You mean the cuffs? I thought you might treat me to a little entertainment. Show me how easily you can get out of them."

"Ah. You are misinformed, Detective. I am not an escape artist."

"I know what you are."

Pathan raised one eyebrow. "Is that so?"

"You can bet on it. We can't hold you forever, but we can keep you cooped up long enough to search your ship. If it's aboard, Horatio will find it—and if it isn't, you're not going to get another chance. Nothing bigger than a breadbox gets loaded aboard that ship from now until it sails without getting the twiceover."

"You know, I still don't have the faintest idea what you're talking about."

"Uh-huh."

Pathan sighed. "I suppose this all seems very dramatic and meaningful to you, but to an innocent man it's—well, it's boring."

"That's a damned shame."

"Perhaps we could do something to pass the time. Do you like games?"

"Oh, I'd *love* to meet you on a football field."

"I was thinking of something a little more cerebral. What the Germans call a *Gedankenexperiment*—a thought experiment. I describe a problem—purely hypothetical, of course—and you tell me how you would deal with it."

Frank's eyes narrowed. "I think you've got enough real problems without creating fake ones—but I guess that's what you do, huh? Okay, *compadre*—let's see what you got."

"Let us say that an individual had a powerful

weapon. Let us further say that said individual planned to use this weapon to cause a great deal of destruction, but he was being hunted by the police. He would have to be extremely careful, don't you agree?"

"Oh, he'd have to be *real* careful. Otherwise, he could end up locked in a room with one of those policemen. Maybe even one on the large side, with anger-management problems."

"So it would make sense to have a contingency plan, yes? To ensure that his plan went forward, even if he were captured?"

"Depends." Tripp leaned forward, putting his forearms on the table. "Just how arrogant *is* this hypothetical genius?"

"Oh, he's no genius, Detective. Just prepared. He has been preparing a very, very long time—his whole life, in fact. That is a very long time to consider possibilities, to think about not just his ultimate goal, but every way a plan might go wrong. Being captured and questioned would seem to be a fairly obvious risk, wouldn't you say?"

"Everything's obvious once it happens. That's called having twenty-twenty hindsight."

"Hindsight is the rationalization of those who fail. Foresight is the hallmark of those who succeed."

"Yeah, I think I heard that on *Oprah* once. This hypothetical planner of yours—you know who he reminds me of? A guy named Alfredo de la Roca. Alfredo was a land developer in Fort Lauderdale, got the bright idea of putting house trailers on old barges, slapping on a coat of paint, trying to sell 'em as offshore condos. 'Course, he ran into all kinds of problems with marina zoning, waste-disposal regulations, that sorta thing—the whole scheme crashed inside of a year, but not before he'd collected a whole bunch of deposits from people who thought they could retire and live like Travis McGee. Alfredo thought he could just pocket the money and disappear . . . but six months later he turned up—what was left of him—in a gator hole down in the 'Glades. Seems old Alfredo made a little miscalculation."

Tripp paused. When he spoke again, his voice had lost its bantering tone. "See, he didn't know who he was dealing with. He thought he was a smooth operator, but he was just another two-bit con man with a movie running in his head. And just like every con man I've ever met—and I've put more of 'em in jail than you've had hot meals—he was a fake. All hat, no cattle. That's all you are, Abdus. You wasted your whole life setting this up, and you're not going to pull it off. You're a one-trick pony with two broken legs, and you don't impress me at all."

Abdus said nothing, but the calm in his eyes had been replaced by a cold blankness. It was, Tripp supposed, the most visible reaction he could expect.

"Now," said Tripp, "I got one for you. I found a corpse in a phone booth once. Bled to death, but he wasn't murdered and he didn't commit suicide. How'd it happen?"

Abdus frowned. "That doesn't—"

"He was on the phone to a friend at the time. Seems he'd just gotten back from a deep-sea-fishing expedition." Tripp stood up and walked around the table. His hands were balled into fists. He slowly spread his arms to either side until they were fully extended, then leaned in close to Abdus. He opened his hands.

"And he'd caught a marlin," said Tripp, "*this* big."

Tripp held Pathan's eyes for a moment, then leaned back and let his arms fall.

"That's what happens to braggarts," said Tripp.

Delko's team of divers had turned up nothing but barnacles. He changed out of his wet suit and was on his way up the dock to help with the internal search when his cell phone rang.

"CSI Delko."

"Eric, it's Marie. Turn around and wave."

"What? Oh." He turned around, spotted her behind the police barricades a little way down the dock. He hung up his cell and walked over; he could see the worry on her face as he got closer.

"Eric, what's going on? I got a call to not come in to rehearsal today—they said the ship's going through some kind of inspection, but the person I talked to said it isn't like any inspection she's ever seen."

"Uh, let's talk over here, okay?"

When she was on the other side of the barricade and they were both out of earshot of anyone else,

Delko said, "Look, I really can't talk about this. We're searching the ship in connection with an ongoing case. Once we find what we're looking for, everybody on the ship can go back to work."

"And if you don't find it?"

"Then there won't be a problem."

"So what you're looking for is dangerous?"

Eric shook his head. "I told you, I can't talk about it. And I never said we were looking for something dangerous."

She narrowed her eyes. "Yeah, right. This has something to do with that magician, doesn't it?"

Delko sighed. "If you say that just a little louder, you could cost me my job."

"Don't worry, I'll keep my mouth shut. How long is this going to take?"

"I don't know. We have to check the whole ship."

"Well . . . be careful, okay?"

"I will, don't worry."

She gave him a quick kiss and then she was gone.

"Careful," Delko murmured. "Right." *And if we aren't careful enough?* How many people, he wondered, would die or get sick?

And would Marie be one of them?

"Mister Wolfe," said Horatio. "Glad to see you're back with us."

Wolfe finished his orange juice and put the glass

down on the hospital tray in front of him. "Thanks, H. Guess I'm not quite as tough as you, though."

"Tough enough." Horatio crossed his arms and studied his CSI; Wolfe was battered and bruised, but his eyes were clear and his voice strong. "I just thought I'd give you a rundown of what's been happening . . ."

He quickly filled Wolfe in on the events of the last twenty-four hours. "We're about halfway through searching the ship right now," he said. "We're sitting on Abdus Pathan for the moment, but the high-powered attorney his father hired won't let that last long."

"Twin terrorists and a suitcase nuke," said Wolfe in a low voice. "You know, I'm not really sure I'm awake anymore . . . you sure the cruise ship's the target?"

"It makes the most sense," said Horatio. "A contained, floating symbol of all the Western decadence and self-indulgence the Hare hates. An environment the Brilliant Batin has access to and is familiar with."

"Sounds like a big job. Need an extra hand?"

"Absolutely, Mister Wolfe. Absolutely."

Delko joined Calleigh as her team was sweeping the casino; she had the wheel off a roulette table and was scanning the base it usually rested on.

"How's it going?" he asked, turning on his own PRD and joining her.

"I wish you had asked me that when I was scanning the craps table."

"Why, you find something?"

"No," she said with a rueful sigh, "but then at least I could have said something witty like 'snake eyes.' With roulette, I got nothing."

"Same here. The underwater sweep came up empty."

"Well, we've still got a lot of boat to search. Give me a hand putting this thing back on, will you?"

Delko grabbed one edge of the wheel while Calleigh hefted the other. Together, they maneuvered it back into place.

"So," said Calleigh, "I've been trying to think like Pathan. You know, get into his head and figure out where he might hide something."

"Any luck?" Delko set down his end carefully.

"I don't know . . . magicians are all about misdirection, right? Make you look at their left hand while the right hand does all the work?"

"Sure—but right now, both of Pathan's hands are in cuffs."

"Doesn't matter. Magic works on preparation; however Pathan's trying to fool us, he set it up a long time ago. The question is, what is it we're *not* paying attention to?"

Delko shook his head. "Beats me. I mean, we're going over this ship inch by inch—we've checked the outside, we're checking the inside. Horatio isn't going to let a single person or piece of cargo onboard without checking it—what's left?"

"Fuel?" she suggested.

"What, you think Pathan's going to pump the bomb aboard in a hose?" Delko grinned. "H already thought of that. All the onboard tanks are being checked—fuel, bilge, water, oil."

Calleigh started scanning the first in a row of video slot machines. "I don't think it'll be as simple as a remote hiding place. Pathan's more the Purloined Letter type—I think it'll be in plain sight but disguised."

Delko started on the row of slots opposite her. "Which narrows it down to anything larger than a suitcase. Terrific."

"Could be worse. We could be searching an actual city instead of an aquatic facsimile."

"Yeah, there is that; worse comes to worst, we can always sail it out into the Atlantic and let it blow up. Hard to do that with a neighborhood."

"You know, I've never understood the whole cruise mentality—I mean, people pay a lot of money for what amounts to a week in a floating mall, then spend most of their time at the buffet table. What's the attraction?"

"Lack of responsibility," said Delko. "When most people say 'I need a vacation,' what they really mean is they need a break from all the pressures in their life. Only thing is, lots of people come back from their vacation even more stressed than they were before—they just traded one set of pressures for another. Foreign food, foreign customs, foreign language; it can get to you after a while."

Calleigh nodded. "The 'I need a vacation from my vacation' syndrome."

"Right. Cruisers have all the comforts of home without any of the hassles; they're paying to be pampered. Most of all, they don't have to think—since they can't go anywhere else, they have a limited number of choices. Add a nice view—just enough to give it an exotic flavor—and you've got a cruise."

Calleigh considered this for a moment. "Limited choices, can't go anywhere else, room and board taken care of—Eric, you just described a prison."

"One major difference, though."

"Fewer tattoos?"

"Nobody gets seasick in prison."

It took them three days to scour the entire vessel.

They found nothing.

They inspected every piece of cargo as it was loaded.

They found nothing.

They allowed passengers and crew to board, not so much because of the lawsuit threatened by the cruise ship line as in a last attempt to locate the bomb. Everyone who came aboard was thoroughly searched.

They found nothing.

"All right," said Horatio, a ragged note of exhaustion in his voice. "Here's where we are."

He looked around the conference room at his

team. Wolfe sat at his right hand; the bandage on his nose and his two black eyes made him look like a football player during a particularily bad half-time. Delko was to his left, Calleigh and Nadira Quadiri on the other side. "We didn't find what we were looking for. That means one of three things: he didn't have the opportunity to plant it, he planned to deliver it in transit, or this was another feint. In any case, the DHS has decided to let the ship sail."

"Probably the wisest choice," said Calleigh. "Whatever's going to happen, better it happen at sea than in Biscayne Bay."

"Tell that to the people onboard the ship," said Eric. "Better yet, don't tell them—just let them sail off into the sunset and die."

"Nobody's getting sacrificed, Eric," said Horatio. "If we didn't find the device, then it isn't onboard. And now that we know what we're dealing with, there's no way for Pathan to get it aboard, either."

"That is not good news," said Nadira. Despite the fact that none of them had had more than a few minutes of sleep in the last seventy-two hours, she looked fresher than any of them. "Deprived of one target, the Hare will surely seek another. Better a cruise ship than downtown Miami."

Delko glared at her. "It's that easy for you, huh? Just write off four thousand people as acceptable losses?"

Nadira glared back. "It's better than the alternative."

Delko got to his feet. "Not to everyone. Not to me." He walked out.

"I'm afraid," said Horatio into the uncomfortable silence that followed, "that it gets worse. Pathan's lawyer has kicked up enough of a fuss that we're being forced to release him."

"Of course," said Wolfe. "Can we at least keep tabs on the guy, or is he going to sue us for that, too?"

"From what I understand," said Nadira, "Mister Pathan intends to honor his previous commitment to performing aboard the *Heart's Voyage*."

"A trouper to the end," said Horatio.

"The question," said Calleigh thoughtfully, "is whether he still plans to go through with whatever he's prepared—or is this just another attempt to distract us?"

"Either way, we're going to have to watch him from a distance," said Horatio. "Once the ship sails past the twelve-mile limit, she'll be in international waters. We have no jurisdiction."

"And no case,"said Wolfe.

"Look," said Delko, "can't you just call in sick or something?"

Marie looked at him as if he'd just suggested she wrestle an alligator. "Are you kidding? You know what they call a dancer with the flu? Unemployed."

They were walking along South Beach, hand in hand. The sun was just above the horizon, sinking behind a pink reef of clouds. The waves gleamed like polished steel.

Delko stopped and faced her. He took both of her hands in his. "I really don't want you to go. I've got your best interests at heart—you know that, right?"

She smiled. "I don't know. I'm not really sure what you've got at heart."

He hesitated. "I—I want you to be safe."

"Safe. Not the most romantic word in the world, but I guess you mean well. Still don't know what the big deal is, though."

"I told you—I can't discuss that."

Her smile faded. "Why? Don't you trust me?"

"That's not it. I just can't."

"Look, you said your guys checked every inch of that ship. It must be safe, because they're letting it sail. If all you're worried about is Batin, I'll stay away from him, okay? I mean, he doesn't have any reason to come after me personally, does he?"

"No. No, of course not."

"Well, unless he turns into a werewolf with a taste for showgirls under the full moon, I should be fine. Right?"

Delko looked into her eyes, then looked away. As much as he wanted to tell her, he knew he couldn't. She had other people she cared about, people she'd want to warn, and if the news got out it would create a panic that would cost lives.

"I'm asking you one last time," he said. "Trust me. Don't get on that ship."

She sighed. "Trust you? How about trusting me? Just tell me what's going on, okay?"

He shook his head. "I'm sorry. I can't."

She pulled her hand away from his. "Huh. Well, that's exactly how I feel. I guess I'll see you in a week—or I won't."

She turned and walked away.

11

The *Heart's Voyage* sailed a day later than it should have, and neither its crew or its passengers was terribly happy about it. The crew had to rush its preparations, meaning some supplies never made it aboard while certain procedures had to be curtailed or skipped entirely; while none of these omissions were critical, it meant that the passengers—many of them already irritated by the delay—were now faced with any number of unpredictable and frustrating changes in their agendas. The pump for the children's pool had been damaged during the search, rendering the pool unusable; parents who had expected a few hours of child-free bliss now had to shepherd their offspring instead of going swimming themselves. Tempers grew short, smiles grew strained, and the feeling that something was building toward critical mass swelled like a bubble.

Or maybe, Delko thought, *it's just me.*

He was in one of the cheaper inside cabins, the kind without a view. He'd paid for it with his own money, knowing that the Miami PD would never condone what he was doing.

What am *I doing? Blowing a big chunk of my savings to follow my girlfriend . . . where? If the ship is clean, it's a wild-goose chase. If it isn't , my goose is cooked—cooked at around three hundred thousand degrees Celsius. Either way, what can I do by myself that hasn't already been done?*

He already knew the answer. He could keep his eyes open, and be prepared.

For anything.

The *Heart's Voyage* was only seventy miles out to sea when a passenger named Horace Ware spotted something off the port bow. He was scanning the surface of the ocean with binoculars for whales or dolphins, but what he saw seemed more like the big, triangular fin of something pale—a white shark, maybe.

Then he realized it was a sail.

Every year, many Cubans tried to cross the ninety miles of water that separated Cuba from the easternmost shore of the United States. Most of the craft that braved the crossing were homemade, including 1950s-era cars that had been converted into something barely seaworthy with the addition of jury-rigged pontoons made from barrels, Styrofoam, or even empty plastic jugs. Not all of them made it; some sank, others were intercepted by the Coast

Guard . . . and some were picked up by cruise ships.

Often, this was not an accident. Cruise ships were a lot like big, aquatic buses; they kept to a regular schedule and a regular route. They also relied largely on their reputation to stay in business, and abandoning a crudely built boat full of refugees in the middle of the ocean was generally not viewed favorably by the thousands of tourists watching from the railing and sipping piña coladas—who would be even less thrilled if the ship were to deviate from its course in order to return said refugees to their home. Therefore, cruise ship policy was to rescue any such unfortunates, give them some food and a place to sleep, and then get rid of them as quickly as possible—preferably at their next port of call.

When Horace Ware excitedly began to shout, "A raft! There's a raft out there!" the crew followed protocol: They stopped the ship's engines and launched a motorized boat to rendezvous with the raft and pick up any survivors.

Eric Delko was unaware of this. If he had been on deck he certainly would have noticed, but the *Heart's Voyage* was a large ship, more like a floating city than a simple means of transport. At the time, he was doing his best to shadow Abdus Sattar Pathan, who was eating in a staff dining lounge. Technically, Delko didn't have the proper ID to access such places, but he had lifted a white kitchen worker's jacket from a laundry bin—that and the proper attitude seemed to be enough to make him invisible. If all else failed he could always show his badge, but he hoped he wouldn't have to; Pathan knew his face, and Delko would prefer to go unnoticed.

Pathan himself seemed utterly unconcerned. He spent most of his time in his room, emerging only to eat or work. Delko had caught both of his performances, hoping for some clue to Pathan's plan.

They began with the Brilliant Batin striding onto the stage of the small lounge he worked in, resplendent in a white tuxedo with a scarlet cummerbund and tie. He introduced himself to the audience, then said something that Delko had never heard a stage magician say before.

"Ladies and gentlemen," Batin said, "if you came here to see a magic show, you will be disappointed. What I do is not magic; it is skill, honed through years of training. It would be an insult to both of us to pretend otherwise, would it not? After all, every one of you is aware of this fact—it's not as if I told you there was no Santa Claus." Scattered laughter. "And to attribute my feats to something like sorcery belittles my own talent and hard work . . . and mocks the Creator of actual miracles."

Delko scanned the audience, but no one seemed to take this statement as anything ominous.

"And so," Batin continued, "prepare to be intrigued, baffled, amazed, and entertained—but not enchanted."

He had been gesturing with both hands during his introduction, and now he extended a hand toward someone in the front row. "Would you mind giving me a hand?"

When the audience member hesitated, Batin smiled broadly and said, "No? Then let me give you one."

He grabbed his own left bicep with his right hand—and ripped his own arm off.

Blood spurted from the socket. Raw red flesh tore apart as the limb pulled free, a single strand of tendon stretching from the white knob of bone at the end of the arm to the socket until it snapped.

Someone screamed. Batin's smile grew wider. He tossed the arm to the side casually, and the thump of it hitting the floor was the audience's cue to burst into nervous laughter.

Delko didn't. He could see how a gag like that could be played for laughs—a fake arm attached by Velcro, for instance—but that wasn't the effect Batin had been trying for. The blood, the raw flesh and bone, had been calculated to shock. From the looks Delko saw on the faces of lounge staff—waiters, bartenders—they were just as taken aback as everyone else. This wasn't part of Batin's regular act.

He hadn't repeated it in his second performance, either, sticking to the same routine of wandering about the audience and performing sleight of hand illusions. He produced people's wallets or jewelry from thin air, then caused them to vanish and reappear somewhere else. While he was extremely accomplished, there was nothing in Batin's repertoire that was particularly brilliant.

And now he was watching the man eat. What Delko was thinking about, though, was what he would say to Marie. He hadn't told her he was aboard yet; he didn't know whether he even should.

At that moment, several decks away, Security Chief Anbar Devkota was observing the crude raft off the port bow through his own high-powered binoculars. Devkota was an ex-Gurkha, as were the ten handpicked men who served under him. Gurkhas were Nepalese mercenaries, or had been when the British army first encountered them in 1814; their fighting skills had impressed the English army so much that they altered their own military policy to allow Gurkhas to serve. Some Gurkha regiments were still part of the British army, but the majority of them had elected to serve under the Indian military when that country gained its independence in 1947. Many ex-Gurkhas now resided in Hong Kong, where they based their own private security firms.

Three of Devkota's men were in the motor launch now approaching the raft; he was in contact with them via walkie-talkie. The *Heart* cruise ship line paid Devkota a great deal of money to anticipate and control situations like this one, and he had been on high alert ever since the authorities had told him what—and who—they suspected.

"We have a head count of twenty-two," reported Lahab Acharya over Devkota's headset. "No weapons visible. Many of them appear incapacitated, possibly dead."

"Proceed with caution." Devkota continued to monitor the scene through his binoculars as Lahab boarded the raft.

There was very little movement on the raft itself; Lahab's assessment appeared to be correct. After a few moments, he reported back. "Only one person conscious, though not rational. He keeps saying *'agua, agua,'* over and over."

"Does he have a white substance encrusted around his mouth?"

"Yes. Many of them do."

"They've been drinking seawater. We'll transport them aboard via the motor launch, a few at a time."

"And the raft?"

"We'll tow it at a safe distance once it's been evacuated."

Devkota continued to watch through his binoculars as the first four men were loaded aboard the launch. He was alert, but not worried; his men were thorough, cautious, and very, very dangerous. Even if the men on the raft were armed with knives and Devkota's had nothing but their bare hands, he knew who would come out on top.

The transfer went smoothly. The men on the raft were dressed in simple, largely homemade clothing, had several days' growth worth of beards, and carried nothing on their persons more dangerous than a penknife—which was promptly taken away.

The activity was watched with much interest from the passenger decks, people leaning over the railing and snapping pictures with digital cameras. Devkota was, as always, intensely aware of their scrutiny; his job had just as much to do with public relations as with security. A cruise ship was kept afloat as much by her reputation as by the sea, and Devkota was always trying to maintain the balance between being visible enough to reassure and invisible enough to prevent worry.

The ship carried several physicians, and one of them—Doctor Oruno—was on hand to examine the survivors as they came aboard. Oruno was a heavyset man from Peru, with a large bushy mustache streaked with gray and a bald patch on the very top of his head. The first man he checked was barely conscious, mouthing unintelligible words in what sounded like Spanish.

"He's badly sunburned, suffering from dehydration and probably heatstroke," Oruno told Devkota. "That we can handle—but if this man has been drinking seawater, he's in danger of renal failure. We don't have the facilities aboard to treat that."

Devkota frowned. He was a small, brown-skinned man, with a military brushcut and a small, neat mustache that he stroked when he was thinking. He stroked it now.

"I'll notify the captain," said Devkota. "We're not

that far out—the worst ones can be taken to Miami via helicopter."

"And the rest?"

"Do your best. We'll see if their condition convinces our next port to take pity on them."

Delko had the decision of whether to tell Marie he was aboard taken out of his hands—he ran into her in one of the ship's corridors.

She didn't say anything for a moment, just stared at him.

"I can explain," said Delko.

"No, no, don't bother," said Marie. "I get it. You're here because you're worried about me—or is this some kind of undercover thing? Is that what you couldn't tell me about?"

"No, you got it right the first time. My boss doesn't even know I'm here."

"Hmmm. You know, I don't know how to feel about this. On one hand, it's sweet—a little overprotective, but sweet. On the other, it feels sort of like being stalked. Plus, I'm *still* pissed at you for not trusting me." She crossed her arms.

"Look, you don't know how hard this is for me. I'm not just following orders; I have very real, specific reasons for not telling you. I promise, once this is over, I'll let you know those reasons."

"Well . . . I suppose that's fair. Except now that I'm not angry, I'm worried. And I don't even know why."

Delko sighed. *Maybe I should just tell her,* he thought. *She's smart, she won't start a panic—*

"I'm sorry, I shouldn't complain," she said. "You're just trying to do your job, and if I wasn't dating you I'd be just as clueless as everyone else aboard. We're all in the same boat, right? Even you."

"I guess I am."

"Hey, don't look so grim. You may be stuck, but at least you're stuck on a big floating amusement park with your girlfriend. Things could be worse—I mean, look at the guys they just rescued from that raft."

"What? What raft?"

"The one full of Cuban refugees. One of the passengers spotted it and we picked them up; I heard they're in pretty bad shape—hey!"

"Stay here!" Delko shouted over his shoulder as he sprinted down the corridor.

The captain of the *Heart's Voyage* was from New Orleans, a tall black man named Henri DuLac. Captain DuLac took a sip of coffee from his white china cup, then set it down on the saucer on his desk. He stared at Eric Delko impassively through a pair of tinted, silver-rimmed sunglasses and said in a deep, French Creole–accented voice, "First of all, Mister Delko, I would like to know what you are doing aboard my ship. Security issues were dealt with in Miami; I am the one in charge now, and I do not recall giving permission for you—or anyone else—to conduct a further investigation at sea."

Delko leaned forward in his chair. "I apologize for that. I'm not onboard in any official capacity, and I'm not telling you how to run your ship. But those men you picked up—"

"What would you suggest we do, Mister Delko? Abandon them to the waves?"

"Of course not. But considering the situation—"

"The situation." Captain DuLac shook his head. "Would you like to know the situation as I see it, Mister Delko? There has been one—and only one—terrorist action against a cruise ship, ever. The *Achille Lauro,* in 1985. That resulted in a single death. Since then, security has improved immeasurably. We have trained military personnel aboard, and they have assured me that these refugees pose no threat. They are barely alive, let alone armed. In fact, one is so badly dehydrated we are having him flown to Miami to save his life."

"What about the raft they were found on?"

"It is being towed behind us, at a safe distance."

"That distance may not be as safe as you think," said Delko. "Has the raft been searched?"

"Of course. Nothing of any import was found."

"What about beneath the raft?"

The captain sighed. "No, Mister Delko. The underside of the raft was not searched. What do you expect might be hidden there—a miniature submarine, perhaps, full of trained killers?"

"I'll let you know," said Delko, getting to his feet, "as soon as I find out."

* * *

One of the shops on the concourse level sold basic skindiving gear. Delko put a mask, snorkel, flippers, and swimming trunks on his credit card, then went to his room to change. He found Marie waiting for him outside his door.

"Okay," she said. "I've got it all figured out. These Cuban refugees are really pirates, right? And Batin is their ringleader. He's gonna give all of them the swords from his act—you know, the ones he usually sticks through a volunteer in a box—and they're all going to start yelling, 'Arr, me matey,' and take over the ship. Right?"

"Very funny. I'll admit a bunch of dehydrated, unarmed men don't seem to pose much of a threat, but the raft they showed up on is another matter."

She eyed the flippers sticking out of the shopping bag he carried. "So you're going to swim out there and check it out yourself?"

"That's right. How'd you find my room, anyway?"

"I have my sources. You're on my turf now, buster."

"Yeah, yours and the captain's." Delko unlocked his door and stepped inside, Marie right behind him. The stateroom was small but comfortable, with a queen-size bed, its own bathroom, a love seat, and a vanity table with chair.

Marie sat down on the edge of the bed. "DuLac not happy with you?"

"He doesn't think there's a problem. And I don't think he's too happy about me being aboard."

Delko kicked off his shoes and started unbuttoning his shirt.

"Captains are like that. They don't like anyone questioning their authority." She leaned back on her elbows and gave him a slow smile. "I'm a little more forgiving."

He stopped as he was about to undo his belt, and grinned. "Does that mean I'm forgiven?"

"Depends on what you do after you drop your pants."

He let loose a mock sigh. "Then I guess I'm still in the doghouse."

"You really think DuLac is going to just let you jump over the side and swim over there?" She pushed herself up off the bed and onto her feet.

"Hey, it's a big ship. I don't think he can stop me."

She stepped in close, put her hands on his bare chest. "I guess I can't either?"

He looked into her eyes, then kissed her.

He was the first to pull away. "No, you can't."

"I didn't think so," she said, but her voice wasn't angry. "I'm just trying to give you a good incentive to come back."

"I will," he said softly. "I promise. Okay?"

"Okay," she said. "Now kiss me one more time—then go do what you have to."

He did.

Getting to the raft was easy; Delko simply walked to the lowest deck with a railing, dressed in his swim trunks and carrying the flippers, snorkel, and mask in the shopping bag. He waited until there were no crew members watching, and then simply dove overboard with the bag in hand.

He slipped his gear on while treading water—a little tricky, but Delko was an experienced diver and had dealt with far worse conditions.

The ship, of course, had continued to move while he did this, but he'd taken that into consideration; the raft was being towed behind the ship at a distance of about a hundred yards, and by the time Delko was ready it was only a few strokes away.

He had to grab onto it quickly—the *Heart's Voyage* was only moving at a few knots, but that was enough to run him over if he didn't get out of the way. He let the raft pass, then caught up to it with a few strong, even strokes.

The raft itself was a ramshackle affair, made of oil barrels, slabs of Styrofoam, and logs. There was a crude structure of two-by-fours and plastic sheeting in the center to provide shelter, and a mast holding a ragged sheet of cloth for a sail.

Delko wasn't interested in what was visible, though. According to the captain the Gurkhas had searched the raft thoroughly, and there was very little space to hide anything—above the surface, anyway.

He was holding on to the edge and letting himself be pulled along with the raft. Now, he took a deep breath and submerged.

Below the surface the pressure of the water

rushing past was much stronger. Fortunately, there were many handholds; he could pull himself along, covering the entire underside of the craft.

There were many nooks and crannies, but nothing big enough to stash what he was looking for. Delko made his way back to his starting point and surfaced, then hauled himself onto the raft itself.

He looked across the water to the ship. People had noticed what he was doing, and it looked like the motor launch was getting ready to cast off and come retrieve him.

There was only one logical place left to look. Quickly, Delko pulled out the PRD he'd sealed in a plastic baggie and stuffed inside the pocket of his trunks. He turned it on, then ran it over the first of the oil barrels being used as a pontoon.

Nothing. There were six barrels in all, three to a side, and he checked them one by one.

Nothing.

The motor launch roared toward him. He could see three brown-skinned faces, and they did not look happy.

It must be shielded. But that would take lead, which would make the barrel much less buoyant.

None of barrels appeared to be floating lower than the others. He did a quick visual inspection and saw that all of them had thick rust lining their seams, indicating they hadn't been opened in a long while.

And then the motor launch pulled alongside, and he didn't have any more time.

"Hey, guys," said Delko. "Can you give me a lift?"

"That," Captain DuLac said, "was extremely foolish."

Delko stared back at him stubbornly. He was still in his swim trunks, having been brought directly to the captain's office by the Gurkhas. "It had to be done. If you wouldn't take the threat seriously, someone had to."

"I see. And what did you find?"

"Nothing," Delko admitted reluctantly. "But that doesn't mean the search shouldn't have been made. A lot of what my lab does is exclude possibilities—"

"Apparently," DuLac interjected, "the one possibility you *haven't* excluded is the fact that you might be *wrong*."

Delko didn't know how to answer that. Of course he could be wrong—but the evidence had to be followed until a definitive conclusion was reached, and he wasn't there yet. "Look, at least cut the craft loose. You already have the refugees' possessions aboard—it's not like it's worth anything."

"I'm not in favor of strewing the seaways with random debris, Mister Delko. But in fact, I agree with you; I had already decided to eliminate the raft when you went off on your little Double-Oh-Seven mission."

"Eliminate?"

"Yes. I had hoped to simply have it mysteriously sink in the middle of the night, but your grandstanding has made that plan unworkable. Too many passengers saw you, too much uproar has been caused."

"You mean you're going to keep on towing it?"

"No, Mister Delko. You may think I'm a stupid man, but I'm simply used to dealing with public opinion as well as fact. I will not endanger my passengers, nor will I cut adrift a potential threat. My security detail will still sink the craft—all you have done is forced me to do so publicly."

DuLac leaned forward across his desk and growled, "I do not appreciate the embarrassment this will cause me, not to mention the potential legal repercussions. Repercussions that, believe me, you will share."

The captain's reprimand was cut short by a familiar sound: the cyclic *whumpwhumpwhump* of rotors.

"That will be the Medevac helicopter from Miami," said DuLac. "Unless you object to a man in critical condition being taken *off* the ship?"

"No, of course not," Delko muttered.

"Then kindly confine your future activities to more mundane pastimes while aboard. May I suggest using one of our pools for swimming?"

Delko sighed.

The Sikorsky S-76A chopper settled onto the helipad on the *Heart's Voyage*'s uppermost deck. It was a transport category helicopter, specially outfitted for medical service, with two Turbomeca Arreil 1S turboshaft engines that were rated at 657.6 pounds of thrust each. As soon as it was on deck, two crew members—Urban and Alderman—rushed forward to secure the landing skids.

The chopper discharged two paramedics, a blond man wearing mirrored sunglasses and a woman with dark hair tied back in a ponytail. The pilot remained in the craft while they grabbed a gurney, already loaded down with medical equipment, and hauled it onto the deck.

"Portable dialysis machine," the woman yelled over the noise of the rotors. "We have to get the patient hooked up as soon as possible."

"I'll take you to him," Urban yelled back.

He led the paramedics down several decks, to the medical clinic where the refugee was being kept. There was a single Gurkha guarding the door, arms folded over his chest, who nodded curtly as they rushed past. Urban, a short man with wiry black hair, got a surprise when he pulled open the clinic door; all twenty-one of the other refugees were clustered around the ill man's bed, on their knees and praying. Doctor Oruno was watching them with a bemused look on his face, but looked up as Urban led the paramedics in.

"Chopper's here," Urban said.

"Patient's ready for transport," Oruno told the woman, who quickly wheeled the gurney next to the bed. "If, that is, his entourage will let him go. They insisted on coming in here to pray for him an hour ago—even the ones with saline drips in their arms—and refuse to leave. Security said it was okay as long as they didn't try to make trouble."

The man in the sunglasses didn't reply. Instead, he grabbed the top of the dialysis machine's console and ripped it off with one smooth gesture.

The interior was full of guns.

12

THE WOMAN WITH THE PONYTAIL was the first to act. She grabbed a large handgun with a silencer from the top of the pile of weapons, strode back to the entrance, and pulled it open. She shot the Gurkha in the head without hesitation. Before the door had swung shut again, the blond man in mirrored sunglasses had begun passing out assault rifles to the refugees.

Urban and Oruno had no chance to react. The refugees—who until now had been behaving like B-movie zombies, shuffling from place to place and moving very slowly if at all—suddenly found tremendous reserves of energy. They grabbed both men, bound and gagged them with surgical tape and strapped them to hospital beds. They did a quick search of the room and their hostages, confiscating two cell phones and disabling the intership phone.

Then, with a quick, practiced efficiency, they moved out of the clinic and into the corridors of the ship.

Delko had gone back to his room, quickly thrown on some clothes, then headed for the upper deck to check out the helicopter. It was pointless, he knew—there was nothing he could accomplish alone that several well-armed Gurkhas couldn't—but he felt he had to do *something*.

There was only one Gurkha keeping an eye on the chopper, though; Delko supposed that between the refugees, the raft, Batin, plus the rest of the ship, they were stretched pretty thin. A number of curious passengers were gathered on the deck below, staring up at the aircraft on the helipad. The Gurkha was motioning the helicopter pilot to step out, and the pilot was indicating that with his headphones on he couldn't hear.

Which doesn't make sense—

Delko and the Gurkha reached the same conclusion at the same instant. Suddenly, there was a gun in the Gurkha's hand—Delko wasn't sure where it came from, since the security agent hadn't been wearing a visible sidearm—and it was aimed squarely at the pilot.

Who smiled.

The shot came from inside the helicopter, through the open cargo bay door. It caught the Gurkha in the throat, a crimson spray exploding from his neck. Even so, he managed to squeeze off a shot before his lifeless body dropped to the deck.

Delko sprinted for the nearest hatch as several screams cut through the air. He knew his only chance was to alert the other Gurkhas before—

"Halt," said a voice. Even over the sound of the helicopter's blades, the speaker didn't sound as if he were shouting; his tone was almost casual.

Delko stopped. The doorway was still nearly twenty feet away, and he knew he'd never make it without getting a bullet between his shoulder blades.

The rotors slowed to a lazy, almost silent whirl. Delko turned around and saw the shooter step out from behind the hanging cargo netting he'd been hiding behind. He was dressed completely in black, including the black scarf that hid his head and face. Only his eyes were visible—that, and the brown-skinned hands that held the assault rifle.

"Greetings," the man said. "My name is *Al-Arnab*—the Hare. Even now, my men are securing this vessel. From this moment on, the *Heart's Voyage*—and every life on it—belongs to *me*."

The primary objective of the Hare's men was the security center. They knew that this was not only where the feeds for the ship's security cameras led, but where the Gurkhas' weapons locker was located. It wasn't possible to monitor every corridor in the massive ship, of course; only the main areas and important entrance and exit points were covered.

Fortunately, the invaders had a map that led them through the areas that were not monitored. They even had an electronic passcard that let them use service corridors off-limits to passengers.

They arrived at their destination within minutes. From the uproar inside, it appeared they had lost the element of surprise; the man in the mirrored sunglasses wasted no time on subtlety.

At his signal, they opened fire on the door. Armor-piercing rounds turned the interior of the room into a blizzard of shrapnel; the men inside never had a chance to even return fire.

Their blond leader used one final shot to blow apart the lock, then kicked the door open. He surveyed the bloody wreckage and shattered monitors inside quickly, then nodded in satisfaction. He counted the bodies, then took out a walkie-talkie and spoke into it.

"Four down," he said in Arabic.

"One here," was the reply. "Six to go."

Of the six remaining Gurkhas, five were currently off-duty and in their quarters. Despite the noise caused by the slaughter of their comrades, the size of the *Heart's Voyage* meant they were basically on the other side of a small town; that, the intervening bulkheads, plus the nearness of the ship's engines to their quarters, meant the sounds of gunfire never reached their ears.

And when it did, it was the last thing they ever heard.

* * *

The Hare kept Delko at gunpoint for several long minutes. The helicopter pilot lay sprawled in a pool of blood at the Hare's feet; he had stumbled out of the chopper and collapsed after killing the engine, the Gurkha's last shot finding a fatal target.

The distant echo of gunfire filled Delko with dread—he knew he was probably hearing more people die. *Please, God,* he prayed silently. *Don't let one of them be Marie.*

"You're crazy if you think you can hold a ship this size," said Delko. "People have learned since the *Achille Lauro.*"

The Hare laughed. "That was over twenty years ago. Any lessons learned have long since been forgotten."

"Maybe. But we've learned a few new ones since then."

"Because of nine-eleven? Of course you have—you no longer allow toenail clippers on airplanes. Such thinking does not impress me."

Delko knew the last thing he should do was antagonize someone holding an assault rifle aimed at his heart, but he felt a rising fury that was hard to control. This was the man who had put Wolfe in a coma . . . the one who'd tried to kill Horatio twice. "You think that's all we've learned? You're not as smart as you think you are."

"No? I'll tell you what you've learned. You've learned to check passengers' identification carefully. You've learned to screen baggage for anything dangerous. You've learned to control access to sensitive areas. All these are lessons learned from nine-eleven . . . and all of them apply to passenger aircraft." The Hare shook his head slowly, his eyes never leaving Delko. "Having been attacked by a bear, you undertake elaborate precautions to protect yourself from further attacks—by other bears. Black bears, brown bears, polar bears—even teddy bears. And while you are carefully guarding against Winnie the Pooh, the wolves circle."

"You're no wolf," said Delko coldly.

"No, I am Al-Arnab—the Hare. Like your Bugs Bunny, you see? I am here, I am there, I make fools of everyone who crosses my path. I am cunning, I am quick, I am elusive."

You're rabbit stew, Delko thought, but said nothing.

"You Americans are so arrogant, so overconfident. What use is scrutinizing ID when your betrayer is already known and trusted? What use is screening baggage when the instrument of your doom is not yet aboard? What good does it do to restrict access to strangers yet grant it to the one who will engineer your destruction?"

Delko understood exactly who and what he was talking about, but decided not to let on how much he knew. "So you've got a spy onboard."

"A spy? Much more than that. One whose mastery of deception almost matches my own—" A walkie-talkie on his belt beeped. He spoke into it in Arabic, listened to the reply, then spoke once more before returning the device to his belt. "Lie on the deck, facedown," he told Delko.

Delko did—he knew that if the Hare wanted to kill him, he would have already done so.

"Interlace your fingers behind your head."

The Hare took a careful step backward, keeping his eyes on Delko. He reached into the chopper and pulled out an object Delko recognized, despite the fact he'd never seen it before.

A battered metal case.

"You will make as good a hostage as any," said the Hare. "Come. We are going to see the captain."

Daldev.

Calleigh had run the word through several databases and search engines, and nothing that came up seemed right. It was an uncommon word, but not so uncommon that it didn't pop up in connection with all sorts of subjects—none of which seemed likely candidates.

Calleigh glared at her monitor in frustration. She needed another word to narrow the search, but she'd already tried everything from *guns* to *radioactive.* The problem was she was firing in the dark, with no idea which way the target was.

It's not the name of a boat. Maybe the name of a company?

She tried that and tracked down a Daldev Inc. in Homestead, a company that imported sugar—but they'd gone out of business four years ago.

"Drat," she muttered.

And that was when Wolfe burst into the lab and said, "The *Heart's Voyage* was just hijacked."

They gathered in the AV lab to watch the news. Horatio stood with his arms crossed, his eyes intent and worried. The screen showed a stock photo of the ship; no reporters were on the scene yet.

"—miles off the coast of Florida, the *Heart's Voyage*, a cruise ship out of Miami, has been taken over by terrorists. No demands have been made, but the hijackers claim to have killed at least a dozen people, all of them security personnel. Their leader, a well-known Islamic militant who calls himself the Hare, says he has the means to destroy the ship and will do so if anyone approaches closer than one mile away. We now go to Harris Cambell, at the Port of Miami."

That was the nut of the story; the rest was network filler, interviews with people who didn't know any more than the reporters but were willing to speculate on camera. Horatio pointed the remote and turned off the monitor.

"We were right," said Wolfe. "For all the good it did us."

"Let's not focus on that right now," said Horatio. "The ship is not available to us, but the evidence still is."

"Which evidence?" said Wolfe.

"All of it, Mister Wolfe—all of it. The Hare may have fled, but he left a trail; we have evidence from at least four crime scenes, not to mention a clue left behind by one of the Hare's victims. Let's see what it can tell us."

"And then what?" said Wolfe. "The Hare's sitting in the middle of the ocean with a rocket launcher, a bunch of guns, and a nuke. What are we supposed to do about that?"

"What we always do, Mister Wolfe. Find the truth . . ."

The hijackers moved swiftly. Once the security office was theirs and the Gurkhas taken care of, they took command of the telecommunications center. All ship-to-shore contact—including the Internet—was cut off. Though the ship was out of range of any cellular network, they brought onboard the same radio-frequency jammer the Hare had used to block Horatio's phone; it would prevent the use of not just cell phones, but satellite phones.

"Attention!" the Hare's voice boomed over the public-address system. "By now, many of you will know that something out of the ordinary is going on. I must inform you that the rumors are true. This ship has been captured by the forces of Allah. This is not a hoax or a joke. Shortly, soldiers will appear and direct you to a holding facility. If you resist, you will be shot as an object lesson to your companions."

And then, working slowly and methodically from stern to bow, they had herded every passenger into the concert hall, one of the largest rooms on the ship. It wasn't designed to hold all twenty-seven hundred passengers at the same time—let alone over a thousand crew as well—but the hijackers weren't concerned about fire regulations.

Delko was among them. He'd been taken to the captain's office first, where the Hare had calmly explained the situation to a visibly shaken DuLac.

"There's no need to kill anyone," DuLac had said. "We'll follow your instructions."

"See that you do," the Hare had replied. Then, Delko's immediate usefulness gone, he had been marched out to join the other passengers.

As soon as he was in the concert hall he began searching frantically for Marie. There were too many people for the terrorists to control in any but the most rudimentary way; once the passengers were inside, they watched them but made no attempt to tell them what to do. The exits had all been secured from the outside and the terrorists knew none of the passengers were armed or could communicate with the outside world—apparently that was all they cared about.

He finally saw her about twenty minutes later, striding through the door and looking more angry than scared. He ran up to her and asked if she was all right.

"Oh, I'm just fine," she snapped. "Kidnapped at sea by pirates. I feel like an *idiot*."

"Just take it easy. We're going to be all right—"

"Well, of course we are. I'm just waiting for Bruce Willis to swing in on a rope and kill all the bad guys. God, I can't *believe* this. No wonder you didn't want to tell me—I wouldn't have taken you seriously!" Her voice was starting to rise, and there was a wavering edge to it. "I mean, come *on*! This is the twenty-first century! You can't just, just steal a ship the size of a city and threaten to kill . . . to *kill*—"

Her voice abruptly broke and she began to sob. Delko put his arms around her and let her cry.

"Listen," he murmured into her ear, "nothing's going to happen to you. You're just one small person in a very large crowd."

He could still hear tears in her voice, but when she replied, "Thanks. Insult my ego when I'm terrified," he knew she'd be all right.

She pulled back and looked him in the eye. "You said 'you.' Not 'we.' You're not going to do something dutiful and stupid, are you?"

"Dutiful, yes—stupid, no." He shook his head at the look on her face. "Don't worry, I'm not going to try to take on a ship full of armed terrorists by myself. I'm no Bruce Willis, all right?"

"Then what *are* you going to do?" she said, her voice dropping to a whisper.

"The same thing I do for a living: collect information."

"How? This isn't your lab, Eric. Even if you brought some of your CSI gear with you, how are you going to use it? You can't exactly ask these guys for their fingerprints or DNA."

Delko glanced up at the two terrorists still ushering people through the main doors. "Doesn't matter—I didn't bring my kit with me, anyway. But that doesn't mean I can't find out a few things on my own."

"Let's say you do—then what?"

"Then I find a way to get a message to Horatio," said Delko. "And hope he can find a way to use whatever I learn."

"Eric's on the ship," said Horatio.

Calleigh and Wolfe stared at him incredulously. They were all in the lab, reviewing evidence from the prior crime scenes.

"What the hell," said Wolfe, "does he think he's doing?"

"Protecting the woman he loves," said Calleigh. "You're sure, H?"

"I am," said Horatio. "He left a timed email message for me, which I just received. He's aboard."

"Is he armed?" asked Wolfe.

"Ship policy wouldn't permit that," said Horatio. "Just as well—he's in no position to launch a counterattack and I wouldn't want him to try. What he can do, hopefully, is give us some inside information on the situation."

"How?" said Wolfe. "He can't exactly place a ship-to-shore call."

"He's resourceful," said Calleigh. "He'll find a way."

"In the meantime," said Horatio, "we have to be ready. Any progress on the message left at the Garenko shooting?"

Calleigh shook her head. "The word Daldev doesn't

match any ship registry I can find. I also struck out on businesses or individuals—except for a sugar-importing business that's been defunct for four years."

Horatio looked at her and narrowed his eyes. "Where were they located?"

"Homestead," said Calleigh. "What are you thinking?"

"I'm thinking that sugar importers always have a warehouse," said Horatio. "And often, they paint the name of the company on the side."

"If the company goes out of business," said Wolfe, "they rarely bother painting over the sign—"

"—and terrorists need a staging area," finished Calleigh. "A large, abandoned warehouse would do nicely."

"If Billy Lee Garenko was ever taken there—even blindfolded," said Horatio, "he might have glimpsed the sign." He was already moving toward the door. "Let's go check it out . . ."

Sonam Lamprahar was the only Gurkha to survive the attack.

This had been due not to vigilance or skill, but—as was often the case—the vagaries of battle. He had been at one of the ship's laundries, picking up his shirts—he was fussy about his appearance and always demanded his uniforms be stiffly starched—when the attack began. He had immediately headed for the source of the shots, the Gurkhas' living quarters.

And arrived too late.

They had left no one to guard the lifeless bodies of his comrades—there was no need. One of the dead was a ship's porter, the only other Nepalese onboard—he visited sometimes, and played cards with them. Now, he was simply another corpse.

Sonam wasted no time on remorse. He was a Gurkha, a member of one of the finest military units on the planet, and he still had a job to do. He located the weapons cache in the cabin—the terrorists had not found it—and armed himself. He disposed of his uniform and slipped into a nondescript pair of baggy jeans, a loose shirt, and sandals.

And then, he went hunting.

The voice that echoed through the empty decks, through the bars and restaurants and corridors and cabins, was not angry. It was amused, with more than a touch of contempt in it. "My men have finished their initial sweep of the ship. We thank everyone in the concert hall for cooperating; you will be treated accordingly. Sadly, that does not include everyone onboard—we performed a head count as people entered, and there are still seven people unaccounted for. In a group of nearly four thousand people, that's not bad.

"It is, however, unacceptable.

"We understand your thinking. In a vessel this size, it is certainly possible to remain hidden—especially if you have firsthand knowledge of the ship. But you must understand, there is very little you can accomplish; we are many and you are few. We are well-armed, while you have—at the most—some kitchen knives or golf clubs.

"Most important, we have hostages.

"We will give you one hour to surrender. Turn yourself in to the guards at the entrance to the concert hall, and you will not be punished. If you do not, we will execute one hostage for every person that remains at large—and we will do so at the top of every hour.

"It is now quarter to three. You have fifteen minutes before the first seven people die."

"*Which* seven people?" Marie whispered to Delko.

Delko looked around the room. Every seat was filled, and groups of people huddled together in the aisles and along the walls, as well. Only the stage was empty; two armed guards stood there, one near each wing, like spear carriers in a play who had tired of their status and decided to do something about it. The crowd was angry and afraid, their voices a constant, indeterminate babble punctuated by the wail of crying children.

"I don't know," said Delko. "He might pick out people he thinks are troublemakers, or he might go for shock value. Leon Klinghoffer—the man killed in the *Achille Lauro* attack—was a seventy-year-old man in a wheelchair."

"Will he—" She paused. "Will he really do it?"

"He might," Delko admitted. "On the other hand, he doesn't want a riot on his hands. He can't shoot four thousand people, no matter how crazy he is—he doesn't have the ammo."

But he does have something else, Delko thought. *Something that can turn this entire ship into scrap. In which case, he doesn't care about a mutiny—at the first sign of trouble, he'll just flip the switch.*

And then, all the voices in the room suddenly died down, leaving only the sobs of children hanging in the air. A man dressed all in black, his face obscured by a black scarf, had just strode out onto the stage. He carried a battered metal suitcase in one hand, which he placed in the exact center of the stage.

"It is time," the Hare announced, "to select those who will pay the price for their fellow passengers' obstinance." His voice boomed out over the audience; Delko realized he was wearing a small cordless microphone. The terrorist pulled a pen-sized device from his pocket: a laser-pointer.

"Sadly, I have no time for fairness," said the Hare. "Those I choose will proceed immediately to the stage—or my men will shoot the people on either side of you."

Brutal but effective, thought Delko.

As were the Hare's choices. He picked men in their fifties or older, always ones with their families with them. Such men were unlikely to risk any harm to their loved ones—and not a single selectee made any trouble. Their wives, children, and grandchildren screamed and sobbed, but it made no difference; at the end of several emotional minutes, the seven men stood at the edge of the stage.

"Before I continue," said the Hare, "there is

something I should explain. You may be thinking that your government will come to your rescue—and indeed, my small group of men could not defend this vessel from a concerted attack. However, the device inside the case you see before you will prevent any such action. Homeland Security is aware that I have this device, and they know I will use it. Its contents need not concern you."

Delko frowned, then nodded to himself. If the Hare had claimed the case contained a nuclear device, many would have disbelieved him; by not revealing its secret, he ensured that people's imaginations would supply whatever they were most afraid of: anthrax, nerve gas, high explosives, it didn't matter.

"Only five minutes left to go," the Hare said. "But I would not count on any last-minute reprieves. After all, the people still missing and the hostages I've chosen are most likely strangers to each other; why should members of one group surrender simply to save people in another they have never met?" He shrugged theatrically. "America, after all, is the land of the individual, ruled by the law of the jungle: only the strongest survive. Those that band together for a common cause, a common belief, might be branded as *communists*—and we all know how that turned out."

Delko bit back an angry reply. *Right. You and your jihadist buddies are the only ones in the world with any sense of community or cooperation. Arrogant piece of—*

And then Delko's reply was made for him.

The back door opened, and a group of people—one woman and five men—came through. Two wore ship's uniforms, four were dressed casually. All of them looked scared but defiant.

"Well, well," the Hare said. "It seems you have some sense after all. Six of you, anyway—but there is still one person missing. And four minutes left to go . . ."

From his hiding spot, Sonam could hear what was transpiring but couldn't see. He was concealed beneath the stage itself, in a small compartment accessible only from inside a storage room currently filled with theater equipment. He knew about it because he had made it his job to search out and identify every such area on the ship—he was aware of spaces even the ship's engineers usually overlooked. The space was small, but he was a small man; he had endured worse.

His mind was calm. He was a soldier, and right now there was no time for doubt or fear or indecision. A paramedic might have diagnosed him as being in shock, but he had none of the physical symptoms—his skin was neither cold nor clammy, his breathing was regular, his pulse strong. He was simply focused in a way few people ever experience, living entirely in the present moment, every sense so alert it was almost hallucinatory.

He considered his course of action. The case that the leader had mentioned was obviously the one Homeland Security had been searching for when the *Heart's Voyage* was in Miami; the ship's security staff had received a full briefing before they sailed. His first priority had to be to get that case and hurl it into the sea.

But how? Sonam was well-armed, but attacking the terrorists head-on was suicide. What he needed was a distraction, something to draw the attention of the guards away from the case long enough for him to grab it. After that, all he would have to do was outrun a hail of bullets . . .

13

"COME ON!" one of the passengers shouted. "There's four thousand people here! Your people could have just miscounted!"

Onstage, the Hare glared out into the audience. "Perhaps someone else would like to take his place, instead?"

Silence.

"I thought not." The Hare had his pistol out, and now he aimed it at each of the seven hostages on-stage in turn. "Who shall it be? Which of you is prepared to pay the price for your missing companion? You? Or you?"

The men he pointed to said nothing. Some of them looked terrified, some angry, some resolute. The Hare had them lined up at the edge of the stage facing outward, like soldiers being inspected.

"But perhaps you're right," the Hare said, his voice casual. "After all, six of you did surrender to me. It would be a shame for people to lose their lives over a small matter of arithmetic . . ."

He brought the pistol up, leveled it at the back of the head of the third man in line.

Delko looked away.

Sonam was almost in position.

He was no longer in the storage space beneath the stage. He had moved, quickly and stealthily, from below to above; he was now perched on a catwalk in the rafters, where he had a clear view of the stage below.

He was waiting for the Hare to fire.

Another death would be regrettable, but it was a small price to pay for eliminating the larger threat. At the moment the Hare's victim died, all eyes would be on the spectacle; it would be the perfect time to grab the case.

He had a rope ready, and could slide down it and be on the stage in a second. He was poised to do exactly that, his escape route already plotted in his mind.

Abruptly, one of the guards shifted his postion as the Hare talked. He was now almost directly below Sonam—there was no way for him to drop down now without involving the guard, and that would lose him the thin edge of surprise he was counting on.

He glanced around, recalculating. There was a black curtain hanging at the rear of the stage, reaching from the floor all the way to the height of the catwalk. If there were space behind it, it would provide enough cover for him to reposition himself at ground level.

He crept slowly along the catwalk until he reached the curtain. Not only was there space, there were support struts he could climb down.

He did so, hoping he wouldn't hear a shot.

Not until he was ready, anyway.

The Daldev warehouse was right next to an empty lot where debris from Hurricane Andrew had been dumped, piles of rubble and splintered wood now overgrown with weeds. Horatio, Calleigh, and Wolfe got out of the Hummer and walked up to the building, a large gray structure with a huge, peeling logo painted over the loading bay.

A sheet of plywood sealed off the front door, spray-painted with the words NO LOOTING. Calleigh inspected it and said, "Old wood—probably salvaged from the lot next door—but new nails."

"Take it down," said Horatio.

Wolfe was already attacking the edge of the sheet with a pry bar. It came off with a protesting screech.

Horatio pushed the door open. The interior was dim, cavernous—and empty.

"Nobody here now," said Wolfe.

"But there was—and recently," said Calleigh. "The floor's been swept. Somebody didn't want to leave any traces behind."

"Then," said Horatio, "let's hope we're better at doing our job than they were at theirs."

They went over the warehouse carefully. Calleigh and Wolfe concentrated on the main floor, while Horatio checked out the office space on the second story.

"Got a casing," said Calleigh. She held it up and inspected it critically. "Nine mill. Could match the spotting rounds from the rocket launcher."

"Not having much luck myself," said Wolfe. He was using his Mag-lite to illuminate some of the darker corners of the room. "Rat droppings and spiderwebs, that's about it . . . hold on." He knelt and picked up something. "Got a piece of red wire."

Horatio made his way down a flight of wooden stairs. "I may have something, as well." He held a folded newspaper in one hand. "Dated a week ago," he said. He handed it to Wolfe.

"There's a spiral scribble in the margin," Wolfe noted. "Like the kind you make when you can't get a pen to work. You can even see where the ink started to flow—before that there's an indented line but no color."

"The scribble," said Horatio, "suggests that the pen was used on something nearby—maybe even a piece of paper lying on top of the newspaper itself. If so, we might be able to lift something."

"All of us are going to be here," said the Hare, "for some time. I want you all to understand exactly the sort of man you are dealing with."

He lowered the gun. "Allah is merciful—and so am I."

In his hiding place behind the curtain at the rear of the stage, Sonam frowned.

"I will not execute a man without a reason," said the Hare. "The hypothetical existence of a single rogue passenger does not warrant this—thus, I will allow you to return to your places."

They didn't have to be told twice. The seven hostages clambered down off the stage, one of them almost falling in his haste. They were met with fierce hugs and tears by their respective families.

Delko had been studying the Hare, and now he whispered to Marie, "Stay here."

"Why?" she whispered back. "What are you going to do?"

"I just want to get a closer look, that's all."

He edged his way through the crowd, moving slowly and stopping whenever he felt a guard's eyes on him. Many people were standing or milling about; it wasn't that hard. He stopped when he was about twenty feet from the edge of the stage.

No deadman switch, he thought. A bomber—especially in a hostage situation—would often rig a trigger that would detonate the explosives if he released his grip on a handheld remote, making it impossible for a police sniper to pick him off. The Hare didn't seem to have one.

He said we were going to be here for a while, though. And the longer a standoff continues, the greater the chance his hand might cramp. Still . . .

Something else was bothering him.

Where's the Brilliant Batin? I haven't seen him in the

crowd, or with any of the terrorists. Are they keeping him as some kind of ace in the hole? You'd think a performer like him would want to be in the spotlight . . .

Which was when the Hare noticed him.

"You," said the terrorist. He pointed straight at Delko. "Get up here. Now."

Delko did as he was told, resisting the urge to look back at Marie.

"You seem very curious," said the Hare. "Perhaps our initial meeting was not as random as I first thought. Search him."

A guard approached and patted Delko down. He didn't have his badge or any ID with him—but he did have the PRD in one pocket. The guard pulled it out, examined it, then handed it to the Hare.

"It's a pager," said Delko tonelessly.

"Really? Strange, most people on vacation leave them at home . . . but then, I suppose you could be a workaholic."

The Hare dropped the detector on the floor and stomped on it, shattering the plastic casing and spilling electronics onto the stage. "There," he said. "Now you can relax . . ."

Behind the Hare, a figure stepped out from behind a black curtain.

Back at the lab, Wolfe used an ESDA—Electrostatic Detection Apparatus—to scan for hidden indentations in the surface of the newpaper. The paper had been in a relatively humid environment, which was good; dampness would help the electrostatic charge.

He fastened the paper to the top of a VacuBox, a rectangular device with a multiholed bronze plate on top, then sealed it with a layer of cellophane. A pump sucked air through the holes, ensuring maximum contact with the bronze plate.

"Now for the fun part," Wolfe muttered. He picked up a short rod with an electrical cable trailing from it and turned it on. The smell of ozone immediately filled the air; the rod generated a high-voltage static charge, which he then transferred to the paper by waving the rod over the surface slowly. It was almost like pouring water over a microscopic landscape; though not visible to the naked eye, there were peaks and valleys in the paper, and—hopefully—some of those valleys had been etched by the movement of a ballpoint pen. The voltage would behave in a manner similar to a liquid, with a higher charge settling into those valleys.

He turned off the rod and set it aside. Next, he sprinkled a fine black powder over the surface of the cellophane, similar to the toner used in dry-process copy machines. The powder was attracted to the static charge still on the paper; the stronger the charge, the more powder would adhere.

Wolfe studied the result and frowned. ESDA could bring out an impression made through multiple sheets of paper—and that's exactly what it had done.

Unfortunately, it couldn't tell him what it *meant*.

Sonam was sure the Hare was going to shoot the passenger.

He had made his move the second he saw the pistol come up. It was obvious to him that a passenger had to die—having established that he could show mercy, the Hare would now demonstrate his ruthlessness. It was elementary psychology, the same pattern that led abused women and children to seek the approval of the abuser; studies had shown that those subjected to random acts of both cruelty and kindness tried harder to win acceptance than those exposed to only rewards or punishment.

But he had made a mistake.

The expected gunshot had not come. He had frozen, exposed, knowing that his minuscule advantage was evaporating by the second. Any moment, one of the guards at the front door would notice him—

The Hare spun around, and fired. Once, twice, three times.

Sonam crumpled to the floor.

The Hare lowered his pistol. "No one steps onto *my* stage without my knowledge," he said.

Delko swallowed.

And then he collapsed.

"It's a chemical formula," said Wolfe, showing the results of the ESDA to Horatio. "Eighty percent nitrogen, fifteen percent carbon dioxide, five percent oxygen. What it's for, though—that I can't tell you."

"Well, I can tell you what it's not," said Horatio. "It wouldn't be pleasant to breathe, but it's not nearly toxic enough to be used as a weapon."

"Not combustible, either," said Wolfe. "It's basically an inert compound gas."

"So what," mused Horatio, "would the Hare want with an inert gas?"

"I'll start checking chemical databases, see what I can find," said Wolfe.

"Do that," said Horatio. "I'm going to see if Ms. Duquesne has made any progress on the bullet casing she found."

The news from Calleigh wasn't much better. "The nine-mill casing matches the ones I found at the rocket attack site," she said. "But we still don't have the weapon that fired them."

"But we know where it probably is," said Horatio. "Onboard the *Heart's Voyage*."

"Maybe," said Calleigh. "You know, H, something's been bothering me."

"What's that?"

"The warehouse. I mean, it's in a fairly isolated area, but not so isolated that automatic gunfire wouldn't get reported. And I didn't find any bullet holes, either."

"You think they trained elsewhere."

"I think they used the warehouse as a staging area, but tried out their firepower somewhere else. You certainly couldn't test a rocket launcher in a warehouse."

"No," said Horatio. "For that you need a couple of CSIs and their transportation."

Calleigh smiled. "Nice to see you still have your sense of humor, H."

"I'd prefer," said Horatio, "to still have my Hummer."

"M-medication," Delko gasped. "Need my—" He rolled his eyes up until the whites showed and went into spasms.

Come on, Delko thought. *Come on, you're a bright woman—*

"Get up!" the Hare shouted. "Get on your feet, right now, or I will shoot you where you lie!"

"Don't hurt him, he's *sick*!" a familiar voice cried. "Let me through, I know him—Eric, hang on, I'm coming!"

Attagirl, Delko thought. *Scratch a dancer, find an actress. Now don't overplay it—*

He heard her land beside him as she vaulted onto the stage. "Medication," he gasped again. "In my cabin . . ."

"He needs his pills," Marie said urgently. "Please! Don't let him die!"

The Hare stared down at her, his eyes cold. He said nothing for a long minute.

"All right," he said at last. "Since our missing passenger has turned up at last, I see no need for any further . . . demonstration."

He glanced pointedly at the body of the Gurkha.

Delko used the opportunity to grab Marie and pull her closer. He whispered a few quick words, then punctuated them with a groan.

"I know where his cabin is," Marie said. "Let me

get them, please. Send a guard with me—I promise I won't try anything."

The Hare nodded to the lone female terrorist, the woman with the ponytail. "Go with her. Kill her if you must."

Marie fumbled in Delko's pocket, found his card-key and pulled it out. "I'll be back in a few minutes," she told him. Her eyes told him she thought he was crazy.

Just bring it back, thought Delko. He said nothing though, just nodded.

The woman with the ponytail grabbed her arm and pulled her away.

Horatio sat alone in his office, thinking. Eventually, he picked up the phone and made a call.

"Nadira?"

"Horatio. I was wondering when you'd call."

"One of my men is on the ship, Nadira."

A pause. "I see. What do you need from me?"

"Just a few minutes of your time. Can we meet?"

"Sure. I'm still at the same hotel—shall we say the restaurant on the main floor, in half an hour?"

"I'll be there."

She was waiting when he arrived, sitting at a table in the back and sipping a ginger ale. "Thanks for coming," he said, pulling up a chair.

"Not at all. Who's onboard?"

"Eric Delko."

She nodded. "Ah. The one with the temper. Not

who I'd have picked as an undercover operative, but—"

"He's not there in an official capacity."

She raised her eyebrows. "No?"

"No. His girlfriend works on the ship. When she insisted on going, he followed her."

"So she doesn't know about the . . . package."

Horatio shook his head. "Eric wouldn't have told her."

"So he felt obligated to try to protect her. Noble. Not very effective, but noble nonetheless."

"He's a good man, Nadira. And a good cop. If there's any way he can help, he will."

"A man inside is always a resource—but only if he's prepared. Do you have any way to contact him? Is he armed?"

"No to both."

She shrugged. "Then what do you want me to do?"

"I'm not sure," Horatio admitted. "But you have connections I don't. If we work together—"

She raised a hand, cutting him off. "I'm not as well-connected as you might think. My superiors aren't happy with the way I've handled things. It was my responsibility to locate the package, and now it's on a hijacked cruise ship. That's why I'm here, getting my updates on CNN in my hotel room instead of being on-site. We blew it, Horatio; the Hare slipped right past us. Again."

She raised her glass and took a long sip, and Horatio realized there was more than just ginger ale in the glass.

"Maybe so," said Horatio, "but it's the last time. He's tried to kill me, he's tried to kill my people, and now he's threatening to execute four thousand innocents."

Horatio got to his feet. "That's not going to happen, Nadira. I won't let it."

She regarded him with an expression that was half-amused, half–something else. "You know—I believe you. Damned if I know why, but if anyone's going to stop the Hare, it will be you." She put down her unfinished drink and stood as well. "Very well. Let's go."

"Not that I don't appreciate the vote of support—but exactly where are we going?"

She grinned. "I was thinking a little ocean voyage . . ."

The female terrorist's name was Fatima. Marie knew this only because she'd overheard another of the hijackers mention it; the woman herself spoke only when she had to. She kept her assault rifle pointed at Marie the entire time they walked, and the dancer had no doubt she would use it.

Girl's got something to prove, Marie thought. *Better not give her the opportunity.*

Not that she had any intention of playing hero. She didn't understand why Delko wanted what he'd asked for, but she was going to do her best to get it—as long as that didn't mean getting shot.

When they got to Delko's cabin, she unlocked it with the card-key. Fatima motioned her to stand a little way down the hall while she peered inside, then gave her the okay to enter.

Marie went straight to Delko's toiletries. He wasn't taking any medication that she knew of, but she'd managed to palm a small vial of antinausea pills she'd had in her pocket. The vial had no label; she hoped it would pass for heart pills or whatever Delko was supposed to have.

The item she was supposed to bring back was on the bedside table, beside his camera. She studied it out of the corner of her eye as she pretended to rummage through Eric's toiletry kit. She held up the vial already in her hand and said, "Here it is!" while taking a step backward.

One of the most difficult things for a performer to do was deliberately screw up—a good singer found it hard to sing off-key on purpose, a good actor found it hard to act badly. As a dancer, Marie was naturally graceful . . . but now she made herself stumble, hitting her heel against the leg of the bed and half-falling. She caught herself with a hand on the bedside table, making a successful grab at the same time. The item was small enough to hide in her hand.

"Sorry," said Marie, "I'm—"

She froze. The muzzle of Fatima's rifle was only inches away from her face.

"Be more careful in the future," said the terrorist softly.

Marie swallowed and pushed herself upright carefully. "I'll—I'll do that."

Fatima's eyes were locked on her own. Marie used the opportunity to slip what was in her hand into her pocket.

This better be worth it, Eric . . .

Nadira still had some pull left. She got herself and Horatio a ride out to the naval blockade parked a mile away from the *Heart's Voyage* on a Coast Guard Hercules transport helicopter. From overhead, the number of ships anchored in a circle around the ship was impressive; the largest of them was the aircraft carrier *John Adams*.

"Half of them are media," said Nadira. "If cameras were lasers we could melt the ship into scrap."

"I don't think lack of firepower is our problem," said Horatio.

They touched down on the flight deck of the carrier. Two sailors came out to escort them into the superstructure itself.

Horatio paused at the hatch, looking over the water at the *Heart's Voyage*. He didn't know what he was doing here, or what he could accomplish that half the Navy couldn't—but he knew it was important that he'd come. "Hang on, Eric," he said softly.

"Take these," said Marie. She crouched beside Delko, who was lying near the base of the stage. He took the pills from her, then asked for some water. Someone handed him a plastic bottle.

"Thanks," he said to Marie after he'd pretended to swallow the pills.

"Glad I could help."

She'd managed to slip him the item from his cabin at the same time, and it was now safely in Eric's pocket. *As long as the Hare doesn't search me again,* he thought.

But this was only the first part of his plan. Now, he had to get close to the case on center stage—and the last person who had tried that lay dead, only a few feet from his objective.

Which gave him an idea.

Captain Leo Novakovic, a burly man with short, wiry brown hair, leaned back in his leather chair and shook his head. "Look," he told Horatio. "I sympathize, I really do. One of your men is on that ship and you're looking out for him. But despite appearances, I'm really just playing host here; I've got a five-star admiral and two presidential security advisors onboard, and unless they decide they want my jets to do more than just flyovers, I may as well ask them what they want in their coffee."

Horatio smiled and leaned forward, his fingers interlaced in front of him. "I understand. I'm not asking for any special treatment; I'd just like to be kept in the loop."

"Lieutenant Caine has been instrumental in the investigation so far," said Nadira. She was seated beside Horatio. "Homeland Security would appreciate—"

The captain held up one thick-fingered hand. "Hold it. I've had Homeland Security waved in my face so many times in the last twenty-four hours I'm thinking of getting it tattooed on my neck. I know who you are and what you do, Ms. Quadiri, and rest assured I'll keep you up to date. All right?"

"Thank you," said Nadira.

"And now, if you don't mind," said the Novakovic, getting to his feet, "I've got to go find out if the secretary of state likes two sugars or three."

Wolfe pounded his fist on the table in frustration. "*Damn* it!"

Calleigh looked up from her workstation. "What's wrong?"

"I can't find anything on this formula. It has no military use, it's not a catalyst for something else, it doesn't seem to be part of a more complex formula—or if it is, I can't figure out what that might be. It's basically useless."

"How about the wire you found?"

"Tool mark on the end matched the cut branches at the Garenko shooting. It confirms that the person who shot Billy Lee was also at the warehouse—but doesn't tell us what he was doing there."

"Well, maybe this'll cheer you up. I have another possible location the Hare might have used."

"Yeah? What have you got?"

"Reports of automatic gunfire out by Markham Park, a week ago."

"Remote enough, I guess."

"That's not the clincher. Person who called to

complain also reported at least one 'substantial' explosion."

"Substantial as in rocket-launched substantial?"

She shrugged. "I don't know. Radio car went to check it out but didn't find anything. What do you say we give it a try?"

"Let's go. Anything beats slamming my head against this stupid formula."

"You know, you sound just like my roommate in college."

"Hey," said Delko. "He moved."

Fatima glared at him from her position at one end of the stage. The guard at the other end was talking quietly to the Hare, who glanced over at Delko's exclamation.

"He *moved,*" Delko insisted, walking up to the edge of the stage. "He's still alive!" *Okay, Eric. Don't think about this next part, just do it . . .*

He vaulted onto the stage. Immediately, every gun in the room swung to target him. He kept his hands low, saying, "Easy! Easy!" and walked quickly over to the Gurkha's body before anyone could move to block him.

He dropped to his knees, expecting to feel a slug slam into his body at any second, and put his hand to the Gurkha's neck as if checking for a pulse.

"You are very close to becoming a dead man," said the Hare. He stood behind Delko, the muzzle of his automatic inches away from the CSI's skull. "Especially if you think you can retrieve one of this man's weapons and use it against me."

"I watched you search the body and take all his guns, just like everybody else," said Delko quietly. "I thought I saw him move. I have some first-responder training, thought I could help."

"This man is beyond help. Or do your impressive first-aid skills tell you otherwise?"

"No," said Delko. He raised his hands slowly, showing the Hare that both of them were empty. "No, I guess I was wrong. He's dead."

"And if you don't want to join him," said the Hare, "I suggest you return to your seat."

The report of gunfire had come from a groundskeeper at the Fair Coast Golf Course, a brand-new eighteen-holer just off the Sawgrass Expressway. Wolfe and Calleigh checked in at the clubhouse, then tracked down the man on the fourteenth tee grooming a sandtrap with a long-handled rake. Jake Tucker was a man in his sixties, lean and spry, with wispy white hair carefully pomaded into a curl over his forehead. He looked up from his work as they approached, shading his eyes from the sun with one hand.

"Mister Tucker?" said Wolfe, pulling out his badge. "I'm Ryan Wolfe and this is Calleigh Duquesne, with the Miami-Dade crime lab. We'd like to ask you some questions about the shooting you reported the other night."

"Shooting? Oh, you mean the gunshots." Tucker

nodded. "Damnfool kids, I expect. There's a place on the edge of the course where they like to hang out, drink beer and so on. They make a mess, but it's off the property so it's not my responsibility."

"Can you tell us where this spot is?" asked Calleigh.

"I can do better than that—I can show you. Come on."

He led them across a broad green, through a swath of tall grass and into a wooded area. The woods ended in a tall chain-link fence, and the carefully manicured appearance of the grounds gave way on the other side to a rougher, more unkempt wilderness. There were the remains of a small campfire there, with broken glass and crushed beer cans scattered around.

"That's it," said Tucker.

Calleigh peered through the chain-link. "I don't see any signs of gunfire."

"Nah, they weren't doing it here," said Tucker. "See the trail, there, leading deeper? There's another, bigger clearing a ways in, with an old wrecked truck sitting there. That's the direction I heard the gunfire from."

"What's the easiest way to get to the other side of this fence?" Wolfe asked.

"There's a gate down by the fifteenth tee. I'll unlock it for you."

"So," Marie whispered, "would you like to tell me what the point of *that* was?"

"Testing a theory," said Delko.

"What—how many times you can tick off a terrorist before he *shoots* you?"

"Not exactly . . ." He leaned in close and whispered a quick explanation in her ear; he didn't want anyone else—passengers or otherwise—to hear.

When he was done, she looked at him and said, "But—I mean, you still have to—and *then* you have to—" She stopped, her look turning into a glare. "That is not a good plan. That isn't even a bad plan. It's like three—no, *four*—bad plans."

"Five, actually," said Delko. "I think you missed the part where I smuggle what I learn off the ship. And in my defense, the first two plans have worked."

"Great—you have a forty percent success rate, so far. With a one hundred percent chance of being killed if you get caught."

"Look, I have to do this," said Delko. "If what I suspect is true, it'll change everything. It's important."

"I know, I know . . ." she sighed. "Okay. How can I help?"

"You've already done your part. The rest is up to me."

"So how are you going to—"

"I'm working on it," said Delko.

"I can see why the radio car didn't find anything," said Calleigh. They were picking their way along a narrow trail beside the fence. "It's a bit of a hike from the road to here, and the trail's not easy to see. If there was no actual gunfire by the time they got here, they probably chalked it up to kids and gave up."

"Plus it was dark," said Wolfe. "Hopefully we'll have better luck."

They reached the campfire site and continued along the second trail. It led through denser, more tangled brush for a good half-mile or so until it abruptly ended at a clearing.

"This looks like it," said Wolfe. "But I don't see any wrecked truck."

"I do," said Calleigh. She pointed to a twisted chunk of metal poking out of a patch of grass. "There. And there. And over there."

"And up here," said Wolfe. He pointed to a rusted chunk of metal embedded about ten feet up a tree trunk. "Looks like the Hare found something to use for target practice."

"He was trying out more than the rocket launcher," said Calleigh. "Those trees over there have been riddled by gunfire." She looked around at her feet. "I've got casings all over the place, too."

"Okay. How do you figure the Hare and his men got out here?"

"The same way that old truck got in. You go left, I'll go right." They skirted the perimeter of the clearing until Wolfe said, "Got it, behind these bushes. Not much of a road, but I can see fresh tire tracks."

"Let's follow it."

The rutted track led out of the woods and onto a dirt road beside a canal. "This must connect with the highway," said Calleigh. "Pretty isolated, though. If it wasn't for the golf course, you could come and go without anyone ever knowing you were here."

"Yeah, but even the groundskeeper didn't actually see anything," pointed out Wolfe. "The only witnesses out here are mosquitoes and mangroves."

"Not necessarily," said Calleigh. "You might be surprised who's watching, even out here . . ."

In the end, it was the body itself that gave Delko his next opportunity.

A middle-aged woman in the crowd raised her hand, then began to wave it when she saw she was being ignored. "Excuse me," she called out. "Excuse me."

"What do you want?" the Hare snapped.

"It's—well, it's *that,*" the woman, a plump, freckled blonde said, pointing at the fallen Gurkha. "I don't want to make any trouble, but—he's really starting to *smell.*"

It was true—it wasn't decomp that was bothering the woman, it was the bodily fluids that had been released when he died and his involuntary muscles relaxed.

"You're right," said the Hare. "I suppose we should dispose of him before he gets any worse. You, you, and . . . you," he said, pointing to Delko last. "Since you were so concerned with his welfare when you thought he was still breathing, you may as well assist now."

Perfect, Delko thought. He made sure he got to the stage before any of the others without seeming too eager. He positioned himself at the head, fumbling for a handhold at the body's neck. He managed to grab the item he'd hidden in the collar without anyone noticing.

"Take him to a cabin and leave him inside," the Hare told one of the guards, a thick-chested man with a jowly, unshaven face. "Leave him there and come back immediately."

The guard motioned them to go first. Delko, at the head, wound up walking backward.

Phase three, Delko thought. *Okay, the easy parts are over . . .*

14

WOLFE TOOK CASTS OF THE TIRE TRACKS while Calleigh processed the clearing. She found multiple casings on the ground and many rounds embedded in the trees, and bagged a few pieces of metal debris to test for traces of explosives back at the lab.

"Double wheels," said Wolfe, showing her the cast. "Truck of some kind."

"They must have used it to transport the hijackers out here from the warehouse," she said. "One vehicle draws less attention than a caravan."

"Yeah, especially when it's loaded with heavily armed terrorists. You finished?"

"Just about. I haven't dug all the slugs out of the trees, but there's too many to process without cutting down half this forest. A representative sample will have to do."

"You know, this is Delko's specialty," said Wolfe, carefully bagging the tire cast. "I'll bet he could figure out a way to ID the truck just from these tracks."

"Well then—I guess you'll have something to brag about to him later, when you do it instead."

Wolfe hesitated. "Yeah," he said. "Sure."

The Gurkha's body didn't weigh much; between the three of them, he seemed as light as a child. The guard stayed a few steps behind them in the corridor until they reached the room they were going to dump him in, one chosen by the Hare at random; he'd simply pointed to a person in the crowd and demanded he give up his key. The guard motioned them a little way past the room, then unlocked it and peered inside.

The moment the guard stuck his head through the doorway, Delko dropped the body and ran.

He was already around the first corner by the time the guard let out a startled shout. He heard the staccato bark of an automatic rifle a second later, but he'd expected that and didn't let it shake him.

Delko had almost had a career in pro baseball, and now he pounded down the corridor like a designated runner trying to stretch a triple into a homer. He knew that if he could get a big enough lead on the guard, he could lose him; to that end, he headed for the Grand Concourse, the mall-like area of the ship that was crowded with shops, boutiques, and bars.

And one of them, he hoped, would also contain a particular piece of equipment.

He came to a staircase and ran up it, taking steps three at a time, hoping the guard would guess wrong and head the other way. A few seconds later he heard footsteps ringing on metal behind him and knew the guard was still with him.

Almost there. Almost there. He heard more shouting from behind him; it sounded like more than one guard was chasing him now.

He burst onto the Grand Concourse and immediately saw that all the shops stood open; he didn't stop but headed straight down the middle. He knew there was no way he could reach the end before the guards hit the Concourse, too, but he needed them to see him; that would mean exposing himself to a bullet, but only for an instant.

The burst of gunfire shredded a tall plant to his left as he reached the end, and he immediately zigged right and down another staircase, this one carpeted in thick red pile. When he hit the bottom, he took a sharp left and ducked under the staircase itself.

A moment later, he heard footsteps pounding overhead.

"All right," said Calleigh. They were back at the lab, Wolfe examining the tire casts and Calleigh at a workstation. "That dirt road runs parallel to a canal and connects to the highway here." She tapped a corner of the screen where a map graphic was laid out. "Right here is pump station S-331. Regulates water flow into the Everglades—and every pump station also has a video camera for security surveillance."

"So if the truck drove past the pump station—"

"We might get a shot of it?" She punched another key. "Like this?"

Wolfe grinned. "Rented panel truck. That logo's hard to miss."

"Not to mention the giant mural of a red-tailed hawk beside it. Not only does it make the truck nicer to look at, it should make it easier to track down."

Wolfe squinted at the screen. "Looks like you've got a partial plate, too."

"First three numbers is all I've been able to make out—should narrow it down considerably, though."

Wolfe nodded. "Let's start calling rental agencies."

The footsteps overhead reached the bottom, and then two guards ran past to the left. Neither of them saw Delko. He waited a few seconds, then ducked out and ran back up the stairs.

The place he wanted was a kiosk, a small, self-contained stall that jutted out from the Concourse like an afterthought. He ducked under the flat-topped gate that served as a counter and inside.

Delko had worked one summer at a one-hour Fotomat just like this one, back in the days before digital cameras were ubiquitous. He'd been worried that the ship might not have such facilities, but apparently enough tourists still used old-fashioned film to make the business viable.

He pulled out the roll of film he'd gone to such trouble to get and loaded it quickly into the processing unit. The machine was largely automatic; all he had to do was hit the button and wait.

Of course, he couldn't just hang around while it was processing. For one thing, the machine made noise; if the guards came back—as they almost certainly would—they'd be sure to check it out. Delko hoped that they'd simply assume the machine was on some sort of preset cycle and not look too closely at what was coming out; most of the roll were pictures of Marie he'd taken last weekend while they were on a picnic. He didn't want any more of the Hare's attention focused on her.

He looked around and spotted a bar on the other side of the Concourse. It would make a good place to hide while he waited for the machine to finish.

And then he heard the voices of the returning guards.

The bar's name was Davy Jones's Locker. It featured a stout oak door for the entrance and large windows on either side. Delko dashed across the Concourse, yanked the door open and darted in.

The interior was fairly large, with a small stage up front, a circular bar in the middle, and thirty or so tables scattered around. There was a row of dartboards along one wall, and something Delko had never expected to see on a ship: a pool table. There were no balls on the table at the moment, but two cues lay on the green felt.

Delko grabbed one and crouched behind the bulk of the table itself. He got a good grip on the cue about three-quarters of the way down its length, with the heavy end at the top, and cocked his arms back so he could get a good swing.

Just like a baseball bat. Visualize the ball, where it's going to be when you're at the apogee of your swing.

The guards would check each of the businesses in turn, but there were quite a few; Delko hoped the guards would split up. If one stood by the door while the other searched, Delko would be in a lot of trouble.

Right. Like where I am now is a walk in the park.

He heard the door open.

He tensed up, and felt one of his calf muscles start to cramp. He gritted his teeth and ignored it.

The carpeted floor muffled the guard's footsteps. *Where is he? I can't tell . . .*

And then he saw the tip of one sneakered foot, poking out just beyond the corner of the table.

He sprang up, swinging the cue in a hard, deadly arc. It connected solidly with the side of the guard's head, and the man went over sideways in a boneless heap.

Delko's eyes went to the door. There was no one there.

He looked down at the guard and came to a

quick decision, grabbing the walkie-talkie clipped to the man's belt but leaving the gun. There was a swinging door leading to a kitchen area in the back; he went through it, then through another door that led to a maintenance hallway.

He found what he was looking for at the end of the hall, an unlocked storage room. He went inside and closed the door, then sank to the floor and tried to get his breathing under control. After the adrenaline rush of the attack, it was hard to simply sit still, but he knew he shouldn't move too far away from the Fotomat booth.

He could hear other guards on the radio, talking in Arabic. Something was bothering him—something beyond the simple fact that he was running for his life—and he suddenly realized what it was: the walkie-talkies shouldn't work. Cell phones had stopped working as soon as the hijacking began, and Delko had been with the captain when the Hare told him they were using a jammer to blanket radio frequencies and kill communications.

Walkie-talkies normally broadcast on a frequency between three hundred and three thousand megahertz. They could have adapted their equipment to use something else—a lower band, probably—and not be jamming that one. It was useful information, but only if he could identify which specific frequency they were using.

A voice suddenly echoed throughout the ship—the Hare's voice, using the public-address system again.

"I understand that a certain troublemaker has eluded his keepers," the Hare said. "This is a most unfortunate choice. I suggest he return to the concert hall immediately . . . or the woman who showed such concern for his health will have concerns about her own."

15

DELKO LOOKED AT HIS WATCH. He still had forty-five minutes to go.

He hit the transmit button of the walkie-talkie. "This is the man you're looking for," he said.

The response was immediate. "You are resourceful," said the Hare. "Where did you get the radio?"

"I took it from one of your men."

"Is he dead?"

"No. I didn't take his gun, either—I don't want this to get ugly."

"How civilized."

Delko hated to do it, but his only chance was to play the part of a scared, selfish tourist. "Look, I'm no hero. I'm not going to do anything to get in your way—I just panicked, okay? I didn't want to get shot."

"I understand. Come back, and all will be forgiven."

"I don't think so. Can't you just leave me alone?"

The Hare laughed. "That's your proposal? It's a big ship, there's room for both of us?"

"Why not?" Delko knew the Hare wouldn't go for it, but the longer he kept him talking, the better.

"For one thing, it would set a very bad example—I can't have someone bolting for the door at every opportunity. For another, you've already demonstrated a disturbing propensity for trouble. I really can't have you running around loose."

"Then let me go. I could jump overboard, swim to one of those ships out there." Delko had no intention of doing so, but it might distract the Hare's men from his true intentions.

"If you intended to do that, you'd already have done so. Why haven't you?"

A dangerous question. "Right, and be a sitting duck for your men."

"If I wanted an easy target, I have a room full of them right here—a fact you shouldn't forget."

Marie's worried face came immediately to mind, but he pushed it away—he had a role to play, and showing concern for her right now could get her killed. "Look, I'm sorry—but I don't care about them. If I turn myself in, you'll kill me. I have to protect myself."

"Then I have no choice but to hunt you down and make an example of you. Is that preferable?"

"No! No, look, can't we work something out? I don't want to die, you don't want to tie up your manpower looking for me—we have to be able to find some kind of compromise here."

"Very well. I'm a reasonable man; what do you suggest?"

Delko looked at his watch. "Give me—give me an hour to think about it. That's all."

"You have twenty minutes."

Delko sighed. Twenty minutes. It would have to be enough.

The panel truck had been rented to an Ahmed Jabbar. Seeing his face and driver's licence information come up on the screen before her gave Calleigh a powerful sense of relief; Jabbar was the first real lead they'd had in a long time.

"You think it'll pan out?" asked Wolfe, leaning over her shoulder.

"Terrorist cells tend to be small," said Calleigh. "The Hare must have called together more than one to get a crew of twenty-five together. I doubt they'd leave anyone behind."

"So he's probably on the ship—and out of reach."

"That may be," said Calleigh, getting to her feet. "But everything he's touched in the last six months is *ours*."

Delko thought about his next move.

The terrorist he'd knocked out would be discovered, sooner or later. He could stay where he was and risk being discovered by a methodical search—or keep moving and risk being spotted in the open.

He opted for the latter. If he was moving, at least he had a chance.

He peered out of the storage room cautiously, then crept down the maintenance corridor. He found another door, marked LOUNGE, and found it unlocked.

The bar on the other side was smaller and dimmer than Davy Jones's Locker. A grand piano dominated the room, with seating around it and a cluster of small tables in a ring beyond that. Porthole-shaped windows looked out on the Concourse. Delko kept low and snuck a look outside through one; he had a good view of the photo kiosk across the way. He hoped anyone who discovered the machinery running would assume it was an automatic process and ignore it—or at least not try to shut it off.

The door to Davy Jones's Locker opened and the guard he'd coldcocked staggered out. He looked both groggy and angry, and demonstrated his feelings by shouting in Arabic and turning his assault rifle on the storefronts across from him. Delko ducked as a spray of bullets shattered the porthole and showered him with broken glass.

The shooting attracted the attention of other guards, who came running. A brief but intense discussion followed—and then they spread out and continued searching the shops.

Ahmed Jabbar was a student at the University of Florida. He shared a dorm room with someone named Fasal Zebramani, but nobody in the dorms had seen them for the previous two weeks.

The resident assistant of the dorm floor let Wolfe and Calleigh in. Their warrant granted them access to anything in the room, and any storage locker or vehicle that the two might have used. Normally, Calleigh would have been surprised at the breadth of the warrant—Fasal hadn't even been directly implicated yet—but these were special circumstances.

The room was orderly, clean, and virtually empty.

"Doesn't look like they were planning on coming back," said Wolfe.

"I'm more interested in where they've been," said Calleigh. She took a step into the room, looking around carefully. "If Jabbar and Fasal are on the ship, they know what the Hare's plans are. Anything they left behind could give us vital information."

"I hate to say it, but the Hare's plans seem pretty clear." Wolfe opened the closet door and looked inside. "Blow up the ship and everyone on it, including himself."

"That would make sense," said Calleigh calmly, running her gloved hands along the underside of the first bed. "But so far, he hasn't done that. He's waiting for something—and I bet our missing roommates know what."

"I do, too," said Wolfe thoughtfully. "But I think we're looking in the wrong place."

Calleigh straightened up. "What do you mean?"

"I mean that the nine-eleven hijackers enrolled themselves in flight school to learn the basics of flying airplanes. What were these guys learning?"

"Good question. We can get a copy of their course schedule and find out."

Delko picked his moment carefully, waiting until all three guards were inside three different shops. He sprinted across the Concourse, keeping low and heading for the photo kiosk.

He almost made it.

He heard a shout behind him as he ducked inside, and then a burst of automatic gunfire. He darted under the counter as bullets slammed into the wall over his head and ricocheted off metal. The machinery gave a screech and a loud clacking noise, and then all the lights on it went out.

It didn't matter. It had already processed the first half of the roll, and the photos were lying on the little conveyor belt that came out of the machine. Delko only had to glance at them to have his suspicions confirmed.

So now I know—won't do much good unless I can tell somebody.

"Come out of there with your hands in plain sight!" one of them called out.

"Sorry," Delko muttered under his breath. "I can't do that—not just yet . . ."

He crept to the back of the kiosk, but there was no exit. The only way out was the way he'd come in.

"Nuclear physics," said Wolfe, studying the course transcript. "And marine engineering."

They were in a small coffee shop on university grounds. Calleigh was sipping a large iced tea, and Wolfe had grabbed a latte. Calleigh was studying Jabbar's transcripts, Wolfe Zebramani's.

"Makes sense," said Calleigh. "They wanted to know as much about the bomb and its target as possible. My guy went a different route, though—chemistry and geology."

Wolfe frowned. "Well, the chemistry might explain the formula we found—but geology? Where does that fit in?"

"Maybe they were planning on mining their own uranium?"

"Uranium is easy to get. It's the enriched stuff and plutonium that make terrorists drool."

"And a degree in geology isn't going to help with that." Calleigh shook her head. "This is important, Ryan—I know it. I just don't know what it *means*."

"Well, we better figure it out," said Wolfe grimly. "Because whatever he's planning, the Hare isn't going to wait forever."

Delko knew there was only one thing to do.

He grabbed the walkie-talkie and said, "Tell your men to hold their fire!"

There was a long pause. Delko waited for the burst of bullets that would end his life.

"Do not kill him," the Hare said. "Yet. Tell me, my quick-footed troublemaker, why should I spare you?"

"Because I know something you need to know,"

said Delko. "Kill me, and you'll never figure it out—until it's too late."

"I find that hard to believe. It has the reek of desperation."

Delko played the only card he could think of. "I know what's in the case. I'm a reporter, I've been following this story ever since the ship was searched in port. I know what they were looking for—a black-market Soviet suitcase nuke."

"How clever of you. But soon enough, the whole world will know."

"Yes, but you're in control here. You could give it whatever spin you want. There are plenty of video cameras aboard—we can shoot an interview. I'll be your spokesman."

The Hare laughed. "Very well. Surrender to my men, and they will bring you back to me. We will discuss our interview."

Delko shouted, "Don't shoot! I'm coming out!" He left the kiosk slowly, hands held over his head.

The man he'd knocked unconscious snarled something in Arabic, and raised his weapon.

Horatio stood on the outside deck of the carrier's flight tower. The gray metal railing was cold in his left hand; the right held a pair of binoculars to his eyes. A mile distant, the *Heart's Voyage* looked as deserted as the *Marie Celeste*; no swimsuit-clad tourists lounged at poolside, no passengers in gaudy tropical shirts roamed its decks. Occasionally a gunman could be seen, but they mostly kept out of sight.

Like rats, skulking in the shadows, thought Horatio.

Nadira climbed the metal steps to the platform and stood beside him. She knew as well as he that watching was pointless, that far keener eyes were observing every angle of the ship every single minute—but she also hadn't pointed that out. She knew why he was here.

"Anything?" she asked.

"No." He lowered the binoculars with a sigh. "I thought I heard shots a few minutes ago, but nobody will confirm that."

She nodded. "Yes. The listening post picked up several bursts of automatic gunfire and some shouting. Our translator says it sounds as if they were yelling for someone to stop."

"Any response?"

"Not that they could tell. Noise from the interior of the ship is almost impossible to make out—we're lucky we heard anything at all."

Horatio nodded. "Somebody making a break for it. Maybe they figure they can hide until this is all over."

"You think it's Delko?"

Horatio smiled. "No, that's . . . not really his style."

She smiled back. "He seemed like a bit of a hothead to me."

"Well, he feels very strongly about certain things. He's passionate and committed. I can't really say I'm surprised he's onboard."

Nadira chose her next words carefully. "How do you think he'll react to being held hostage?"

"You mean, do I think he'll do something stupid." Horatio shook his head. "Not a chance. Eric's got a cool head under pressure. If he sees a chance, he'll take it—but he won't put anyone else at risk."

"What about his girlfriend? The one he followed?"

"I don't know her well, I'm afraid. From what Eric's said, she seems levelheaded . . . but there's no telling how she'll react to the situation."

Or, Horatio didn't add, *how Eric will react to her being threatened.*

There was a long, tense moment. Finally, the guard spat out, "If you try to run again, I will shoot you—no matter what Al-Arnab says."

Delko believed him. "Whatever you say," he said.

They marched him to the end of the Concourse and up a flight of metal stairs. Delko was thinking furiously, but the only solution he could think of wasn't one he liked.

If the Hare doesn't just kill me in front of the audience to make a point, they'll probably restrain me or lock me in a closet. This is the last chance I'll have.

It would depend on the route they took back to the concert hall. Fortunately, the quickest way seemed to be along an outside passageway, one that looked out on the ocean.

He needed a distraction, something that diverted the guard's attention for just a second . . . and at that moment, a fighter jet screamed by overhead, seeming only yards away. Delko heard one of the guards curse.

He dove over the railing.

It wasn't his most graceful dive, though it certainly seemed to last the longest. All the way down he expected to feel bullets ripping into his body . . . but he didn't even hear a cry of alarm until the instant before he hit the water. The guards must have been looking at the jet instead of him.

He struck at a reasonably clean angle, slicing into the sea headfirst. He kicked even deeper, immediately angling toward the ship. He heard the strange, distinctive noise of bullets penetrating water, but it was behind him and he didn't worry. If they hadn't gotten him in midair, the density of good old H-2-O would protect him.

He dove under the keel, glad the engines weren't running. It was a fair ways to go, but Delko was a good swimmer; he knew he could hold his breath and cover the distance before the guards could make it to the other side of the ship—though they'd probably wait for him to surface near where he dove, thinking they could pick him off then.

Of course, if there *were* guards waiting for him on the other side, his next breath would be his last.

Nadira suddenly put a hand to the wireless earpiece she wore. "I'm getting an alert," she said calmly. "Observers on the opposite side just reported a body being dumped into the ocean."

"Description?"

"Dark-skinned male. Hold on, they're saying it appears he jumped himself. The hostage takers are firing at the water . . . it looks like an escape attempt. They can't tell whether or not he was hit."

Horatio immediately focused the binoculars on the waterline of the ship. "Eric's a trained police diver. If he went into the water, he'll come out where they least expect it . . ."

"What makes you think it's Delko?"

Horatio didn't answer. He was too busy concentrating on scanning the water—and then he saw it. Little more than a dark dot on the water, near the prow of the ship. He couldn't tell if it was a person's head or not.

And then he saw the flash.

Delko came up on the other side, took a quick gulp of air, and submerged again. This time, he struck out for the bow; he knew that the prow of the ship would provide a slight overhang that he could hide beneath—it would make him harder to see from above, anyway.

He surfaced, trying not to make too much noise, and then reached into the waistband of his shorts. He pulled out the shard of mirrored glass he'd salvaged from the photo kiosk, and thanked God that this side of the ship was in direct sunlight. It would make him easier to spot . . . but now, that was a good thing.

Delko had been a Boy Scout. One of the first badges he'd ever earned had been in signaling, twenty letters per minute. He could do it in semaphore—or in Morse. He also knew that the heliograph, one of the oldest signaling devices in the world, consisted basically of nothing more than sunlight and a mirror.

He focused his improvised heliograph on the aircraft carrier, and hoped someone was paying attention.

"It's Morse code," said Horatio. "B—O—M—B . . . it's stopped." Horatio moved the binoculars slightly and saw a guard leaning over the railing at the prow, studying the water.

"Keep your head down, Eric," Horatio muttered. "I know you can hold your breath for at least three minutes, so just be patient . . ."

The seconds crawled by. The guard left—but returned a moment later, apparently still not satisfied.

"Just a little longer," Horatio murmured. "You can do it, pal . . ."

The guard finally gave up and stalked off. Not ten seconds later, a dark head broke the surface.

"He's signaling again," said Horatio. Only four more letters followed . . . but they were all Horatio needed to know.

"Good job, Eric," Horatio said, lowering the binoculars. "Now get yourself to safety, my friend . . ."

The last four letters Delko sent were F, A, K, and E.

Whatever was in that case, it wasn't radioactive. Delko knew that, because radioactivity fogged photographic film—and the pictures he'd run through the photo processor had turned out just fine, without so much as a streak or a spot. From the readings he and Calleigh had gotten before, he knew the real bomb was giving off enough gamma particles to affect film a few feet away—which was why he'd planted the canister on the Gurkha's body and then retrieved it.

That meant that the real bomb was still out there—and Horatio was the only one with any hope of finding it.

There was a loud splash behind him, and he turned his head to realize the motor launch was in the water. They were going to search for him in a more direct way.

He took a deep breath and submerged to think about his options. He could swim for the nearest boat—a mile wasn't that far, and he could do most of it underwater where he wouldn't be seen. If he was seen, though, they wouldn't hesitate to shoot him; he'd been lucky so far, but if the motor launch spotted him it was all over. They could cut him off, wait for him to surface, and kill him. If the ship was still towing the raft he might have been able to use it as a halfway point, but he'd noticed it was no longer there—the hijackers must have cut it loose.

Or he could surrender—which was probably a death sentence. His choice seemed clear.

He came back to the surface to recharge his lungs and take a quick fix on where the motor launch was. It was a calculated risk; unless one of the terrorists was looking right at the spot where he surfaced, he could gulp some air and dive again in an instant.

Then he saw the launch, and all his options vanished.

Marie was perched on the prow like an unwilling figurehead. The Hare held her there with one hand on the back of her neck; the other held a gun to her head.

"—make a decision, little troublemaker!" the Hare shouted. "Surrender now, or I will put a bullet in her skull!"

"I'm over here!" Delko yelled. "Don't shoot! I give up!"

The Hare turned toward the sound of his voice. He motioned to his guards.

"They're taking him into the boat," said Horatio. He lowered the binoculars. "He surrendered once they threatened a hostage."

"They may kill him anyway," Nadira said. Her voice was neutral. "As an example."

"Then let's make sure his message wasn't delivered in vain," said Horatio.

Their news was met with skepticism, but once Horatio explained who Delko was and what he knew about the case, opinions shifted. Horatio left the brass to argue about what to do next—he trusted Delko's information as much as he trusted the man himself, and that information had just changed the entire direction of the investigation.

Unbelievable as it sounded, the cruise ship was just a distraction. The real target—the real crime—was something even bigger.

Horatio didn't know what it could be, but he knew the chemical formula they'd found at the abandoned warehouse must have something to do with it. And—despite the increased danger Delko was now in personally—there was nothing more Horatio could do for him by waiting on the sidelines. Wherever the bomb was going to be used, it wasn't out here.

"I'm going back to Miami," he told Nadira.

"I know," she said. "I've already got a chopper waiting. I'm staying here."

He eyed her speculatively as he zipped up his windbreaker. "Even though the bomb's not here?"

She shrugged. "Somebody's got to keep an eye out for Delko. In case anything happens."

He nodded. "Thank you, Nadira."

"Good luck. Keep me apprised."

"I will."

They brought Delko back to the stage and made him and Marie kneel. Delko took Marie's hand; she was shaking badly, but she tried to give him a smile all the same. "Just take it easy," he told her. "Take deep breaths, let them out slow."

"You have left me with little choice," the Hare said. He had his automatic out, and now he tapped it thoughtfully against his chin. "You understand, don't you?"

"More than you think," said Delko.

"Oh, I doubt that. In fact, I doubt you're a reporter at all. You're what—Homeland Security? An agent, sent to spy on—" The Hare paused. "—the ship? I knew there had to be agents aboard."

"I'm not with Homeland Security."

"He's my *boyfriend,* okay?" Marie blurted. "I work on the ship, I'm a dancer, you can check—"

"I know who you are," said the Hare.

"Of course you do," said Delko. *"Abdus."*

The Hare glared at Delko. He leveled the gun at Delko's temple. "What did you say?"

"If you kill me," said Delko carefully, "you'll never find out how much I know. Or what I managed to communicate to the aircraft carrier while I was free."

"You didn't communicate a thing. All radio transmissions are being jammed—"

"Except the frequency you're using for your walkie-talkies," Delko said. "I guess my commanding officer couldn't have told me anything useful. Like what the Hare's real target is."

The Hare reached up and tore the wireless microphone off his throat. He tossed it aside, then leaned in to talk in a low, urgent voice. "You are a fool. Every word out of your mouth is another reason for me to silence you forever."

"Maybe. But you won't kill me until you find out how many words I have left." Delko met the Hare's eyes with a cold, steady gaze. "This is just another show, Abdus—but it's not *your* show. You don't know what you're doing. Your brother would torture me without a second thought—but you're not him, are you? You're a fake, a decoy. We may be on a stage, but you're about to find out just how real this all is."

"Shut *up*," Abdus Sattar Pathan hissed.

"Nice trick, getting aboard that helicopter. Guess nobody expected someone to jump on instead of off—at least, nobody on the ship. What did you use, a hidden door? Or did you just slip in dressed as a crew member and then change outfits?"

"You have obviously gone mad," Pathan said. "Take him away and lock him in a cabin. Bind him thoroughly."

A guard came over and jerked Delko to his feet by one arm.

"And do the same to this one," said Pathan, indicating Marie. "Not the same cabin. I will be by shortly."

He met Delko's eyes. "And then, my little troublemaker, we will talk further. And I will show you just how wrong about me you are . . ."

16

Calleigh and Wolfe met Horatio at the airport's helipad. Horatio had called them from the chopper and brought them up to speed; Calleigh had filled Horatio in on what she and Wolfe had learned.

"I'll drive," said Horatio. Calleigh tossed him the keys to the Hummer and got in on the passenger side. Wolfe got in the back. "Hey, when do I get to ride shotgun?"

"When you own as many as I do," said Calleigh. "Horatio, do you really think Eric will be all right?"

"I don't know," said Horatio, starting the engine. "But one thing I am sure of—whatever the Hare has planned for the cruise ship, he'll hold off until his real target has been acquired."

"I have to admit, it fits his pattern," said Wolfe, leaning forward between the seats. "The Brilliant Batin's pattern, I mean."

"That it does," said Horatio. "And I think that's

exactly what's going on here—Abdus Pathan is standing in for his brother one more time."

"I'll bet Billy Lee was the one who built the fake bomb," said Calleigh. "They'd want something that looked reasonably convincing if it were ever examined up close."

"You know," said Wolfe, "even if we do manage to find and stop the Hare, we may be putting Eric—and everyone else on that ship—at even greater risk."

"It's a chance we'll have to take," said Horatio.

They tied Delko to a chair with nylon rope, and gagged him with duct tape. He didn't struggle. He knew that any physical resistance at this point would get him shot; he'd pushed his luck as far as it could go on that front. No, the conflict that was about to occur was going to take place on an entirely different battleground.

He wondered what method Pathan would use first—simple brute force seemed most likely. Pathan was in a highly stressful situation, and he wasn't used to dealing with it the way his brother was. Delko would have to be careful not to push him too hard; Pathan was a control freak, and Delko had frustrated that control more than once. A beating Delko could survive, but a bullet to the head was a much different threat.

But nothing happened for the next hour. Delko recognized the technique; he'd used it himself more than once. Make the subject sweat, let his own imagination build the fear. By the time you sat down on the other side of the table, you had a room full of imaginary demons crowding your back.

And then the screaming started from the cabin next door.

He recognized Marie's voice immediately. The guard sitting on the bed chuckled at the look on Delko's face. "Too bad for your girlfriend," he said. "Maybe I go in there next, huh? That okay with you?"

Calm down, he told himself. *Pathan is a showman, a master of illusion. Those screams aren't real—they probably just told her to scream, and she did.*

He almost believed it.

Horatio studied the class transcripts. At one end of the lab, Wolfe was on the phone, talking to one of the students' professors, trying to gain any additional information. Across the room, Calleigh was scrolling through a materials database, trying to find some relevance to the chemical formula. It was strange—they had all scattered as soon as they'd gotten back to the lab, each one trying a different approach . . . but none of them talking much to the others.

None of them saying what was really on their minds.

Horatio put down the papers and looked first at Calleigh, then at Wolfe. Wolfe had hung up and was now staring off into space, an intense, frustrated look on his face.

"Mister Wolfe," said Horatio. "Calleigh. He's going to be okay."

Calleigh turned away from her monitor, her expression troubled, but didn't say anything.

Wolfe shook his head. "How can you say that, Horatio? I mean, Pathan claims he's already killed every security officer on that ship. After what Eric did, I don't see why he would keep him alive."

"You're forgetting something, Mister Wolfe. Eric himself. He's managed to keep himself alive so far, and even get a message out. We have to have faith in him."

"I just wish there was something we could *do,*" said Wolfe.

"If Eric were here," Calleigh asked Wolfe, "what do you think *he'd* be doing?"

Wolfe sighed. "His job?"

"Absolutely," said Horatio. "We're all worried about him—but he's going to get through this. We all are."

He met Calleigh's eyes, then Wolfe's. Calleigh nodded silently; Wolfe looked away, then back. "Yeah. Yeah, all right."

"Good. Now . . . I've been looking at these transcripts, and something bothers me."

"The geology course?" said Calleigh. "We were wondering about that, too."

Wolfe got to his feet. "Maybe they want to use the nuke on a physical feature of the landscape—start a landslide or something."

"In Florida?" said Calleigh. "I doubt it."

"It's not that," said Horatio. "It's the marine engineering course. If the target isn't the cruise ship, why research engineering details? You'd think Batin would have provided them with all the information they needed."

"Unless the target is still something nautical," said Wolfe. "It'd be a real coup if they could take down something big—like an aircraft carrier."

"Not practical," said Horatio, crossing his arms. "I was on that carrier. Nadira told me they were surveilling the entire area around the cruise ship with every kind of monitoring equipment they had—there's no way to get a nuke close enough, no matter how small it is."

"Then what?" said Wolfe. "I mean, I'm having a hard time imagining a target more prominent than a cruise ship filled with four thousand people."

"That's because you're not thinking like a showman," said Horatio. "None of us are. The question isn't just what the target is—it's why the cruise ship is being used as a distraction. Calleigh, can you call up a chart of the shipping lanes for the East Coast?"

"Sure, H." She turned and started tapping on the keyboard. Wolfe and Horatio joined her in front of the screen.

"Okay," said Horatio. "Here's where the *Heart's Voyage* is right now." He pointed to the screen. "What does that suggest?"

Wolfe and Calleigh studied the monitor carefully. "A lot of shipping routes go right through there," said Calleigh.

"Or used to," said Wolfe. "The navy has that whole area blockaded now. Nothing's getting through."

"Exactly," said Horatio. "Ships that should be in transit are still sitting in port. Ships in transit have been diverted to other ports."

"You think that's the Hare's plan?" asked Wolfe. "Disrupt shipping?"

"No, I think it goes a lot further than that," said Horatio. "Remember the deal that the Hare made with Pierce Madigan? He claimed the target wouldn't be on American soil. And one of the ports that will get some of those diverted ships is right . . . *here.*"

Calleigh and Wolfe stared. "Oh, my God," said Calleigh softly. "Of course . . ."

It was one of the longest nights of Eric Delko's life.

The screaming hadn't gone on for long. It was replaced by pleading—Marie's voice, begging for them to stop, for Eric to tell them whatever he knew. He would have, too—except that he was still gagged, and couldn't say a word.

The pleading gave way to sobbing, and then abruptly stopped.

Shortly after that, Abdus Pathan walked in. His hands were covered in blood; he walked past Delko and into the small bathroom, where he washed them. He also removed the black scarf that covered his face, folding it neatly and tucking it into a back pocket. He told the guard watching Delko to go with a nod of his head, then sat down on the bed, facing Delko. He regarded his captive with a slight smile on his face.

"So," he said. "You know who I am. And I, of course, know who you are, as well."

Delko stared at him impassively.

"You're wondering why I didn't kill you earlier. Why I allowed things to go on as long as they did." Pathan's smile grew wider. "I did so because I wanted to see what you would do. A leash, no matter how long it is, is still a leash. As long as I had your woman, I had you. You were never a threat to me."

Just keep thinking that, Delko thought.

"The insufferable Lieutenant Caine made a mistake, sending you to spy on me; a mistake he will come to regret."

Abruptly, Pathan leaned forward and ripped the tape off Delko's mouth.

"Horatio didn't send me," Delko spat. He wanted to scream *What have you done with Marie?* but forced himself not to. *Can't let him use her against me,* he thought. *Love is not my friend, not here. Love is the enemy.*

"So you came on your own? To protect your lady fair, no doubt. A job you seem to be doing rather badly."

"I didn't come for her. I came for *you.*" *Got to change his focus. Make this about me and him, not Marie.*

"Oh? You thought you could stop me on your own, perhaps get a promotion?"

"Something like that."

"You are an *idiot.*" Abdus leaned forward, his voice suddenly filled with venom. "From an entire *country* of idiots. I have lived among you my entire life, and every day I marvel at the colossal, incredible *stupidity* you wallow in. Every time I perform I see it; the bovine incomprehension on the faces of my audience. Some of them actually believe what I do is magic." He shook his head. "It is your culture, your values. Western civilization is *built* on lies and illusions. You paint them like a whore's face and call them dreams, but they are as false and evil as any demon."

"You're not making any sense." *Got to keep him talking, keep him focused on me.*

"Sense? What do you know about sense? For an American, sense is believing that you will all grow up to be rich and famous, that it's your right to have your every urge fulfilled, no matter how blasphemous or obscene. You dishonor Allah by your very existence."

"So do you," said Delko. "No magician will ever pass through the gates of Heaven—"

Without warning, the gun came up.

And fired.

"Which ship is the Hare going to use?" said Calleigh. "It's a major shipping route, there must be dozens of possibilities—"

"But only a few scheduled to be in those particular waters at this exact time," said Wolfe. He was already at another workstation, calling up a nautical database. "I can narrow down the possibilities—"

"Geology," said Horatio thoughtfully. "Ahmed Jabbar was studying geology and chemistry. And I think I just figured out why."

Wolfe stared at the charts he'd just accessed and reached the same conclusion a second later. "Because they're the kind of courses you'd take if you were planning—or trying to make people *think* you were planning—a career in a particular industry."

Calleigh got it, too. "Which would let you apply for a training position on a particular type of ship."

"Any number of which," said Horatio, "pass through those shipping lanes."

"An oil tanker," said Calleigh. "The Hare's planning on using the nuke on an oil tanker."

Delko opened his eyes. He wasn't dead.

The bullet had passed beside his head, so close he felt it go by. Abdus was still holding the smoking muzzle in his face, the smell of gunpowder sharp in Delko's nostrils.

"I am not a magician!" Abdus roared. "I am a true servant of Allah! I do not break the *hadith,* I do not practice *Istidraj*! I have devoted my entire life—my entire *being*—to my faith!"

Delko swallowed. "Okay," he said carefully. "I didn't mean to offend you."

Abdus stared at him, the gun in his hand trembling, his breath coming hard. "I have waited for *so long,"* Abdus hissed. "You have no idea what I have endured. Other children are taught to be honest, to be good—I was taught to *deceive*. My father rewarded me for every lie, every bit of trickery I could conceive—unless I was caught. Then I was beaten."

Delko said nothing, just eyed Abdus warily. He wasn't sure what the correct response was, or if there even was one.

"But I did not complain, did not whine about my rights or desires. I followed the will of Allah, and I came to understand that my suffering would be rewarded in another life. I came to understand the great evil I was preparing to do battle with. Oh, how I envied my brother; to be able to strike back directly, with bullet and bomb and blade . . . I would lie alone in the dark sometimes, thinking about him, wondering if he were spilling the blood of some blasphemer at that very moment. You cannot imagine how proud I am, how *honored,* that my last and greatest illusion will be to stand in his place."

His last illusion.

Delko didn't like the sound of that.

"Why an oil tanker?" said Wolfe. "I mean—considering the target—causing an ecological disaster doesn't really make sense—"

"He's not going to cause an oil spill," said Horatio grimly. "He'll go after an empty tanker, not a full one."

"A fuel-air bomb?" said Wolfe. He understood

the concept: the fumes inside a sealed container—like the hold of a ship—were far more explosive than the liquid fuel they were generated by. "Okay, that's a scary thought—but empty tankers dock at ports all the time. There must be some kind of safety protocol to prevent accidents—"

"There is," said Calleigh. The shipping channels had disappeared off her monitor; she was into another database entirely. "According to this, they pipe the exhaust from the engines into the empty fuel bays, where it forms a layer of inert gas that won't combust. Guess what the formula for the gas is?"

"Eighty percent nitrogen, fifteen percent carbon dioxide, five percent oxygen," said Horatio.

"But easy to replace," said Calleigh. "Flood the tanks with ordinary air instead, and you have a two-hundred-thousand-ton seagoing bomb."

"And if you set it off with an atomic device," said Horatio, "it's a dirty bomb as well. Ground zero will be uninhabitable for decades."

"Exactly what the Hare wants," said Calleigh.

Delko understood why Abdus was talking to him instead of questioning him or simply executing him. The magician's existence was one of conflicting extremes: raised to be a professional extrovert, he had always been forbidden to discuss his deepest feelings. In Delko he literally had a captive audience, and Abdus would take full advantage of that fact—even if he was unaware of what he was doing.

"They say twins have a bond," said Delko.

"It is a bond created by Allah. We are of the same flesh, the same soul. It is, I have always believed, what has given me the strength to continue in my mission."

He regarded Delko more calmly. "You have not asked me about the fate of your woman. Perhaps you already know."

"She's not my woman," said Delko as coldly as he could manage. "She's just someone I met aboard. Something to occupy my time while I watched you."

Abdus narrowed his eyes and smiled. "I see. Then her death will mean nothing to you."

Delko said nothing.

Love is the enemy, he repeated silently to himself. *Love is the enemy . . .*

Ahmed Jabbar sat on his small bunk and regarded the gun he held. It was a Micro Uzi machine pistol, capable of firing 1,250 rounds a minute, and it had been absurdly easy to smuggle aboard. A VLCC—Very Large Crude Container—tanker didn't have the kind of security that cruise ships enforced, and despite their immense size they were only staffed by a crew of twenty-five.

His job was simple. Disable radio communications, secure the bridge, and kill anyone who got in his way.

It was 3:00 A.M. Most of the crew were asleep in their bunks, aside from the night shift. He would take the bridge first, handcuffing the wheelman to the controls and making sure no alarm was raised. He had plastic flexicuffs to restrain as many as ten people, but he didn't think he'd need them all. Once he didn't have to worry about the people in the wheelhouse warning the rest of the crew, he would simply shoot them in their bunks.

The ship had already received orders redirecting them; they would be expected at their new port of call . . . but the harbormaster there would have no idea that the tanker *Venerated*, supposedly empty, would in fact be carrying a very deadly cargo indeed.

Abdus was on his feet now, pacing back and forth. He seemed to be talking more to himself now than Delko. "I have prepared, and I am ready. The eyes of the world are upon me, and they shall be opened to the truth."

"But not by you," said Delko.

Abdus stopped and glared at Delko.

"It's your brother who will get all the glory," said Delko. "You're just creating one more illusion. Performing a trick. You think that's going to impress anyone after what the *real* Hare does?"

Delko knew it was dangerous to bait him—the more he decried Abdus's efforts the more likely the man was to do something to prove himself, and that proof would no doubt be lethal—but Delko understood the perverse relationship he and Abdus were forming. If he could make the magician equate his prisoner with the outside world, it would become more important to Abdus to impress him than kill him.

"You don't understand at all," said Abdus. "This isn't about me. It isn't about my brother. It's about the will of Allah. There is a stain upon the honor of Islam, and Al-Arnab will remove it."

Delko's stomach was empty and growling. His skin was raw and chafed from the ropes, and his muscles ached. He was exhausted, hungry, and part of his mind kept screaming that Marie was dead. "I don't think so. His plan is crazy—there's no way it'll work."

The punch broke Delko's nose. Pain exploded through his head and everything turned flat and gray for a few seconds. When his focus returned, the first thing he was aware of was the blood running across his lips and down his chin.

"You are the fake. You are the phony," said Abdus coldly. "You have no idea what our plan is, and I will not enlighten you. Why should I? You will die as your whore died, ignorant and in pain."

He turned and strode out of the door. His last words burned in Delko's brain.

"Marie!" he screamed, hoping she could hear, could respond. "Marie? Say something! *Marie!*"

The only answer was laughter from the other side of the wall, and a mocking imitation of his own pain.

"If there's a nuclear device aboard an oil tanker, our options just shrank down to zero," said Wolfe. "It'll have to be destroyed before it reaches port."

"Maybe not," said Horatio. "There's a slim chance the bomb isn't aboard yet. Abdus delivered a terrorist strike team at sea because that's where security was weakest, and the Hare will probably do the same."

"Makes logistical sense," said Calleigh. "The nine-eleven hijackers didn't have to learn how to take off in a plane, or land it; they just had to know how to steer toward their target. Same principle would apply with a tanker—and it eliminates the risk of a search in port."

"So the tanker," said Wolfe, "will probably rendezvous with a smaller craft. How do they get aboard?"

Calleigh was scanning maritime schedules on her monitor. "Ahmed Jabbar. An internship with one of the petrochemical corporations could have gotten him onto a ship—and it only takes one guy to drop a rope ladder."

"One guy to steal an oil tanker?" said Wolfe. "That's hard to believe."

"Even the big ones only have a crew of about two dozen," said Calleigh. "Time it for when most of the crew are asleep, and you only have to subdue a few people."

"Calleigh," asked Horatio, "is that a list of vessels currently in the shipping lanes?"

"Yes. Got several possibles, but this database doesn't tell me if they're empty or full."

"Okay." Horatio studied the monitor closely. "The *Heart's Voyage* was hijacked here, right at the mouth of the Nicholas and Santaren channels. That's an effective choke point for anything coming around the southernmost point of Cuba, through the Windward Passage."

"Sure," said Wolfe. "Forces them to either go all the way around the Turks and Caicos Islands, or even farther west around Cuba."

"There are several tankers headed through that passage from Venezuela," said Calleigh.

"Yes," said Horatio. "The question now is, where is the Hare going to make his rendezvous . . . I don't think he'd risk flying, which means he'll take a boat. The only route that makes sense is through the Gulf of Mexico and around the north end of Cuba."

"We may be able to head him off," said Calleigh.

"Mister Wolfe, get on the phone and find out which of those ships has Mister Jabbar aboard. Calleigh, come with me."

"I have to stay behind?" said Wolfe.

"You've already been blown up, Mister Wolfe," said Horatio. "It's Calleigh's turn. We wouldn't want anyone to think I'm playing favorites, would we?"

"Ready to go, H," said Calleigh.

"Not quite, you're not. We have a stop to make at your gun locker, first."

Calleigh smiled, but her eyes were hard. "Good idea, H. Think I know just what we need, too."

The Brilliant Batin left the cabin and walked down the corridor. He didn't travel very far; his destination was another cabin on the other side of the hall, one identical in almost every respect to the one he'd just left.

Except for its lone occupant.

"He does not know," Batin said, closing the door softly behind him. "He is an intelligent man, but he is not well-versed in deception. The screams you can hear right now have the sincerity of anguish; his studied indifference did not."

There was no reply from the figure on the bed.

"Some might say that telling him his girlfriend is dead is a mistake," continued Batin. He walked over to the bedside table and picked up a bottle of water. "That she is too valuable a lever to be thrown away so casually." He unscrewed the cap and took a long drink, almost emptying the bottle. "Ah. But they do not truly understand the mechanics of emotional manipulation. My father does; he is a master at it. I was his only pupil, and I knew more about bargaining strategies and negotiation psychology by the time I was ten than Machiavelli himself."

He pulled the chair out of the kneehole of the desk, reversed it, and sat down. "Manipulating a person in a heightened state of emotion is like directing the course of a river. You must place a dam here, a waterfall there. Right now, Mister Delko is experiencing shock and horror; he will combat this with fury, which will burn brightly for a while and then gutter out into the ashes of despair. There is still much ahead of him . . ."

* * *

Horatio had Calleigh drive; he had phone calls to make. The first was to Nadira Quadiri. He filled her in on what they'd learned, and the Hare's true target.

"You have proof?" said Nadira.

"Wolfe's working on finding the ship Jabbar's on, but the navy has to throw up a blockade, and fast."

"I'll tell them—but this is going to be a hard sell, Horatio. We're talking about an independent country here; blockading one of their major ports is not going to be something the navy does without serious consideration."

"They'll be taking it a lot more seriously if that nuke goes off."

She sighed. "You're sure about this? It's not just a theory?"

"It makes sense, Nadira. You know it does."

"Yes, it does," she said. "With one blow, they can eliminate a major American military asset and close a legal loophole the U.S. has been exploiting for years."

"Which is exactly why," said Horatio grimly, "we have to prevent that oil tanker from reaching Guantanamo Bay."

17

GUANTANAMO BAY, on the southernmost tip of Cuba, contains not only the oldest U.S. Naval base not in the continental States, but the only one in a hostile country. It is completely self-sufficent in terms of water supply and power—a condition made necessary after Castro cut off supplies in 1964—and encapsulates a microcosm of American life: it holds a library, a gas station, a hospital, a bank, and a youth center; it has teaching facilities that range from kindergarten to a community college. It has a dry cleaner, a bowling alley, even a furniture store, and it is home to approximately eight and a half thousand people.

This does not include the prisoners of Camp Delta.

Camp Delta was built to replace Camp X-Ray, the original holding facility for suspected terrorists. It is divided into eight subcamps: camps one through six classify prisoners based on the level of their cooperation, while Camp Iguana is a lower-security facility used for prisoners under the age of sixteen and those classified as noncombatants. Camp Echo is reserved for detainees regarded as being of high value by the Department of Defense, the CIA, or the president. Originally designed to hold 641 prisoners, Camp Delta can in fact hold many more.

The Hare intended to reduce the entire thing to radioactive rubble.

In order to do so, he had to rendezvous with the *Venerated* at sea, approximately two hundred miles away from its final destination. He would deliver the bomb himself, ensure that it was properly placed, and then leave. The glory of being Allah's messenger would belong to Ahmed Jabbar, at the controls as the *Venerated* bore down toward her target; he envied the boy that, but the Hare was already assured of his place in Heaven—and his work on Earth was not yet done.

Not while a single blasphemer still drew breath.

The craft he intended to use for the transfer was a Cigarette boat, a long and sleek vessel favored by drug traffickers for its speed; its twin supercharged nine-hundred-horsepower Mercury SC V-8 motors could push it to over a hundred miles an hour. At the helm would be a young man named Mohammed Jawi. The Hare would have preferred a more experienced operative, but his resources were stretched thin—his best men had been required for the cruise ship mission.

Not that it mattered. His brother had done a

masterful job, and the world's attention was centered upon him. Transferring the device itself should be the easiest part of the entire operation, and Jawi would be more than adequate for that task. All he had to do was pilot the boat, and he had already demonstrated his skill at that.

But if other difficulties should arise . . . the Hare was prepared for that, as well.

Natalia Boa Vista lay alone in the dark, unable to sleep. She was thinking about Eric Delko.

She and Eric had had a brief relationship, one that she had hoped could turn into something deeper. But there had been miscommunication and crossed signals on both sides, and in the end it simply hadn't worked out. That was fine; she was an adult, and both of them had moved on. From what she understood, he was happy with the woman he was dating. More than happy.

She rolled over and hugged her pillow, trying to get comfortable.

Talk around the lab was that Delko had stowed away aboard the ship in order to protect his new girlfriend. That sounded like Eric, she had to admit, except for the stowing away part; he would have insisted on buying a ticket. It was one of the things that had attracted her in the first place, besides his obvious good looks and charm: that Boy Scout–like morality underneath his *La Vida Loca* attitude. Eric played at being a playboy, but that wasn't who he really was.

Maybe that's why we didn't work out, she thought. *Because of who I really am.*

Natalia headed the Justice Project, an adjunct to the CSI lab that specialized in using DNA techniques to re-examine old cases. It was good work, work she was proud of, responsible for freeing a number of falsely imprisoned men—but it had come with a price, something she wasn't so proud of. She'd been asked to provide inside information on the lab by Internal Affairs as part of a corruption probe. She'd agreed to do so, but that was before she'd actually begun working with Horatio and his team.

Now, she knew she'd made a horrible mistake. Every day felt like a betrayal, and she couldn't see any way out.

She wondered if Eric would have followed her onto that ship. She wondered what he would say to her right now, if he knew what she'd done.

It was a long night.

Dawn broke over the bow of the *Heart's Voyage* with a cold, gray light. Most of the thousands of passengers locked in the concert hall were asleep, huddled together on the floor or on a few of the longer tables. Two gunmen patrolled back and forth on the stage, their eyes roaming over their prisoners restlessly, their movements jerky and nervous; they had broken into the ship's pharmacy and taken some of the stimulants they'd discovered.

Delko had finally passed out, still tied to the

chair in the cabin, exhausted by the aftereffects of sorrow and adrenaline. He slept fitfully, haunted by images of Marie's face hovering in a fog bank, begging him to save her, crying tears of blood as her face slowly receded into the mist.

He woke with a start and an involuntary cry. The room was dark, but he couldn't feel the presence of anyone else; he was alone. The dried blood on his face itched. He managed to rub his chin against his shoulder, but he couldn't reach his upper lip.

He wondered how long Pathan would keep him alive. It was impossible to tell; by all rights, he should be dead already. Pathan seemed convinced Delko knew nothing useful, and had proven it by killing Marie instead of using her against him.

There was only one reason for that, Delko knew. Sheer sadism. He'd wanted Delko to know, to blame himself, to wallow in grief and guilt. It was far worse than any physical torture he could have devised.

But only if he let it.

What would Horatio do? he thought to himself. His boss was the strongest man Delko knew when it came to handling pain; nothing ever seemed to stop him.

He'd embrace it. He'd accept the loss, swallow the agony, and somehow turn it into strength.

Delko didn't know if he could do that. Horatio's ability to not just face suffering but draw power from it had always seemed slightly unbelievable to him, almost supernatural. Almost like—

Almost like a magic trick.

He laughed out loud, the sound shocking to his own ears. *That's not it, Eric,* he could hear H say. *Dealing with your problems by going into hysterics is not a good strategy.*

"Then what is, H?" he whispered. "I'm not you, I can't just—just shake hands with death and smile."

Is that what I do, Eric? Smile at other people's pain?

"No. 'Course not. You're always looking out for others. Always."

That's the secret, Eric. The more you concentrate on other people's pain . . . the less you notice your own.

"You're right. Have to think about everybody else on the boat. I have to—have to—"

It's all right, Eric. I'm coming to get you. You know that, don't you?

"Yeah. Yeah, H, I know that. Never doubted it for a minute."

Just hang in there, pal. I know you can do it . . . The voice faded away, leaving Delko in the dark.

Ahmed Jabbar crept down the corridor, the Micro Uzi clutched in his hand. He was only nineteen years old, but he was the one who had been chosen. He felt the weight of responsibility in the pit of his stomach like a hard, cold stone.

He swallowed and told himself to calm down. After this, he would be the most famous of all martyrs, the one who delivered all those imprisoned by the Great Satan into the hands of merciful Allah. They would welcome it, he knew; no more interrogations, no more humiliation. And after the blow was struck, America would no longer be able to imprison his people without charging them, without legal representation. Guantanamo Bay would become a blasted, radioactive wasteland, uninhabitable by anyone. The Americans would be forced to abandon it—and by the terms of their treaty with Cuba, once they left they could not come back.

A door opened in front of him. It was Pablo, the ship's cook, a short, squat man who—despite missing a front tooth—always seemed to have a smile on his face. He was carrying a tray of food, evidently on his way to deliver some early breakfast to the wheelhouse.

He saw Ahmed immediately, and the smile froze on his face as he registered the gun an instant later. "What—what is that?" he asked, his voice more confused than scared.

Ahmed brought the muzzle up, his hand trembling. "It is your death," he said. "Unless you do exactly as I say."

Calleigh and Horatio caught a ride on an MH-68A Sting Ray helicopter out of Jacksonville. The chopper was one of the Coast Guard's Helicopter Interdiction Tactical Squadron units, a heavily armed craft equipped with laser-sighted fifty-caliber rifles that could destroy a boat's engine with a single precise shot. The HITRON unit was specifically tasked with intercepting small, fast, drug-running boats that could outrun most other ships.

Their destination was a Coast Guard cutter just off Grand Cayman Island; the helo would land on the boat itself, keeping Horatio from worrying about extranational jurisdiction. He knew the Hare would likely have to stop in the Caymans for fuel, and if he was lucky he could pick up the trail there.

Calleigh was on the phone, talking to Wolfe. She kept the conversation brief—it was hard to hear over the racket of the rotors. "Jabbar is on a tanker called the *Venerated*," she told Horatio, snapping her phone shut. "Quadiri has the information, but she's having a hard time getting through to the brass. The tanker isn't responding to radio communication."

"Then it's already been commandeered," said Horatio. "Nothing we can do about that—so we have to stop the Hare before he can deliver his package."

Wolfe wished for the hundredth time that he'd insisted on going along. "Delko didn't follow protocol," he grumbled to himself. "Why should I? I don't always have to follow the rules . . ." He sighed. "At least I've stopped counting things. Guess being blown up by a rocket has *some* positive effects . . ."

"Talkin' to yourself, kid?" said Tripp, walking into the lab. "Not a good sign."

"At least I listen," said Wolfe.

Tripp stopped and slapped the folder he held with one hand. "Horatio around? Got some information he might be interested in."

"He's not here. He and Calleigh think they have a line on the Hare."

"Yeah? Whereabouts?"

Wolfe told him, and Tripp whistled. "Whoa. Cayman Islands? Kind of out of Horatio's jurisdiction, isn't it?"

"He's using a Coast Guard boat—they're authorized to interdict smugglers."

"And you got stuck holding down the fort?" Tripp shook his head. "Well, you know what they say about those also serving who stand and wait."

"Yeah—they say it sucks." Wolfe slouched lower in his chair.

"Buck up, kid. You guys are supposed to provide us with evidence, not foot soldiers."

"Yeah? Maybe someone should have told H."

"Not this cowboy. Horatio makes his own rules when he has to—and when that happens, better not get in his road. You should be glad you didn't get to go, anyway."

"Why? Because I might wind up as a radioactive corpse?"

"No—because with you the only CSI around, you're the one that gets a first look at this." He handed the folder to Wolfe, who took it and opened it.

"What is this?"

Tripp grinned. "Read it and see for yourself."

Wolfe scanned it quickly. "This is a list of Khasib Pathan's assets," he said. "Impressive, but I don't see how it helps us."

"Khasib's out of the country, right? Supposedly took off when the fat hit the fire."

"Supposedly?"

"Way I figure it, there's not a chance in hell Papa's gonna run while all the fireworks go off. At the very least, he's gonna want a ringside seat—a rich guy like that, more like a private box."

Wolfe took another look at the list—and then broke into a grin. "Wait a minute. This says he owns a yacht."

"So it does. A yacht that just happens to be currently anchored off Key West."

"Box seats," said Wolfe.

"Terrorist assets," said Tripp. "I think we should organize a little social call, don't you?"

"Hell, yes," said Wolfe.

The Coast Guard cutter *Navaho* had a crew of a hundred. The chopper was lashed down to the helipad that took up most of the rear deck; a storm was rolling in and the waves were getting choppy. Calleigh was crouched down admiring the Sting Ray's weaponry when Horatio hunkered down beside her.

"Force From Above," said Calleigh. "That's their motto. These M240 7.62-millimeter machine guns let them deliver it, too."

"As long as there's something to shoot at," said Horatio. "If the Hare is using a boat with a low radar signature he could be difficult to locate."

"Like a go-fast, you mean?" Go-fast was the

slang term for a Cigarette boat; they were notoriously difficult to track.

"Exactly. This gunship can keep up with one, but first we have to find it."

"True. Guess that's up to the Coast Guard, now."

"Not necessarily," said Horatio thoughtfully. He straightened up and walked to the rail, Calleigh following him. "A Cigarette boat is an expensive item."

"Not a problem if you're being bankrolled by someone like Khasib Pathan."

"No . . . but these days, the higher the price tag the more likely it is to be tagged in another way."

"LoJacked, you mean?"

"LoJacking uses a radio frequency," said Horatio. "I was thinking more along the lines of a GPS system—more practical in isolated areas."

"Wouldn't they have disabled it?"

"If they were aware of it, yes," said Horatio. The sea was rough and gray, the sky almost the same color. "But Khasib Pathan inhabits one world, and his sons inhabit another. Communication between the two is guaranteed to not be perfect . . . and a tracking device designed to remain hidden might just be overlooked."

"It's possible," she conceded. "Especially if Khasib paid for the boat and the Hare just took possession. I'll check into it."

Horatio stared out over the choppy waves. Somewhere out there, the Hare was still running . . .

* * *

Onboard the *Heart's Voyage,* things were getting ugly.

Cold food—bread, fruits, vegetables—had been passed out from the kitchens, but many of the passengers, especially the older ones, were on special diets or even diabetic. Guards had been sent a dozen more times to fetch medication. People were growing restless.

It is time, Abdus Sattar Pathan thought, *for a demonstration.*

He strode onto the stage and regarded his captives. He felt the same cold hatred he always felt when he looked out over a cruise ship audience; they were like pigs that had learned to walk upright. *Overfed, ignorant, wallowing in the excrement of their pathetic culture.* Pigs were omnivorous, not only able but willing to eat almost anything—including their own kind—and that was the kind of mindless hunger he always saw in the eyes of those he was supposed to perform for.

You come here to consume, he thought. *Endless buffets, endless gambling, endless shallow entertainment in your little floating bubble of a world.*

Not anymore. Now, you are in my *world.*

They had fallen silent at his arrival. Now, a pale man with short gray hair and a double chin raised one meaty arm. "Uh, 'scuse me," he called out. His voice carried clearly to Abdus's ears; the hall had excellent acoustics.

"What is it?" said Abdus.

"My mother," said the man, indicating a frail-looking woman sitting beside him. "She's ninety-two. She can't take sleeping on the floor—can we get maybe a cot or something?"

"I can certainly do something about that," said Abdus. "But I will require a volunteer to move the bed."

Several men put up their hands. Abdus picked one at random, a slender young man with thinning blond hair and glasses. "You. Come up here."

The man made his way to the front and climbed onto the stage.

Abdus pointed to the wings. "Back there."

Abdus let the man take four steps before he drew his pistol and shot him.

He smiled beneath his concealing scarf at the screams of horror. The man crumpled to the ground, limbs twitching, trying to speak but only managing to spew blood from his lips.

"QUIET!" Abdus roared.

The only sound to be heard was a muffled sobbing. That, and the dying man trying to draw air through a punctured lung.

"I will now explain why I did that," said Abdus. "Because . . ."

Abruptly, he plucked the scarf from his face and tossed it aside. He smiled brilliantly, chuckling at the gasps of those who recognized him.

"It was only a *trick,*" he said. He paused, letting his statement sink in.

"Don't you recognize me? The Brilliant, Baffling Batin? This, you see, is my *greatest* illusion. Convincing an entire cruise ship that they've been hijacked . . . but relax! *It's not real!"*

More gasps. A few bursts of hysterical laughter.

"Look, there's a camera hidden right there!" he said, pointing to a planter. "And another in the chandelier, and one over there! This is my new television show—and you're all going to be famous!"

Now there was scattered applause, along with more laughter and some swearing.

"And this man here, he's not really dead," said Abdus. He strode over to the man he'd just shot, bent down, and grabbed him by the hair. He lifted him high enough so the audience could see his face.

And then he emptied the gun into it.

This time, the silence following the gunshots was absolute.

"*Now* he is," said Abdus.

Someone cursed, but it sounded more like a sob.

"Every one of you disgusts me," said Abdus. "You would rather live in a world that would degrade you with such an idea than face the truth. I am telling you the truth now. I chose that man purely at random—but I killed him because *you* dared to complain." He pointed at the double-chinned man with his elderly mother. "And I will do so again, if another complaint is raised. Another life, chosen at random and erased in an instant. Think about that the next time you bother me—and watch your neighbors closely . . ."

* * *

"H," said Calleigh, sitting down across from Horatio, "you are not going to believe this." Horatio was at a small table with a scarred plastic top, in the cabin that served the cutter as a mess hall. He'd come inside to get out of the weather; it was starting to squall, sputters of rain driven by increasingly fierce winds. The up-and-down motion of the boat was strong enough to make Horatio glad there was a lid on the cup of coffee he was sipping from.

"I borrowed one of their workstations, did some checking," she said. "Khasib Pathan bought a Cigarette boat six months ago from a private dealer in Fort Lauderdale. I talked to the dealer, and he told me the craft had a GPS transponder built into the hull. It's monitored by a company called SeaPilot, who specialize in marine security. They confirmed that the transponder was installed by them, but never activated; you have to subscribe to their service first."

"Then we're out of luck?"

"Not yet. The tracking unit can be turned on remotely, as long as they know the approximate location. Basically, it's already powered up, just not officially in their system. I talked to someone at SeaPilot, and they said they'd broadcast the activation code."

Horatio took a careful sip of his coffee through the hole in the lid. "So if the Hare is in range—and hasn't found and disabled the tracker—we'll know it."

"To within ten feet," said Calleigh.

* * *

Ahmed marched the cook ahead of him to the wheelhouse. He hadn't counted on another person in the mix, but he couldn't just shoot the man—too much risk of the shot waking the rest of the crew.

"You are a terrorist," said Pablo. His voice sounded more sad than scared. "Aren't you."

"Shut up!" said Ahmed. "Just keep moving!"

"You don't understand," said Pablo. He had stopped. "I'm going to turn around now, very slowly. Please don't shoot."

"What? No!" This was not in his plan, not at all.

Pablo turned slowly, his tray of sandwiches held at waist level in both hands. "It will not work."

Ahmed took a nervous step backward. "If you move, I will kill you."

"People are not stupid. You think we are—stupid and weak—but we learn." Pablo's gap-toothed smile had been replaced with a resigned sort of dignity. "If you are not stopped, we are all dead, anyway. Unless you are stopped."

"And who will stop me? You?"

Pablo's reply was to thrust the tray at him. There were two sealed cups of coffee on the tray, and one of them hit Ahmed in the chest and burst open, scalding him with hot liquid. Pablo was already charging, holding the tray in front of him like a shield.

Ahmed shot him, the bullet punching through the tray and hitting Pablo square in the chest. The cook's momentum carried him forward, but he was dead before his body slammed into his assassin, carrying them both down to the deck.

Ahmed cursed and shoved the corpse off him. He stood quickly and looked around, panting. Only a single shot. Had it been heard? He looked down at his gun and saw that he had forgotten to set it to full auto; otherwise, it would have released a spray of bullets.

He had no choice, now. He sprinted down the corridor, toward the wheelhouse, trying to ignore the searing pain of his burned chest.

"We've got a hit," said Calleigh.

She and Horatio were belowdeck, in the command center of the cutter. A row of technicians sat in front of a gleaming metal bulkhead, embedded with state-of-the-art monitors and more old-fashioned dials and gauges. Calleigh and Horatio studied one monitor in particular.

"Got a bogey approximately ten nautical miles east," said the technician, a young woman with her brown hair in a tight bun. "Steady signal on the same frequency you gave us."

"Get the chopper in the air," said Horatio.

The crew jumped into action, moving smoothly into a well-practiced routine that had to be performed as quickly and efficiently as possible. Within minutes, the helo was lifting off the rear deck into the stormy sky.

"The weather's getting worse," said Calleigh.

"If we're lucky, it'll do the job for us," said Horatio. "I'd rather see that case at the bottom of the ocean than in anyone's hands . . ."

"Doesn't look like he's moving too fast," said Calleigh. "Storm's slowing him down."

Horatio pointed to a red dot on the upper right-hand corner of the screen. "Maybe not enough. That's the *Venerated,* right there."

"The chopper'll get there before we do," said Calleigh. She turned around and headed for the door.

"Where are you going?" asked Horatio.

"To get my gun," said Calleigh.

Ahmed Jabbar stared around at the blood-soaked wheelhouse and wondered where it had all gone wrong.

It had been a simple plan. Take the pilot and the mate on duty hostage, secure them in the wheelhouse, then eliminate the crew. The Hare himself had instructed Ahmed in this, telling him what to say, how to act. "The key is to convince them that if they surrender control, you will grant them their lives," said the Hare. "Once you have control, their lives are yours to dispose of as you wish. Theft is the best excuse; even though no one would be mad enough to steal an empty tanker for profit, they will believe such a story—because belief in the story gives them the belief they will survive the experience."

"You were wrong," Ahmed whispered. "So very, very wrong . . ."

The first mate, a long-faced, taciturn Swede named

Parsival, had been the officer on duty. He had turned when Ahmed came in, froze when he saw the gun, and seemed to grasp the situation quickly. The pilot, a broad-shouldered New Englander with a bushy handlebar mustache, had thought it was a joke at first.

Or so it had seemed. When Ahmed had thrust the plastic handcuffs at the pilot, the man had made a grab for the Micro Uzi. Ahmed, already nervous, had reacted with a long burst of gunfire that had sprayed blood everywhere.

Parsival had seemed more reasonable. "No need for that, no need," he'd said, clearly terrified. "Don't kill me, dear God, don't kill me."

"I'm not going to kill you," said Ahmed. "I'm stealing the ship. Cooperate and you can live through this."

But when he'd held out the handcuffs, Parsival had stared at them like they were live scorpions. His eyes had come up and met Ahmed's, and an understanding had passed between them, a moment of truth that could not be denied.

"Ah, hell," said Parsival softly, and he'd lunged forward.

Now both of them were dead. The noise had awakened the crew, and they'd come to investigate. He'd held them off with bursts of gunfire, but sooner or later they'd find a way in.

He'd disabled the radio, though, and thought he could keep the ship on the right heading. If he could just hold on until the Hare arrived, they could dispose of the crew and resume their course.

If he could just hold on . . .

Lieutenant Floyd Ulysses Durango had been with HITRON since the early days of the operation, when they were still flying MD900 Enforcers. He was one of the pilots who had helped perfect night-time landing techniques for the new Sting Rays—though he'd never tried landing in chop quite this rough—on the deck of a cutter.

The three other members of his flight crew were Rudy Gerber, his copilot, and Bernard Kopeckni and Duane Shulman, his gunners. The technique they used to catch go-fasts was first to locate the craft and match speeds with it. This often took place at night, when many smugglers made their runs, but the ANVIS-9 night-vision goggles the HITRON crew used gave them a perfect view; Durango loved to see the expression on a drug-runner's face when he suddenly realized the noise he'd been hearing over the roar of his own engines was a helicopter that was suddenly pacing his "uncatchable" craft at eighty miles an hour.

At that point, they would try to get the boat to stop, broadcasting instructions over the radio and a loudspeaker. If that didn't work, they'd get closer and try using hand signals. If there was still no response, they would fire a few warning shots to get his attention.

That was the smuggler's last chance to stop on

his own. If he didn't, it was up to one of the gunners to stop him.

The go-fast speeding beneath them had already failed to heed the verbal warnings. Now, Durango brought the Sting Ray down within a few feet of the waves and parallel to the speeding craft.

"Put a few across his bow, Duane," said Durango.

The gun Petty Officer Duane Shulman had in his hands was an RC50 precision sniper rifle, capable of putting a fifty-caliber slug into a bull's-eye at a range of two thousand yards. It was a big gun, weighing twenty-five pounds, with a barrel that measured almost thirty inches in length. He used a rope slung across the Sting Ray's open door as a muzzle rest, and snapped off two thunderous shots.

"I don't think he wants to pull over," Duane said. "License must be expired or something."

Durango grinned. "Then I guess we'll just have to persuade him, won't we?"

18

THE HITRON STRATEGY for getting a go-fast to kill its engines was a simple three-step process. First, they would ask politely. Then they would fire a few not-so-polite warning shots.

Then they would shoot the engine.

The emptiness of the open ocean was what made this maneuver possible; they didn't have to worry about hitting civilians, and the chopper could position itself in such a way that there was very little chance they'd hit the smugglers, either. A fifty-caliber "ball" bullet—originally designed to take out armored vehicles—could penetrate an inch of concrete, six inches of sand, and twenty-one inches of clay at a range of over sixteen hundred yards. It would tear through an engine block like it was made of papier-mâché.

Sometimes the smugglers even fired back, though the range and power of the Sting Ray's weapons soon made it clear to even the most crazed Tony Montana wannabe that he had no chance of winning a firefight.

But then, Tony Montana never had a rocket launcher.

While a go-fast was not built with comfort in mind, it was designed to carry cargo; it had both storage space and a small cabin belowdecks. The Hare had ducked down when the helicopter showed up, and now he reappeared—with the SMAW perched on one shoulder.

He fired before either of the gunners had time to realize what they were seeing.

"What the—" Duane Shulman began, and then screamed as the Sting Ray exploded in a fireball.

Calleigh and Horatio saw the fireball go up. The cutter was heading for the go-fast as quickly as it could, but the rough weather was slowing them down. The Hare was still at least half a mile away; there was no way they could catch him—and he knew it.

Horatio had a pair of binoculars trained on the boat, and he could see a pair looking back at him. The Hare lowered his pair first, and let Horatio see his eyes. Then the terrorist turned and went belowdecks.

When he reappeared a moment later, he had a metal briefcase in his hands.

"Here!" the Hare yelled. "This is what you have been pursuing, American! I want you to see it! You cannot catch me, you cannot stop me! I am Al-Arnab, the Hare, and I will rejoice as my brothers in your hated concentration camp give their lives for Allah!"

"Can you make out what he's saying?" asked Calleigh.

"Not a word," said Horatio. "Take him out."

Calleigh brought the sniper rifle up from below the railing in one smooth move, socketing it against her shoulder and sighting through the scope. It was a nearly impossible shot—both boats were moving, rain and wind reduced visibility, and the Hare was nearly a thousand yards away.

She blew his hand off at the wrist. He was using both hands to brandish the briefcase over his head, and the abrupt loss of one of them made him drop what he was holding. The case bounced off the hull and into the water, disappearing beneath the waves.

"You could have just shot the case," said Horatio.

"That's what I was aiming for," said Calleigh. "Close enough, I guess."

"You want to kill me, don't you?" said Abdus.

Delko stared at him. "Yes," he said.

"I applaud your honesty. Most men would have lied."

"I don't give a damn for your applause."

"Oh? But you should. Applause is like currency in America. The more you receive, the more valuable your culture considers you. And as much as I loathe the people I performed for, I was still very good at evoking that response."

"Yeah? You get a lot of applause in the last twenty-four hours?"

"Oh, I'm sure I have," Abdus said, leaning back in his chair. "Not here, not in your country—but in other places, they are singing my praises. Or rather—as you've already pointed out—my brother's. But it's *my* performance that should impress you."

Delko's stare turned colder. "Nothing you do impresses me."

"No? Not even resurrecting the dead?"

Abdus clapped his hands, once. The door to the cabin opened. There, bound to a chair identical to Delko's, was Marie.

She was alive.

"I hope you know what you're doing, Caine." The speaker was a rear admiral, and he didn't look happy about handing the reins of a large military operation over to local law enforcement.

Horatio nodded. "I'll do my best, sir." The two of them were in the captain's at-sea quarters onboard the USS *John Adams*, the admiral seated behind a desk and Horatio in front of it. Horatio had managed—with Nadira's help—to convince the brass to let him try negotiating with the hostage takers. So far, Pathan had remained stubbornly incommunicado—but Horatio had information he thought would get a response.

The first problem was getting a message through;

the jamming device the hijackers were employing meant that radio signals were useless. Horatio thought he had a solution.

"First," he'd said, "we have to get their attention. If we can convince them they *want* to talk to us, they'll turn off the jammer. The only reason they used one in the first place was to prevent information leaking out while they established control. They have that now."

Horatio had paused, then looked out the porthole at the distant cruise ship. "Besides," he'd added softly, "I think the man in charge is dying for a bigger audience . . . and I intend to give him one."

They used large white plastic tarps, battleship-gray paint, and rope. A dozen sailors were given instructions on what to paint, and the tarps were laid flat on the flight deck and weighted against the wind so they wouldn't sail away. The entire operation, Horatio thought, looked like a military school making banners for a parade—except this particular banner was going to be half the size of a football field, and its message was less than celebratory.

When it was ready, it went up in stages; the top layer was strung between two poles on the superstructure like clothes from a line, with four subsequent layers suspended from that. There were gaps between the layers to allow the passage of air, alleviating the tendency of the thing to act like a giant sail. The letters themselves were each about fifteen feet tall.

The banner read: G-BAY DESTROYED. UHF FREQ. 460 MHZ.

"You got what you wanted," Horatio murmured to himself. "Let's see what you do next."

"Marie! Are you okay?" Delko blurted before he could stop himself.

Marie was gagged, but the guard removed it when Abdus gestured.

"I'm sorry," she said miserably. "I didn't want to scream, but—"

"It's okay," said Delko. "It's okay."

"Such a lovely reunion," said Abdus. "But so short . . ." He nodded, and the guard dragged Marie's chair out of sight down the hall. "Eric!" she cried out.

"Just—just hang on!" he called back. He didn't know what else to say.

Abdus closed the door. "Happy Valentine's Day," he said. He chuckled at the look on Delko's face. "Yes, today is February fourteenth. What a lovely gift I have given you, eh? I suppose I'm just a sentimentalist at heart."

"Don't hurt her."

"I'm not going to hurt her, Mister Delko. I'm going to kill her."

Delko's breath caught in his throat. "Why?" he managed.

"Because the first time you thought she was dead, you descended into a pit of despair. I raised you up from that pit mere moments ago, did I not?

The look on your face, in your eyes . . . the sheer relief you felt was palpable. And *I* put it there."

Abdus paused. "I told you before that the only thing that kept me going through all the years of deception was my connection to my brother. That is not strictly true. I also drew strength from pride in my craft. It takes tremendous dedication, many hundreds of hours of practice, to become truly good at sleight of hand. But even though I shunned the traditional trappings of so-called 'magic' shows—the juvenile insistence that such tricks are the result of sorcery and not skill—I always knew that the audience was essentially responding to an illusion . . . something that was not real."

Delko said nothing. There was a tone in Abdus's voice he hadn't heard before; the angry undertone of contempt was gone.

"There is no prohibition on Muslim singers or actors, you know," Abdus continued. "I have always envied the great ones. The emotions they can provoke—love, sadness, anger, laughter—are genuine. They are revealing a part of their soul through their performance, not duping their audience. They are touching God . . . not hiding from him."

Abdus smiled, and to Delko's amazement there were tears in his eyes. "Such a connection has always been denied to me. Even now, my greatest performance is simply another illusion. But what you felt when you saw that your lover was still alive . . . that was *real*."

There was an edge in Abdus's voice now, but it

wasn't one of hatred. It had the quavery, intense sound of someone a little too close to the brink of insanity.

"And when I kill her in front of you," said Abdus, "*that* feeling will be real, too."

When the guard brought him the message, Abdus left Delko alone in the cabin and made his way onto the deck. He read the banner with his own eyes, and laughed.

"Could it be?" he asked. "Would they admit to such a thing?"

The guard, a man named Butrus, shook his head. "It could be a trick."

"Perhaps. But the only ones who knew of our plans would die before betraying us."

Butrus was their electronics expert. "I know that frequency. It is one used for television channels."

"Obviously, they are offering confirmation." Abdus shrugged. "Perhaps we should switch off the jammer and see for ourselves. What can they do, kill us with bad TV?"

Butrus laughed nervously. "Yes, yes, you're right. What could be the harm?"

He had Butrus turn off the device, then found a lounge with a television and turned it on. There was nothing but static on every channel but one. He tried his walkie-talkie and found it disabled as well.

"They are using a jammer of their own," Abdus observed to Butrus. "Controlling our access to the media, only letting through a single channel."

The woman he saw was a local Miami news anchor, with the logo of her program across the bottom of the screen. She was standing on the deck of a boat, with the immense, lighted bulk of an aircraft carrier behind her.

"—no word yet on response from the military. Again, the world is in shock after the first confirmed nuclear terrorist attack. An atomic device was apparently detonated in the hold of an empty oil tanker in Guantanamo Bay, completely destroying the naval base there. There is no official death toll, but officials fear that over ten thousand lives may have been lost, including all the detainees held at Camp Delta."

The reporter continued to talk while her image was replaced with the outline of a mushroom cloud shot from a video camera, already dissipating in the distance. "So far, no one has come forward to claim responsibility for the attack, though there is widespread speculation that the hijacking of the cruise ship *Heart's Voyage* in the waters off the northern coast of Cuba is connected. The hijackers have yet to make any demands, leading many to wonder if capturing the vessel was simply intended to distract authorities from the real target—Guantanamo Bay."

"Praise Allah," said Butrus. "We have won."

"Have we?" said Abdus. He felt curiously hollow, not filled with triumph as he had expected. The plan had worked; the hated Camp Delta was no more. And yet . . .

The reporter disappeared from the screen. The face that replaced her was that of Lieutenant Horatio Caine.

"The news report you just saw," said Caine, "was taped this morning at eleven-thirty A.M., from Channel Five in Miami. We're rebroadcasting it from the aircraft carrier *John Adams,* to show you that your plan has succeeded. There are other factors at work now, factors you're unaware of; please, use the following frequency to contact me if you'd like to know more." A number appeared on the bottom of the screen. "It concerns your brother . . ."

The screen returned to the beginning of the news report. Abdus watched for another few minutes until he'd seen the whole thing, then reached up and switched off the TV.

"We must—" began Butrus, but Abdus cut him off with a raised hand.

"I am aware of what we must do," said Abdus. "But I wish to know what Caine has to say about my brother."

"We were not supposed to have any contact—"

"It does not matter now. We have accomplished our grand design. Nothing Caine could say or do will change that . . . and I want to hear him say that himself."

Butrus nodded. "Very well. I will adjust one of our communication units to the frequency."

"You really think he'll buy it?" Calleigh asked. She and Horatio were sitting in a corner of one of the immense mess halls that fed the crew, having a quick meal.

"I do," said Horatio. He added some pepper to his clam chowder. "It's always easier to make people believe what they want to believe . . . and right now, Abdus wants to believe that he's just as valuable as his brother."

Calleigh took a bite of her sandwich and thought about it. "But if Abdus thinks the Hare just wiped out Gitmo, what's he going to do to one-up him?"

"It's risky, I know. But I think Abdus wants to step out of his brother's shadow and do something on his own, something memorable. Destroying Guantanamo makes the Hare a military hero; killing everyone on a cruise ship just makes Abdus a mass murderer. We need to give him a better option."

Calleigh nodded. "One that makes him look good."

"One that makes him look like a hero. Because that's the choice he's going to have to make; hero, or monster . . ."

A sailor approached them at a trot. "Excuse me, sir. You're wanted in the communications room—it's urgent."

Horatio got to his feet quickly. "Showtime," he said.

"Break a leg, H. Preferably one of his."

"This is Horatio Caine," Horatio said. They'd given him a headset with a small attached mike.

"Lieutenant Caine," said a familiar voice. "How pleasant to talk to you again."

"Hello, Abdus," said Horatio. "Or would you prefer the Brilliant Batin?"

Abdus chuckled. "Oh, I think my career in that field is over. It would be hard to top an illusion of this size, anyway; my greatest feat will also be my last."

"Is that how you want to be remembered? As the world's most famous fake?"

"There is nothing *fake* about my control of this ship and its passengers, Lieutenant." Abdus's voice was brittle.

"But is it really *you* in control? Or is it your brother?"

"My brother is not aboard."

"But he's still in charge. He was the one who planned the hijacking, acquired the weapons, trained the men. He's the soldier, not you."

"Do you have a point, Lieutenant, or are you simply trying to anger me?"

"My point," said Horatio, "is this. You don't have to follow your brother's orders anymore. You can make your own decisions. Create your own legacy."

"And I suppose this legacy would have something to do with surrendering."

"Hear me out. Killing the passengers gains you nothing but a footnote in the history books. Letting them live puts you on a different path altogether—a path different from your brother's."

"Yes—the path of a coward."

"No. The path of the merciful. Isn't Allah a merciful God?"

"Do not speak to me of Allah—you know nothing of Him or His truth. And you know nothing of mercy."

"That's not true, Abdus. We're prepared to show you a great deal of leniency in return for the lives of the hostages."

"Oh? I know the kind of treatment 'enemy combatants' receive."

And there it is, thought Horatio. *At last . . .*

"Abdus," said Horatio carefully, "I don't think you're really thinking this through. *Guantanamo Bay is gone."*

Horatio paused. When there was no reply, he continued. "No naval base. No Camp Delta. In fact, no American presence at all. What you and your brother have done has changed the rules . . . you've closed the loophole that allowed the U.S. to hold prisoners in legal limbo."

"Are you saying," said Abdus slowly, "that I would be tried in the U.S.? In an American court of law?"

"We would have no other choice. And as much as you despise it, the Western system does have its advantages—you would have full access to legal counsel, maybe even the media. You could tell your story to the world."

"And end up with a needle in my arm."

"I doubt it. We don't need another martyr; you'd wind up in prison, where you'd be a celebrity. You could give interviews, write a book—and then there's the inevitable movie."

"Certainly. I could do talk shows, chat with Oprah from my cell." Abdus laughed. "Really, Lieutenant, this is a most bizarre offer."

"It's better than the alternative, Abdus. And the offer is conditional."

"I can guess what the condition is, Lieutenant. Don't worry, your man is still alive."

Horatio closed his eyes for a second, then opened them. "That's good to hear, but that's not the condition I was referring to."

"And what would that be?"

"That you're actually in command."

"What?"

"You're not a soldier, Abdus. Do you really think the Hare would trust you to make a soldier's decisions—especially the hard ones? He needed you as a figurehead, but that's all."

Abdus's voice was cold. "I am the leader of this mission. These men follow my orders, and will die for me if necessary. Do not doubt it."

"I'm sure they're ready to die. But can you make them turn their backs on death? Will they follow your wishes . . . or your brother's?"

There was a long silence. Then, "This conversation is over. Good-bye, Lieutenant." The hiss of static followed.

"That didn't sound good," the admiral seated beside Horatio said.

"Actually, it's about what I hoped for," said Horatio. "We've planted a seed. Now, we give it a little time to grow . . ."

Loyalty. That was what it came down to.

Abdus Sattar Pathan knew exactly where his loyalties lay: to the greater glory of Allah. His father, his brother, his comrades-in-arms—all of them had the very same dedication and faith burning in their hearts.

But Allah relied on men to interpret his wisdom, and men were fallible. What one man saw as the will of God, another might see differently. And if those men were leaders, then the men who followed them would be divided as well.

Abdus sat in a chair in the empty lounge and brooded. He had asked that he be left alone to think, and though Butrus had given him an odd look, they had acceded to his wishes.

But would they continue to do so?

The next part of the plan was clear. They were to do their best to ram the largest navy ship they could, ideally taking both ships down to the depths. The *Heart's Voyage*, in fact, massed about the same as an aircraft carrier; a collision between the two would be catastrophic.

That would never happen, of course. Once the navy understood their intentions, they would be forced to sink the cruise ship. That would be even better; to have the Americans killing their own tourists in full view of the world's media. It would be a glorious death.

But it would still be a death.

He was not afraid to die, nor were the men who accompanied him. But Caine had presented him with an alternative he hadn't considered—

No.

If he were to be honest with himself, he *had* considered it. And why not? What was the point in sacrificing himself? His brother had enjoyed years of infamy, cloaked in the mystique of the uncatchable, unkillable Hare. Al-Arnab's plan did not require him to die, either—he would simply slip away to one of the islands in the West Indies. And from then on, he would be regarded as the greatest of Allah's heroes, the mightiest warrior of Islam alive.

I could be a spokesman, thought Abdus. *A voice for Allah. With Camp Delta gone, they could not keep me locked away from the world. They could not silence me.*

But his brother would still see it as a betrayal.

"It's risky," said Nadira. She and Horatio were talking on the flight deck of the carrier, having been asked to step outside while the upper links of the command chain argued over Horatio's idea. "If we push him too hard, he could go the wrong way."

"I agree," said Horatio. "But I've dealt with this man before. I know the size of his ego. For all his posturing, he's a kitchen-table revolutionary—

when push comes to shove, he'll show his true colors."

"And if they're bloodred?"

Horatio looked down, but didn't reply for a long moment. "Then Eric dies," he said softly. "And so do a great many other people."

"I'm sorry," said Nadira. "I didn't mean to put it quite that harshly."

"It's a harsh situation, Nadira. One way or the other, Pathan is going to jump. This is our only chance to give him somewhere else to land."

She sighed. "You're right. I just hate risking everything on a single turn of the cards."

"Sometimes," said Horatio, "that's the only way to win."

"Lieutenant Caine." The voice crackled from the radio speaker. Horatio was instantly alert, putting down his Styrofoam cup of coffee and leaning forward in his chair in the communications center.

"I'm here," he said.

"I have given your proposal some thought."

"I'm glad to hear that."

"You will be less glad to hear my response. Do you really believe I could be so easily manipulated, Lieutenant? Seduced by promises of celebrity?"

"That wasn't my intention—"

"No. You want to save those lives I hold hostage. Perhaps one in particular is in your thoughts, even now?"

"This is bigger than a single life, Abdus."

"You hear that, Mister Delko? Your boss doesn't think you worth saving."

Horatio's eyes widened. "Eric? Are you all right?"

A long pause. Then, "I'm okay, Lieutenant."

Horatio couldn't remember the last time Eric had called him lieutenant, but there was no mistaking Delko's voice. "I get the message," Horatio said. "Loud and clear. Whatever you want, just let me know."

"Do not fool yourself," said Abdus. "This is not a negotiation. It is a demonstration."

Horatio knew what was coming next, and he forced his voice to stay calm. "Before you do anything, Abdus, there's a very important piece of information you need to have."

Beside him, Nadira was shaking her head violently. *No,* she mouthed silently. *Not now, it's the wrong move—*

"Your brother is dead," said Horatio.

This time, the silence that followed seemed to last forever.

"I don't believe you," said Abdus flatly.

"He was intercepted by a Coast Guard cutter off the coast of Bermuda. There was a firefight and he was shot. He tried to run and bled out before anyone could get to him."

"That is a transparent lie—"

"You have a gun to my friend's head," Horatio snapped. "Do you really think I'd give you an excuse to pull the trigger?"

Horatio held his breath.

A long moment later, Abdus said, "Why would you tell me this?"

"Because it's the truth, Abdus. Because I want you to make your decisions based on facts—not on the agenda of a dead man."

"I see. You think that with my brother dead, I will simply abandon my ideals?"

"No. I think you'll fight harder for them. And you can't do that from the grave."

"I—I still require proof."

"You'll have it," said Horatio. "Turn on your television."

The same channel that broadcast the news clip was now showing a two-minute video loop. The footage was shot with a handheld camera and had no sound. Its subject was the corpse of a man missing his right hand.

Abdus stared at the screen, feeling a sick sense of horror and surreality. It was like looking at his own death, broadcast somehow from the future; his face, his body.

His fate.

He did not feel the anger he knew he should. He had admired his brother, but he had never known him. Now, he never would. For that he felt grief, but it was a distant thing. The impact of coming face to face with his own mortality resonated through his very soul, drowning out everything else.

For the first time since events had began to unfold, it all felt real.

This is no performance. This is no illusion. This is the end.

He did not want to die.

It was that abrupt, that simple. The most insidious illusions, he knew, were the ones you believed in the most. He had based his whole life, his whole existence, on a romantic view of who he was, what his grand purpose would be. That view crumbled now, under the weight of a single image.

He reached up and shut off the TV. He had viewed it alone, not allowing anyone else in the room. His men would be expecting him to give the order now to turn the ship, to get the engines running at full bore.

He had one final performance to give.

They locked the doors to the concert hall, leaving all the hostages inside. Abdus gathered his men in the same lounge he'd used to view his brother's body and addressed them as a group.

"My brothers," he said. "Praise be to Allah and the prophet Mohammed. We have succeeded; the abomination known as Camp Delta has been obliterated."

Though the news had already traveled through their ranks, they still cheered and embraced and cried their thanks to Allah.

"That is not all," said Abdus. "I have heard from my brother."

"How?" asked Butrus. "There is no way to receive such a message—"

"There is," said Abdus, "if you have an operative on one of the ships not half a mile away."

Butrus looked confused. "But—"

"You were not told because this information was privileged," said Abdus. "I can reveal our true objective only now."

"Our true objective?" asked one of the men.

"Yes. We—all of us—are to become *imams,* holy teachers. Our task will be much harder; all of us will be called on by Allah to endure much suffering."

"We will endure anything!" one of the men shouted. "Tell us what we must do!"

"We must live," said Abdus. "We must surrender to the Americans."

Shocked silence—and then a chorus of angry denial.

"WE MUST!" roared Abdus, using every ounce of projection he'd learned from a lifetime onstage. The voices fell silent. "We *must* let them jail us—*because those jail cells will be in America.* Guantanamo Bay is no more—they can imprison us, they can torture us, but they will reap the whirlwind! We will expose their lies with their own media, hamstring them with their own rules!" He pointed at each shocked face in turn. "You and you and you—you are called by *Allah himself* to tell the story of what we have done, of the mercy we showed when we could have caused a bloodbath. So says my brother, and those he answers to. I will not dispute their wisdom—will you?"

Another hushed silence, broken by the noise of a jet screaming by overhead.

"No," said Butrus at last. "If this is the burden we must bear, then we shall."

"Praise to Allah," said another, and then all of them were saying it.

"Yes," said Abdus. "Praise Allah . . ."

Delko hadn't seen Abdus since he'd returned with a walkie-talkie in hand. The conversation that followed between Abdus and Horatio had been nerve-wracking; Delko knew the only reason Abdus had chosen to talk in front of him was to put H through the same kind of torture Delko had endured when he heard Marie screaming. He gritted his teeth and resolved to not make a sound, relenting only enough to let Horatio know he was still alive.

I get the message, H had said. *Loud and clear.* Those words had been meant for Delko, to let him know that his heliographed code had been received and understood.

So. H knows the bomb is phony. But does he know because I told him, or because the Hare used the real one to destroy Guantanamo Bay?

The Hare was dead, of that much he was sure. Horatio had said he could prove it, and he wouldn't make a statement like that unless he was prepared to back it up. He didn't know how Abdus would react to his brother's death, but Delko trusted Horatio's judgment.

"Hope you know what you're doing, H," he whispered to himself. *Because if Abdus doesn't jump the way you think he will, he'll turn this ship into a slaughterhouse.*

And so he waited. He tried calling for Marie a few times, but either she was gagged or she'd been moved to a more distant room. They hadn't even left a guard with him, trusting that his bonds would hold.

At last, he heard footsteps outside. The door opened.

Horatio stood there, gun in hand. He nodded silently toward the bathroom, and Delko blurted, "Nobody's in there. Man, am I glad to see you . . ."

Horatio holstered his weapon, stepped into the room and called back over his shoulder, "I need a medic!" He pulled a multitool out of his pocket and had Delko free in seconds.

He almost fell out of the chair, but Horatio caught him by the shoulders. "Easy, pal," he said.

"I'm all right," said Delko. "Been tied up so long—Marie! Where's Marie?"

"She's fine," said Horatio firmly. "We found her in a cabin at the end of the hall. Shaken up and a little bruised, but that's all. Paramedics are treating her for shock and dehydration."

Delko nodded. His head was whirling dizzily. "I didn't hear any shots."

"Abdus surrendered. Convinced his men to do the same. They're all in military custody."

"And Gitmo?"

Horatio smiled. "Still there."

"Does Abdus know?"

"Not yet. I figured I'd let you tell him . . ."

Horatio draped Delko's arm across his shoulders and helped him to his feet. "C'mon, pal," he said. "Let's go home."

Abdus Sattar Pathan surveyed his new home.

The cell was eight feet in length and less than that in width. The walls were made of steel mesh, like a cage. There was a metal toilet, a sink, and a metal bedframe with a thin foam pad for a mattress.

He carried in his arms the only items he was allowed to possess: two sheets, two blankets, two towels, a washcloth, a canteen, some basic toiletries, a prayer cap and mat, and a copy of the Quran. He wore flip-flops, a pair of orange shorts, and an orange shirt.

He had been processed in a building that looked like an unfinished wooden shack. He had been subjected to a thorough search, a chest X-ray, and a delousing. He had been fingerprinted and photographed and issued a plastic bracelet that snapped around his wrist.

"You get two fifteen-minute showers a week," said the guard behind him. "Try not to sweat too much—there's twenty-three other cells in this unit, and your neighbors won't appreciate it. Speaking of which, we have a little surprise right next door to you."

Abdus entered the cell and put his items down on the bed. "Torture, you mean," he said flatly.

"That's not what I mean at all," said the guard. "More like a family reunion. New guy, came in just after you did. Look, here he is now . . ."

Abdus turned around and saw another prisoner in orange, his hands shackled in front of him, being led down the corridor. Khasib Pathan met his son's eyes for a brief second, then looked down.

"Heard they nabbed him just off Key West. Took him off his own yacht, seized all his assets. Guess money can't buy everything."

Khasib entered his own cell. He wouldn't look at Abdus.

Both doors slammed shut. The sound echoed down the corridor like the ghost of applause.